'Good morning, Miss Finsham.'

The smile Hugh turned upon her appeared warm and almost caressing. Louisa wondered whether she had been forgiven her excursion to Waterloo. She decided it could do no harm to return his good humour. Being in high spirits herself after her exercise, she positively beamed back.

For a split-second the sight of her radiant face seemed to shock him into immobility. In that moment, something almost tangible seemed to flow between them. . .

Sarah Westleigh has enjoyed a varied life. Working as a local government officer in London, she qualified as a chartered quantity surveyor. She assisted her husband in his chartered accountancy practice, at the same time managing an employment agency. Moving to Devon, she finally found time to write, publishing short stories and articles, before discovering historical novels.

Recent titles by the same author:

ESCAPE TO DESTINY
A MOST EXCEPTIONAL QUEST

A LADY OF INDEPENDENT MEANS

Sarah Westleigh

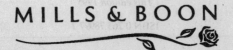

MILLS & BOON

MILLS & BOON LIMITED
ETON HOUSE, 18–24 PARADISE ROAD
RICHMOND, SURREY, TW9 1SR

MILLS & BOON, the Rose Device and LEGACY OF LOVE are trademarks of the publisher.

First published in Great Britain 1995
by Mills & Boon Limited

© Sarah Westleigh 1995

Australian copyright 1995   Philippine copyright 1995
This edition 1995

ISBN 0 263 78997 7

Set in 10 on 12 pt Linotron Times
04-9503-77829

Typeset in Great Britain by Centracet, Cambridge
Printed in Great Britain by
BPC Paperbacks Ltd

CHAPTER ONE

Louisa hung over the rail of the packet boat knowing she was about to die and wanting to. Wind, rain and salty spray lashed at her, soaking her garments and whipping her disordered hair into dripping rat's-tails. Her stylish bonnet hung from its ribbons, the feathers dripping poppy-red dye which spread into the silk and dropped on to her new pelisse, but she scarcely noticed any of these discomforts.

Her stomach heaved again but it had long been empty. A trickle of bile rose to her mouth and she wiped her lips for the hundredth time, wielding a sodden handkerchief with a shaking hand.

Why had she allowed Aunt Nazeby to cozen her into coming? She would die long before she reached France.

'Are you ill? May I help?'

The sound of the deep, rather languid voice, which carried clearly above the howl of the wind, the lashing of the waves and the creaking of the rigging, merely made her shudder. 'Go away,' she croaked. Apart from the crew, who after a shout of warning had paid her no attention at all, and the deck passengers huddled in a bunch towards the stern, she was alone, having sought solitude in which to endure her misery. She wanted no one to witness her present distress.

But instead of obeying her the man moved nearer, peering round to glimpse a fine brow, a bony nose and

5

a wide mouth set in an oval face presently pale and tinged with green.

'You would feel better lying down,' he advised. 'Allow me——'

Louisa cut him short. 'Thank you, but no! I will not return to that cabin.'

The sentence finished on a gulp. She did not see the compassionate if rather amused smile that crossed his face, being busily engaged in trying to bring up the non-existent contents of her stomach.

'Then lie on the deck,' he suggested, placing a strong hand on her shoulder. 'Come, ma'am, you will be much better off.'

She seemed unable to resist the gentle pressure he exerted. Reluctantly, she relinquished her grip upon the rail and allowed him to turn her round.

'Wrap yourself in my greatcoat,' he urged, removing the garment as he spoke. 'Be thankful that the wind is driving us towards France, for otherwise we might be doomed to a long and stormy passage, running wherever it dictated.'

Louise felt the heavy garment descend about her shoulders. She looked up to protest and met concerned grey eyes under a furrowed brow, which yet held a glimmer of wry amusement. He, curse him, was not in the slightest bit affected by the tossing motion of the little vessel. Under a wide-brimmed tall hat, which he had somehow managed to keep on despite the gale, his broad face, made distinctive by strong, anything but regular features, held no trace of the sickly tinge she knew must be evident in hers. For an instant, as she saw his gaze wander over her, she regretted the disastrous state of her clothes and toilette, but by the next had forgotten everything but another attack of nausea.

He waited patiently in the soaking rain and spray until it had passed. Then strong arms picked up her not inconsiderable weight to carry her across the heaving deck. He staggered slightly but managed to keep his balance with admirable skill.

Feebly, she struggled, knowing such intimacy with a complete stranger to be quite improper. But she knew she was fighting against the comforting feel of solid man as much as convention. 'Put me down!' she moaned.

He chuckled. She could feel the laugh reverberate through his chest and on through her own body. 'Immediately, ma'am.'

He laid her down carefully, wedging her between the coaming surrounding the hatchway to the cabin and some deck tackle. His own clothes had suffered quite abominably, she noticed abstractedly. Since he had taken off his caped greatcoat to wrap it around her, his superfine coat and buff pantaloons had become exceedingly damp. The brocade of his waistcoat had suffered from contact with her wet pelisse and his cravat hung in limp folds which would be the despair of his valet. But at least his hair must have remained dry under the hat.

She realised suddenly that lying down did help. Her head had stopped swimming. She had been incapable of thinking as clearly as this while leaning over the rail. A small smile of gratitude touched her lips.

'Thank you, sir,' she managed.

'Remain where you are. I will secure you something to drink.'

He departed abruptly and Louisa felt bereft. She had noticed him earlier, sitting alone in the cabin, aloof and somewhat bored, scanning a newspaper. That had been before the sudden summer storm hit the packet, rendering most of its passengers incapable.

She wondered how Aunt Nazeby was feeling. That lady, used to the crossing to Ireland where her son, the present earl, possessed estates brought to him by his wife, had declared herself immune to seasickness; but she had not altogether escaped the effects of this storm. Louisa had left her in the midst of other stricken passengers, looking decidedly sickly herself while attempting to brace their wretched lady's-maids.

Not, of course, that her rescuer had been in the least stricken. She wondered who he could be, but with only vague interest. She felt too ill to concentrate on anything but her own misery.

He returned quickly. He had another greatcoat draped around his shoulders—his servant's, she surmised by the cut and inferior quality, and why he hadn't sent his man up to tend her she couldn't imagine. Unless that individual was ill, too. But his master had come bringing a bowl and towel as well as a goblet of watered wine acquired, presumably, from a steward below.

'Drink this,' he instructed, squatting as nearly at her side as he could get. His top boots and damp pantaloons seemed overwhelmingly near her face.

'I can't. I'll be ill again,' moaned Louisa, who did not want to move for fear of bringing back the nausea.

'Yes, you can. Even if you bring most of it up again, it will do you good. Come, now, ma'am, let me lift your head.'

He put a square, capable hand under her wet curls and urged her up. Reluctantly, but without the strength to resist, Louisa allowed him to raise her head, eventually putting down an elbow to support herself. He held the goblet to her lips and she drank. At least it took the taste of bile from her mouth.

And then, of course, it all came surging up again. He held the bowl for her.

'I told you so,' she gasped when she was able. She had never felt so wretchedly mortified in her life.

'I know. But you will feel better now.'

He stood up and went to the lee rail, paddling through the water surging in and out of the scuppers as the packet heeled in a strong gust. When he came back he placed the empty bowl near at hand, jammed among the tackle.

'I will leave you to recover now, ma'am. The storm is almost over and I fear I am needed below in the cabin. We shall be in Calais within the hour if this wind prevails. I will inform Lady Nazeby that you are safely resting, and come back to assist you to disembark. Your servant, ma'am.'

With a courteous bow, just as though they were in a drawing-room instead of on a streaming, heaving deck, he withdrew. She heard him descend the companion-way and close the hatch behind him.

She did feel better. In fact Louisa suspected afterwards that she dozed off, because the sound of barked orders and renewed activity all around made her start up. The sun had appeared again and its warmth was making the wet deck steam. The motion of the ship had lessened. Because the wind had abated and veered the crew were engaged in shaking out the reefs and resetting the sails.

Slowly, Louisa stirred. She sat up, leaning her back against the coaming. His coat was still about her shoulders. Her own garments were soaked beneath its comforting warmth. On land the day had been warm, but the storm and the wind at sea had caused the temperature to drop alarmingly. Now it was rising sharply again. Perhaps she should try to dry herself off. She moved cautiously, still feeling queasy, then staggered across to sit upon the barrel of one of several cannons carried as defence against attack by pirates. Spreading her skirts, she lifted her face to the sun, careless of her complexion. She needed to dry her hair as well as her clothes.

Who was he? The question returned to nag at her mind. She ought to know him, for he spoke as a gentleman and his garments were of top quality and cut even although he could not be described as a glass of fashion, tending rather to conservative tastes. He must move in first circles, for he apparently knew the Dowager, yet she could not remember seeing him in either drawing-room or ballroom. Not, she thought, that he seemed the sort to be comfortable in either. He hid himself in the card-rooms, perhaps. If he attended such functions at all.

She drowsed, soaking up the warmth of the sun. And awoke again to hear her aunt's anxious voice.

'There you are, Louisa, my love. I had thought you would return to the cabin once the storm abated, but here you sit as though you were nothing but a deck passenger! Have you no regard for your complexion? Where is your parasol?'

Shrugging, Louisa said, 'In the cabin, I suppose.'

'Then we must make sure to recover it! Come, my love, we must make ready to disembark!'

'Are we there already?' Louisa looked ahead and saw the coast of France looming near. 'I must have dozed off,' she explained ruefully. 'This seat is quite comfortable, you know, and I needed to dry off.'

She ran her fingers through her short curls and replaced her stained, misshapen hat, tying the ribbons securely beneath her chin.

'The feathers are in a sad state,' she observed, 'but the hat will have to do until we reach the shore. Who was that man, Aunt? The one who came to my aid.' She stroked the cape of his greatcoat, her fingers lingering on the damp, expensive material.

'Didn't you know? No, I suppose you might not. I did not recognise him at first. He's the Duke of Chadford's son. We had met before, so did not need further introduction.'

'Not Alnbridge,' said Louisa decidedly. 'I'd have recognised him.'

'No. Lord Hugh Deverill, the Earl's brother. Did a Season once, before you came out, but none of the belles could fix his interest, though plenty tried, despite Deverill's only being a younger son. Then he practically retired from Society, attached to the Foreign Office, so they say, no time for idling about in drawing-rooms, which is why I did not recognise him at once.'

'But plenty of time to conduct an *affaire*, if rumour is true. I have heard of him, though I've never met him, as far as I know. Isn't Lady Kingslea his latest flirt?'

'Possibly. Rumours did circulate when he was in

London last. Mostly to the effect that he had become
Maria Kingslea's latest victim. Don't sound so disapproving, Louisa. Most unmarried men have a mistress;
there'd be something wrong with 'em if they didn't, in
my opinion——'

'Married men have them, too,' interrupted Louisa
bitterly, 'but gentlemen have no need to attach other
men's wives. There must be plenty of widows or
members of the muslin company available to meet their
needs.'

'Really, Louisa, you shouldn't use such terms,'
scolded Lady Nazeby, her eyes twinkling. 'And it takes
two, you know. No one forces a woman to be unfaithful
to her husband.'

'I know, or a man to his wife. When I remember the
misery poor Mamma suffered. . . .'

'Don't refine upon it too much, my dear Louisa. your
father was a rake, no one denies that, but few men are
such bad lots as he turned out to be, and I'm sure Hugh
Deverill is not one of 'em. I'd have heard.'

'I wonder where he's bound?' muttered Louisa as
she rose reluctantly to her feet. Her shoes were still
wet, her pelisse damp and her skirts inclined to drip.
She had never felt so wretchedly turned out in her life.
She thrust his lordship's greatcoat into her aunt's
hands. 'Are you climbing down into the cabin again?
Take this back and give it to him,' she begged. 'I do
not wish to speak with him again.'

'My dear, you must offer your thanks——'

'You can do that for me, Aunt Nazeby. I'll wait here
until it is time to go ashore. I cannot face that cabin
again. I do declare, next time I cross the Channel I
shall travel as a deck passenger!'

'And be herded behind the mast with only a tarpaulin to shelter you from the elements?'

'Infinitely better than that stuffy cabin!' laughed Louisa. Please God, next time she took to the sea it would remain calm!

'I'm glad you're feeling more cheerful, my dear,' smiled Lady Nazeby fondly. 'I'll go back and deliver this coat and thank his lordship, then. Rose and Betty should be feeling up to scratch by now. I wonder how Dench is?'

'Wet, I should think,' said Louisa. Their footman had chosen to be an outside passenger.

'I hope not. And if he was sick I hope he has recovered. We need him to help carry our hand luggage.'

So saying, Lady Nazeby swayed back to descend the companionway and return Lord Hugh Deverill's coat to its owner.

Sighing, Louisa went to the rail to watch Calais draw nearer. A further trying time lay ahead. She did not mind so much going to Paris, where the *ton* was taking up residence *en masse*, but she did wish her aunt had not insisted on visiting Brussels and Waterloo first. The very thought of viewing the field of battle turned her cold. Such a ghoulish desire, she considered it, to wish to see the spot where over forty thousand men had died, many of the Englishmen among them the young, gallant officers who had graced the ballrooms of London, Brighton and Bath over the past years. Yet it was the thing to do, so her aunt insisted. One simply had to inspect the site of Wellington's famous victory or be deemed unpatriotic.

The packet began to dock. Luckily the tide was up,

so they would not need to take to the faring boats to land. Louisa moved from the rail to join her aunt as the latter emerged from the cabin and handed her her parasol. Together, the two women, followed by servants laden with bandboxes and a trail of porters humping trunks, prepared to cross the gangplank to French soil.

'Are you quite recovered, Miss Finsham?'

Louisa recognised the voice immediately. She swung round, determined not to blush. At five and twenty she was far too old and seasoned to be overset, at however much of a disadvantage fate had placed her. Her parasol, at least, had not suffered, and she twirled it defiantly.

He did not wait for a reply, but turned immediately to her aunt. 'I would account it a great honour, Lady Nazeby, if you would introduce me to your companion.'

'Not my companion, my lord. Louisa is my niece, though she has chosen to reside with me and keep me company. Louisa, my love, may I introduce Lord Hugh Deverill?' Her eyes twinkled. 'I believe you have already met informally. My lord, Miss Louisa Finsham.'

'Servant, Miss Finsham.' His lordship bowed with easy grace despite his large frame. He was not stout, she conceded, but solidly built, with broad shoulders under the superfine coat. And her inspection confirmed her previous impression of strong, shapely limbs stretching the fawn pantaloons. To her mortification she noticed a spot of poppy-red marring the perfect whiteness of his crumpled cravat.

'My lord.' Louisa returned his bow with a neat curtsy, formally polite.

Other passengers, anxious to disembark, jostled behind them. Dench, loaded with several bandboxes, nevertheless proved himself quite able to help his employer down the narrow gangway. Louisa found Lord Hugh hovering at her elbow.

'Allow me, Miss Finsham.'

Without asking, he relieved her of the damp pelisse, which she had removed and was carrying, and offered his arm. Louisa could scarcely refuse to take it, though she wished she were not so aware of the muscles hidden beneath the tight-fitting sleeve. His man followed them down, carrying his master's greatcoat, like her own pelisse no longer required, and a large valise.

All was bustle on the quay, where a number of carriages awaited the packet's passengers and a contingent of surly-looking, armed *douaniers* in dark green uniforms and cocked hats stood ready to inspect passports, collect duty and intercept any contraband.

'I will see your luggage through Customs and loaded on the chaise, my lord,' said Deverill's man impassively, for his master showed little inclination to oversee the disposition of his trunks himself.

Deverill nodded. 'I'll not be long.' He smiled down at the woman on his arm, apparently not at all disturbed by her dishevelled appearance. 'Do you have your passport handy?'

'I have it here.' Louisa delved into her reticule and produced a damp document. 'I hope it will be readable!'

Deverill glanced at it briefly. 'Eminently. The paper is merely moist. The man will not question it.' He handed both documents to a waiting *douanier*. As the man returned the papers and he handed hers back, he asked, 'Are you bound for Paris too, Miss Finsham?'

'Eventually, my lord. We are to travel via Brussels.'

A frown immediately formed between his intelligent, deep-set eyes. 'Indeed, ma'am. You are making an excursion to view the battlefield?'

Distaste informed his voice and expression. Resenting his implied criticism, Louisa removed her hand from his arm.

'Indeed, sir. It is quite the thing, you know. We should be considered quite out if we did not.'

'And that would matter to you?' he enquired coldly.

'But of course. My aunt would never forgive me were I to shirk such an obvious duty. To see where our brave young men died, you know.'

'Forgive me if I cannot admire such a sentiment, Miss Finsham. To me this passion for viewing the site of tragedy on such a grand scale is nothing short of repulsive.'

'Perhaps you do not rejoice in the great victory, my lord? You would prefer that monster Napoleon to remain in power? To see Europe in constant turmoil?'

He shook his head. 'Not at all.'

'But then,' she said kindly, 'you are not a soldier, I collect. Perhaps you resent the admiration our army and its commander have so deservedly gathered to themselves.'

He executed a frigid bow. 'You must think as you wish, Miss Finsham. If your desire is to tread upon the bones of the dead I have nothing to say. No doubt we shall meet again in Paris. Until then, I will bid you adieu.'

He turned on his heel and strode to where Amelia, the Dowager Countess of Nazeby, was busy instructing the maids and Dench upon the best disposition of their mountain of luggage. The *douaniers* appeared to have lost interest in their possessions, Louisa was relieved to see.

She watched as Deverill made his devoirs to Lady Nazeby. It seemed his displeasure did not extend to that lady.

Why had she reacted so defiantly? wondered Louisa, feeling rather guilty. After all, it seemed their opinions on the subject were similar. She had allowed his inexcusable attitude to provoke her into asserting her aunt's views, not her own.

Well, it hardly mattered. If he appeared as much in Society in Paris as he did in London they would scarcely be likely to meet. He had done her a service but cancelled any debt by his censorious words. Tread upon bones, indeed! No, she would not mind if she never set eyes on Lord Hugh Deverill again.

Brussels reeked of gangrene and typhus. Wounded soldiers, most of them French, still lay about the streets begging for help. A few people were doing what they could to relieve the suffering, but it was little enough. And the majority carried on with their lives as though the poor fellows did not exist. In particular, those members of the *ton* still in residence there seemed determined to exact the last fragment of enjoyment from their social activities. On the very day of arrival they received a number of visitors at the rooms they had rented for their stay, cards were left and invitations to several soirées and drums delivered.

Louisa was appalled. 'How can they, Aunt?' she wailed, thinking how Hugh Deverill's lips would curl in disgust.

'Life must go on, my love,' Amelia pointed out. 'The world cannot come to a halt because some poor souls have died and others are suffering.'

But she did not look as though she believed what she said. Louisa eyed her aunt anxiously. Since arriving in Brussels a kind of pall seemed to have descended to dampen her usually ebullient spirits.

'Do you wish to attend the Richmonds' soirée tonight?'

Amelia sighed. 'No, my dear, I do not believe I do. The journey has been most trying. But if you would like——'

Louisa cut her off quickly. 'No, Aunt. It is the last thing I want to do. There is too much suffering in this city for me to contemplate such a frivolous occupation.'

'Then we will remain in. Dench shall go out and bring back Ordinaries from the nearest inn.'

Next day, while her aunt continued to rest, Louisa dispensed considerable sums of money to help some of the poor derelicts find shelter and others to pay their way home. The following morning after breakfast she announced her intention of visiting the hospital in order to volunteer her services there.

'I cannot possibly countenance such a thing, Louisa,' cried her aunt, scandalised. 'Nursing men! Besides, you could so easily catch the fever and die, and what good would that do to anyone, I'd like to know? I wish I had listened to you and not come here, but no one had told me what Brussels would be like. We have a hired

house—an *hôtel*, as the French call it—waiting for us in Paris. We will leave for there tomorrow.'

'Without viewing the battlefield?' asked Louisa in relief.

'By no means! That was our reason for coming here and I am quite determined to do so. But once we have seen it we may go.'

The set of Lady Nazeby's jaw indicated the impossibility of arguing with her. Louisa tried all the same.

'But——'

Lady Nazeby continued as though she had not spoken. 'We will drive out there this morning. There will be plenty of time before dinner. I will ring for Dench and send him to acquire a hired carriage immediately. By the time he returns we shall be ready.'

As her aunt suited actions to words, Louisa swallowed her disappointment. She owed Lady Nazeby so much; she had been the only one to care for her since her mother's death, and she loved the old lady dearly. She could not argue more against this expedition, which for some reason she seemed so determined to make. Nor could she bring herself to refuse to accompany the Dowager.

The hired coachman, well used to such expeditions, took them to join a string of other sightseeing vehicles lined up on the road just below the ridge the Allied army had defended so bravely. He pointed out Wellington's strong points, the château of Hugemont to the west, the farm of La Haye Sainte with its orchard in the centre, and the farm of Papelotte to the east. Beneath them stretched the trampled cornfields across which Napoleon had thrown all his men into the attack. In the distance they fancied they could see the knoll near

La Belle Alliance from which Napoleon had directed his army.

Lady Nazeby made no attempt to descend from the landaulet and stroll about, as the driver expected and the other visitors were doing. Their voices, the high-pitched shrieks of the women, floated up to them, incongruous in that otherwise empty landscape. The hood of their carriage was down since it was another fine day. The Dowager Countess simply sat and stared. As she did so the tears began to gather and then to fall.

Louisa, hardly able to bear to look upon the ruined buildings, the devastated countryside which even yet bore the debris of battle, traces of those who had died there, kept her eyes steadfastly fixed on the silk gloves covering hands gripped together in her lap.

So at first she did not notice her companion's distress. Eventually, though, her aunt's silence made her look up. Despite the concealing brim of a large bonnet she saw the tears streaming down the lined cheeks and immediately her own feelings were forgotten.

'Dear Aunt,' she cried, 'I should have tried harder to dissuade you from coming here! Do not fret yourself so, I beg you! Coachman,' she called in schoolroom French, which was all she knew, 'return to Brussels at once, if you please!'

The man, who had been holding his horses' heads, returned to the box and set the carriage in motion. Louisa took hold of Lady Nazeby's hand and clasped it in both of hers, not understanding her aunt's distress and afraid to speak for fear of making things worse.

'I'm sorry to be such a watering pot, m'dear,' wavered Lady Nazeby. 'I declare, I cannot imagine what has come over me!'

She did not seem able to stem her tears, however, and the return journey was accomplished in silence. With Dench sitting impassively beside the driver Louisa did not feel free to speak as she would have liked.

Once they were settled in their own private sitting-room, however, Louisa could restrain herself no longer. Her aunt's eyes were still suspiciously moist and she seemed upset beyond all comprehension.

'Dear Aunt,' she began, 'do please tell me what is amiss. I do not like to see you so overset. You appeared so determined, so anxious to follow everyone else to the battlefield. You must have known it would be a harrowing experience. What can have caused you such distress?'

Lady Nazeby dabbed at her eyes with a dainty lace handkerchief and sniffed the tears back with sudden determination. Her voice, however, still wavered.

'Did I seem so very heartless to you, my love? I knew, of course, that it would not be pleasant. But I had my own reasons for wishing to see the field of battle for myself. 'Twas not simply a desire to be in the fashion.'

'Was it not, Aunt? Then what was your reason?' asked Louisa gently.

'I have never confided this to anyone before,' sighed Amelia, who, now she had started, seemed to have gained a better command over her voice, 'apart, of course, from the dear friend who adopted him. I had a son, Louisa. He—was not Nazeby's.'

Louisa caught her breath. 'You did, Aunt?'

'Yes, my love. Your respectable aunt. I fell in love, you see. Perhaps that is why I can understand other wives. . . But no matter. When I discovered my state I went into retirement and had my lover's son. I travelled with a friend, a woman who desperately needed a son to keep the love of her husband. She had a property up in Yorkshire and we announced we were going there to rusticate. Our husbands did not mind. Thought it rather a joke, left 'em free to live bachelor lives for a while.'

'And you did not mind that?'

'Nothing new. Trouble with arranged marriages is if you don't suit it's hard on a man. Has to find his pleasure elsewhere. Love's worse, though. Plays the very devil with the emotions. Raises too many problems.'

'Unless you're free to marry the person you love,' murmured Louisa.

'I know very well why you've hung out for someone special but you mustn't delay too long, my dear Louisa; you're not quite past your last prayers yet, but you're not getting any younger——'

'I have no need to marry,' put in Louisa quickly. 'Thanks to the foresight of my grandmother I have enough fortune to live in reasonable style for the remainder of my life, and do not intend to allow some rake to drink and gamble it away. I know my husband will not control my fortune, thank God, but I would be hard pressed to refuse him help should he demand it. But do go on, Aunt. What happened?'

'Together, we planned everything and no one suspected the child was not my friend's. Wrote back to say she was increasing a month after we arrived. Her husband posted up with all haste, but since it was too early for anything to show it didn't matter. Told him we were set on remaining in Yorkshire and not to come again, babies were a woman's affair. With which he thoroughly agreed. He'd see it soon enough after it was born.'

'And he did as he was told?'

'Of course. Men ain't much interested in a woman when she's in a delicate condition. After that we were left to ourselves. Had it been a girl my friend would have been disappointed, but she would still have taken her, for she would at least have had a child to love even if it weren't the son her husband wanted.'

'But it was a boy,' prompted Louisa, since her aunt had fallen into a reverie.

'Yes. Such a beautiful baby. Very like his father, you know.'

'Who was he?'

'The father?' A wistful smile lit Amelia's face for a moment. 'That I will never divulge. Even my friend who brought him up did not know. But he was a peer. The boy's pedigree could in no way be considered at odds with his supposed father's consequence.'

'What became of him?'

'He inherited the title. Wed and produced an heir. And died honourably on the field we have just seen.'

'Oh, Aunt!'

Compassion filled Louisa's voice as she dropped to her knees at Amelia's side. However much she might dislike infidelity there was something about her aunt's story that caught at her emotions. Amelia had not been happy with Nazeby and had not mourned his death. How many women suffered a lifetime of unhappiness because their husbands had been chosen for them by parents blind to the consequences of forcing conflicting characters into a marriage devoid of affection, let alone love? And were the ones who took lovers simply

seeking consolation, hoping to find that joy and close-
ness denied them in their lawful union? How thankful
she was that her father had died before he could
arrange such a joyless match for her.

After a moment of silent sympathy Louisa returned
to her questions.

'So your grandson has inherited. How old is he?'

'Twelve,' said Amelia baldly.

'Poor little fellow! So much consequence to bear! Is
his mother sensible?'

'Only marginally. I could never understand why
R——' She cut herself off quickly. 'Why my son married
her. She was pretty, of course, in an insipid way. No
accountin' for a man's taste. And my friend, the boy's
grandmother, is no longer able to follow his progress
as she would like.'

'She is ill?'

'Not precisely. But she suffers considerably with her
joints and can no longer travel. We have both outlived
our spouses. They were much older than us, of course.'

'You are still able to keep an eye on him.'

The words were spoken quietly. Amelia glanced at
her niece, a flush of colour staining her cheekbones.
'Why we're goin' to Paris,' she muttered. 'Standin' in
for her. His mother insisted on taking the boy there.
Wanted diversion to take her out of her mopes, she
said. Didn't want to miss the chance of catching another
husband, in my opinion.'

'You don't like her,' observed Louisa wryly.

'Don't think anything about her. Just hope she don't
spoil the boy.'

'Dear Aunt, if you could bring yourself to tell me
who he is, I'd look out for him, too.'

Amelia's eyes filled with tears again. 'I could happily trust him to your care, my love. I am getting to be an old woman.'

'Nonsense, Aunt! That's not what I meant at all! You are going to live for years and years yet! What would I do without you? But I thought we might share the burden, in the way we share so much else.'

'It's true, though. And I would feel happier about the boy if I knew you were keeping an eye on his welfare after Muriel and I are gone. James Grade. Thurrock.'

Louisa's eyes widened. 'The new Earl of Thurrock? His must be one of the richest inheritances in the kingdom! I trust his wealth is securely tied up in trusts!'

'You may depend upon it. The Thurrock fortune always is. Families are beginning to show some sense. No good preserving the entail to prevent estates being split up if there ain't any money left to run 'em.'

'No,' agreed Louisa. 'Though it is hard on the younger sons,' she added thoughtfully. 'I often think they must resent the eldest inheriting everything.'

'I suppose they may. Most go into the army. As heir, Robert should never have been allowed to purchase his pair of colours, but there was no stopping him. Mad on it. Ensign at seventeen. Fought all through the Peninsula. Couldn't resist Wellington's call when Napoleon returned. Rallied to the flag and, like Tom Picton, got himself killed.'

'At least he left an heir.'

The glamour of the red coat had never attracted Louisa. She knew fighting was necessary to stop someone like Napoleon, but men seemed to glory in it and that she could not understand.

Yet, despite holding these sentiments herself, she had taunted Lord Hugh Deverill on not being a military man. And he had been piqued. Had climbed up on his high ropes and taken a disdainful leave.

Why should she think of Hugh Deverill now? she asked herself in irritation. She hoped never to see him again. Such an encounter could only prove too mortifying to be endured.

CHAPTER TWO

PARIS had changed. Or so said those who had known it before the Revolution. Amelia, who had visited in her youth, decided that little had physically altered. But the large mansions of the *aristos*, once so splendid, were mostly dilapidated from years of shuttered neglect or, worse, had suffered wanton destruction. A few had been used by the Revolutionary movement as centres of government or had been lived in by its leaders. But their treatment had not been kind and with but few exceptions all exuded an air of decay.

However, the city was far from dead. The *ton* of several countries had gathered there and social life in the highest circles had never been more lively. Horsemen and carriages thronged the streets. For the lower orders of Parisian inhabitants, however, life was far from rosy. With a combined force of sixty thousand encamped near by, soldiers from the victorious Prussian, Russian and Austrian armies were everywhere, terrorising the ordinary inhabitants and leaving a trail of broken lives and shattered homes behind them.

'Thank God,' remarked Louisa, shuddering as they watched a poor, weeping woman being deprived of her furniture, 'there are no redcoats among them.'

'Prussians, I believe,' grunted Amelia, noting the blue jackets, white breeches and knee-boots of the offenders. 'The guard on the gate did say that the

27

British soldiers needed passes to enter the city and have orders to pay for whatever they take.'

'I trust the commanders will ensure that their men obey the order,' said Louisa fervently. 'I should hate for our army to be guilty of such conduct. By what I've heard, many of our senior officers have taken up residence within the city so they should be able to keep an eye on the lower ranks.' As the carriage passed on towards the centre of the town she felt constrained to remark, 'It doesn't appear too difficult to obtain a pass, judging by the number of red coats to be seen on the streets.'

'True, but note, my love, they are behaving exactly as they would in London.'

'Parading to display their uniforms,' chuckled Louisa. 'Particularly the officers!'

The Duke of Wellington had taken over Marshal Junot's house, situated on the corner of Place Louis XV near the Place Vendôme. The Dowager Countess's hired residence stood near by. The procession which drew to a halt before its ornate if dilapidated façade consisted of two carriages, each drawn by four horses, escorted by six outriders. Dench, in bob wig and the Duchess's blue and white livery, the coat lavishly decorated with gold frogging, sat up behind his mistress in the first. The second vehicle accommodated their maids and most of the luggage.

As the Dowager's train drew up before their temporary residence Louisa was so absorbed in looking up at the elaborate carvings and decorative ironwork smothering the front of the building that at first she failed to see the party gathered on the step before the double doors. Even when she did lower her fascinated gaze her eyes alighted first on Lady Nazeby's groom, Pershaw, who ran forward to hold the leaders' heads.

He was quickly relieved of this task by others and, as Dench sprang down to help his mistress alight, Pershaw bowed to her respectfully.

'Well, Pershaw! So you are arrived! My horses are safe, I trust?'

'Indeed, your ladyship. We had a pleasant crossing, and I took the journey here in easy stages, you may be sure. The bays arrived in splendid condition, Miss Finsham's black, too.'

He made another bow, in Louisa's direction this time, and she smiled at the wiry little man, who had served the old Earl before his death and had continued in the employ of the Dowager, to whom he was devoted. She suspected he was only slightly less devoted to herself. She seemed to have known him forever; it was he who had taught her to ride and afterwards all she wanted to know about horses, for she had been a frequent visitor with the Countess ever since her mother's early death, and it was Lady Nazeby who had brought her out. When her father's demise, some three years ago, had finally left her a lady of independent means able to indulge her independent whims and live the way she chose, it had seemed natural to make her permanent home with her aunt Nazeby.

'Hello, Pershaw,' she greeted the groom. 'How nice it is to have a familiar face to welcome us! Have Prince Hal saddled and ready for me at seven tomorrow morning, will you? And be ready to accompany me. I know I can trust you to have discovered the best rides.'

Pershaw returned her smile. She knew that not only

was he always happy to accompany her on her spirited excursions, he positively enjoyed them, feeling supremely superior to those poor grooms forced to idle along behind a mistress barely able to control a docile hack. They shared a moment of complete understanding.

'Certainly, miss. There are still some excellent rides in the Bois de Boulogne despite part of our army's being encamped there.'

They could not linger long with Pershaw, however, for the party on the doorstep had moved forward to greet them.

For the first time, Louisa consciously registered its presence. She immediately recognised the elegant figure of Sir Charles Stuart, the British Ambassador, for they had often met in London. He was already making his devoirs to the Countess. Over his bent head her eyes passed on to the tall man standing at his shoulder, waiting to make his bow.

It couldn't be. But it was.

She crushed down the mortification threatening to overwhelm her. Remembered gratefully the style in which they had arrived. Lifted her chin under the fashionable bonnet with its frilled brim and bunch of blue ribbons, the colour of which exactly matched the smart pelisse-robe she had chosen to wear for the journey. On this occasion she had absolutely no cause to feel at a disadvantage.

So there could be no possible reason for sight of him to put her to the blush. She was in full command of herself now, and if he chose to condemn her for visiting Waterloo it could scarcely signify.

She stepped forward with deliberate dignity and

apparent aloof calm to receive the ambassador's greeting and made a curtsy which included both men. Lord Hugh Deverill had already swept a dutiful bow, removing his tall, curly-brimmed hat to reveal thick black wavy hair. His deep-set eyes held little expression, though she was close enough and fit enough to see that the grey of the iris became a mottled blue near his pupil. She had never before seen eyes quite like them and found it surprisingly difficult to tear her own away. There appeared to be something mesmerising in their neutral depths.

She had been feeling too ill to take in his appearance aboard the packet properly. Now, having at last managed to detach her gaze from his, she dazedly appreciated how attractive his smile was, lighting his ruggedly handsome face despite the fact that it did not reach his eyes.

'Miss Finsham.' His deep voice touched some nerve inside her, causing it to vibrate. 'You are fully recovered, I collect?'

'Indeed, my lord.' She met his gaze again bravely. She would *not* quake! 'Seasickness soon passes once the motion ceases, as I am certain you are aware. I must thank you again for your timely assistance on the packet boat.'

He acknowledged her thanks with a slight inclination of his head. 'It was nothing. I trust you will enjoy your residence in Paris.'

She returned his polite gesture with the merest movement of her own head, feeling such a formal welcome required no verbal response, and was glad when Sir Charles intervened.

'Deverill has been sent by the Foreign Office to assist

me here, now the numbers of English visitors have increased so dramatically. If you ladies have need of advice or help at any time, you have only to call upon either of us and we will be entirely at your service.' He swept another deep bow.

'That is most kind of you, Sir Charles,' Amelia replied for them both, 'and I greatly appreciate the courtesy of your being here to greet us. But do let us go inside! I am vastly curious to see what manner of mansion my agent has chosen.'

'One of the best available, Lady Nazeby, I do assure you.' Sir Charles gave another bow, less flourishing this time. 'I think you will find the *maître d'hôtel* highly efficient. I recommended him myself.'

He ushered the Dowager forward and Louisa found herself mounting the steps beside Lord Hugh Deverill. Unaccountably, she stumbled. Instantly, his hand, warm and sustaining, grasped her elbow. The effect took her breath as currents of sensation flowed up her arm and through her body.

'Thank you,' she gasped as she recovered her balance. His hand was immediately removed. 'Such a shallow step! You must think me inordinately weak and foolish!'

His reserved manner broke. He laughed. 'Really, Miss Finsham! *You*, weak and foolish?'

His manner teased and she could not resist smiling back. 'Well, I always seem to be thanking you for your assistance, my lord!'

'Which it gives me great pleasure to afford.'

She had reminded him of their previous encounter. The laughter left his face and he regarded her thoughtfully as they passed through the entrance doors.

'I was surprised to be informed of your imminent arrival,' he remarked. 'I had imagined you to be planning on a longer stay in Brussels.'

'We found nothing to delay us there, my lord,' responded Louisa neutrally. The pleasant intimacy of moments earlier had deserted them. Louisa knew the reason and regretted the loss.

'Your journey was agreeable, I trust?'

'Tolerable, I thank you. We had feared molestation by vagrants or mayhap by revolutionary peasants who resented our presence, but fortunately our fears proved groundless.'

'You were right to be cautious and to travel well-protected.'

He had the air of a man forcing himself to keep up the polite conversation. His continued reservations over her movements irked. Yet she would be lacking in conduct were she to allow her irritation to show in public.

'Even in England there are dangers,' he was going on, 'but here the nation is somewhat naturally still in turmoil. Napoleon may be finally defeated but the Bourbon dynasty has never been popular and the people suffer its restoration only because they have no choice.'

Her interest caught, her pique forgotten, she asked sharply, 'The return of King Louis is not welcome?'

He shook his head. 'No. Most Frenchmen cherish the freedom they have purchased with their blood. Many acquiesced in the Terror which so shocked us—'

'How could they?' shuddered Louisa, appalled at the very idea.

'It is perhaps difficult for you to understand, but at first it was their feudal lords and oppressors who went to the guillotine. In the end, of course, the holocaust swallowed up even its own creators.'

She turned to him indignantly. 'You have the right of it, my lord! I find it impossibly difficult to understand! The *émigrés* I have met have all been highly civilised people——'

'But haughty?' he demanded with a quizzical smile. His manner had relaxed again. This was no longer a conversation conducted for the sake of courtesy. 'A little high in the instep? Imperious in the demands made upon their inferiors?'

Louisa flushed. 'Some, my lord,' she admitted. 'But others——'

'There are good and bad in every circle, Miss Finsham. And many of the *émigrés* had of necessity to practise humility, being dependent upon the charity of others. You must know that there are plenty of Englishmen who would welcome a revolution there.'

'The Jacobins!' exclaimed Louisa scathingly.

To her relief they had caught up with Sir Charles and Amelia, who was about to greet a long line of servants gathered in the hall for her inspection. The conversation, which had threatened to become a heated argument, ended.

The tall, spare major-domo stepped forward and bowed, all stiff formality from his bewigged head to his white-stockinged legs and polished shoes. '*Bonjour, mesdames*. Welcome to the Hôtel des Fleurs, milady.'

'This,' said Sir Charles, 'is Chausson, the *maître d'hôtel*.'

The Frenchman bowed again. 'Me, myself and my staff are entirely at your service, milady.'

'Chausson gained an excellent command of English during his service in England, where he sought refuge with his master during the Revolution,' Sir Charles went on to explain. 'His master unfortunately died in exile. I believe several of the more senior servants, including the chef, are likewise able to speak our language, for similar reasons.'

Amelia beamed happily. 'Capital! For I know scarcely any French! What I learned in the schoolroom many years ago has long since been forgotten!'

'Most ladies find the knowledge returns to them when required, ma'am.'

'I do not count on it,' muttered Amelia, who considered herself too old to be re-learning old tricks.

Having booked from afar, the ladies had scarcely known what to expect of their accommodation. The agent had assured them that the house would be large enough for modest entertaining but they had not expected such lavish, if rather tarnished opulence. Nor under-servants who, without appearing obsequious, were so obviously eager to please and employed in such numbers.

'My!' exclaimed the Countess as they passed along the row acknowledging bows and curtsies. 'Where did you find all these people to staff the house, Chausson?'

'Many were employed in great households before ze Revolution, milady, and are pleased to resume zair former tasks. Eet was not ze work zey ab'orred, but zair masters. The feudal system 'as at last been abolished in France and will not return. France, she is free.'

'I see,' returned the Duchess drily. 'I trust they will not come to abhor us!'

'I sink not, milady. Ze English are more considerate.' He bowed in the direction of the two men from the embassy.

'We have a reputation to live up to, I collect,' said Louisa, unable to repress a wry grin.

'I am sure you will not find that difficult,' murmured Hugh Deverill, still seemingly glued to her side.

'And should we fail you would no doubt rejoice to see us sent to the guillotine!' returned Louisa sharply.

'Me, Miss Finsham?' He sounded startled. 'Why should you think that?'

'You speak like a Jacobin, my lord.'

She knew he was not. Some devilish imp had made her accuse him. The mischief sparked from her eyes.

He grinned. 'In my profession I must appreciate every point of view,' he defended himself lightly. 'There is always more than one side to any question. I cannot afford to be blinkered in my outlook.'

Implying that I am? wondered Louisa. If so, she had only herself to blame. But she had gone too far in this enlivening conversation to back down now. 'And one of them must be right!' she retorted smartly.

He shook his head, the smile still lingering on his lips. 'There you mistake, Miss Finsham. Both sides often have much to recommend them. That is where diplomatic compromise is required.'

'Ah, yes! Compromise!'

What scathing remark she would have made next neither of them knew, for before she could think of one, 'We must take our leave,' announced Sir Charles. 'We have already delayed your settling in for too long.

But before I go I am commissioned by Lady Stuart to extend an invitation to you both to attend a reception she is giving tomorrow evening, at the embassy. There, you will meet everyone who is anyone in Paris at the present moment.'

'The pleasure will be ours,' responded Amelia, delighted. 'Where have you set up your embassy?'

'In the building Lord Wellington chose, last year. The Hôtel de Charost, in the Rue du Faubourg St Honoré. It was acquired by Napoleon. His sister used to live there and it is one of the few mansions not sadly in need of repair. I will see that cards are sent to you immediately, my lady. May I also send a carriage for you tomorrow evening?'

'Thank you, but that will not be necessary. I have instructed Pershaw to hire an adequate coach, and I have my own horses already here. We will look forward to tomorrow.'

The men made their formal farewells. Louisa watched their retreat, her eyes lingering on the form of Hugh Deverill. Most of the men she met were either podgy or willowy. She could not imagine why. Lord Hugh was neither. Broad shoulders tapered to slim hips which allowed the square tails of his frock-coat to hang with exquisite elegance. He wore narrow trousers, she noted, with a stirrup under his shoes to keep them taut. Quietly attired rather than dressed in the first stare of fashion, he nevertheless cut an admirable figure.

She had enjoyed their sparring once he had dropped his insufferably critical attitude. She could even begin to think him attractive.

* * *

For days now Hugh's mind had been filled with pictures of an urchin-like creature dealing courageously with the discomforts of seasickness. Now he found his mental vision completely engaged by a bewitching face peeping from beneath the brim of an outrageously becoming bonnet to challenge and tease him.

After the instinctive revulsion he had felt at the discovery of her intention to follow fashion and make a macabre visit to Waterloo, he should have put her firmly from his mind. Somehow he had not been able to. Now, such a course seemed even more impossible. Had it not been for that—— He pulled his thoughts up short. They were leading to realms he would rather not contemplate, situated as he was.

Thankfully, he turned to Sir Charles, who was demanding his attention with an ironic enquiry as to whether Lord Hugh would stop wool-gathering and pay attention to the point under discussion.

As Chausson led the two ladies up the impressive curved staircase with its ornate balustrade Hugh Deverill continued to dominate Louisa's thoughts. Throughout their recent exchange she had sensed the reserve underlying his manner towards her. She resented it. Men did not normally take exception to her or her opinions. What right had he to condemn her, whatever she chose to do or think? She should not let his opinion concern her. Yet, perversely, it did.

On the first floor Chausson paused and she had to jerk her mind back to what he was saying.

'Ze withdrawing-room is 'ere, milady, and through those doors the dining-room. Behind is ze morning-room and over there a smaller reception-room. And now please allow me to show you up to the bedrooms. François!' He called imperiously to a footman labouring up under the weight of several pieces of luggage, and went on to address him in French. 'Stand aside for the Countess!'

The Dowager was shown into the master bedroom, which had a dressing-room and boudoir attached. Both ladies exclaimed over its size and the elegance of its furnishings.

'You have always loved pink and cream!' cried Louisa. 'I cannot wait to see what my room is like!'

Shown into a large, airy chamber overlooking the gardens which, judging by the profusion of blooms in the neglected beds, must have given the house its name, Louisa expressed her delight.

'Green and silver are so cool and restful! Do you not think it delightful, dear Aunt?'

'I must confess to being quite in raptures over the entire establishment, Louisa, but now I must leave you. Chausson informs me dinner will be ready to be served within the hour so we must make haste to change.'

Betty soon had the huge canopied bed buried under garments extracted from travelling boxes, piling them up ready for ironing and hanging. As the older woman left what she was doing to assist her to change, Louisa realised that her maid's normally cheerful countenance wore a gloomy expression.

'Come, Betty, what is the matter?' she chided. 'Do you not find Paris to your liking? You did not object to Brussels, I collect, despite its sad state. Paris appears to be a fine city, with plenty of sights to see and no immediate aftermath of battle to render it uncongenial.

Or is it this establishment which you find not to your liking?'

'It's not anything like that, Miss Louisa,' Betty confessed. 'Though I could do without seeing that Bastille place and the prison where the poor King and Queen were locked up before they were murdered. And I hope they've taken that dreadful guillotine away.'

'I'm sure they have,' Louisa reassured her. 'But what is it, then? You do not normally wear such a glum look.'

'Well, Miss Louisa, if the truth be told I'm worried. It seems to Rose and me that there must be plenty of smart French lady's-maids out of work over here, and both you and the Countess might prefer to have one of them to look after you.'

Astonished, Louisa spread her hands in a helpless gesture. 'Do not be foolish, Betty,' she chided. 'Have I ever shown the slightest displeasure with your work? Are we not on the best of terms? How should I be able to confide in a French maid, when I do not speak the language above a word or two?'

'I am getting old, Miss Louisa,' muttered Betty. 'You might prefer someone younger, more up-to-date in her ways.'

'Nonsense, you ridiculous creature!' Louisa gave the older woman a warm hug. 'You are scarcely in your dotage yet! Have you not been with me since I was deemed old enough to need a maid? Did you not see me through my come-out? We know each other's ways. I should dislike vastly to have anyone else look after me, I can assure you! Come now, arrange my hair and stop fretting. Do your best to see that I present a splendid appearance at dinner, even though we are to dine alone. Show these French servants what an English one can do!'

Thus reassured and challenged, Betty excelled herself. So far Louisa had not taken to wearing a cap, not having entirely resigned herself to spinsterhood. She descended the stairs dressed in fine white muslin over cornflower-blue silk, her curls threaded with matching blue ribbon in a most becoming style. A pity, she thought with a soft chuckle, that there would be no guests to enjoy the undoubted excellence of her *toilette*. And if one particular guest she had in mind happened to be Hugh Deverill that was simply because of the challenge he presented. She wished to force him to admire her, to break through his coolly critical attitude. The gentleman was altogether too sure of himself. He badly needed to have his self-consequence shaken.

The lack of guests had not daunted the French chef, who, anxious to impress his new if temporary employer, had prepared a splendid dinner which Chausson saw served with great formality in a dining-room which would accommodate a minor banquet. A huge expanse of table stretched between the two ladies as they were ushered to their allotted places.

'This looks quite delicious, Chausson,' observed Lady Nazeby, 'and the covers are laid out beautifully, but in future when we dine alone we will have the meal served in the small dining-room. Meanwhile, please have Miss Finsham's place removed to this end of the table, or we shall be unable to converse.'

Chausson bowed his acquiescence and Louisa, shaking with mirth internally while maintaining a dignified outward appearance with some difficulty, took her place at her aunt's right hand. Servants often stood upon protocol and dignity far more stiffly than did their masters.

Lady Nazeby had survived the journey well, considering her age. She, too, looked the picture of elegance in a gown of rose-pink, the colour suiting her fair complexion and the white hair escaping the confines of a matching turban. She had kept her figure remarkably well and the low neckline revealed skin only slightly dried and baggy with age.

'You,' pronounced the Dowager, eyeing her niece critically as she sat, 'will take Paris by storm, my love.'

'I hardly think so, Aunt. You are prejudiced. I still lack looks, just as I did at seventeen.'

'Nonsense!' snorted Amelia. 'You never lacked looks, though I admit you are no classical beauty. You possess something far more valuable, my dear: individuality and character. And now you are older your looks have matured into striking perfection. What man of sense wants to take a beautiful simpleton to wife?'

'Your son, for one,' muttered Louisa defensively, and then could have bitten out her tongue. The last thing she wished to do was to hurt her mentor.

But Amelia brushed the remark aside. 'Amy is no simpleton, though I must admit Robert was led astray by what he considered to be a diamond of the first water. She has sad defects of character, not brain. However, you are evading the issue, my love. You have had plenty of offers, you just refuse to consider them.'

'One I did not,' Louisa reminded her aunt quietly.

Amelia snorted again. 'Do not tell me you are still

refining over that worthless stripling Radburn! He has his just deserts. A shrewish wife——'

'Who brought him twenty thousand a year,' inserted Louisa grimly. 'I thought he loved me, Aunt. It seems he loved money more.'

'Most young men hang out for a rich bride; *you're* no simpleton, you know that. Besides, his uncle arranged the match, if you remember, against his will and over his head. There was not much he could do.'

'Except stand on his own two feet and refuse to be coerced! We could have managed quite well on my five thousand.'

'So you thought, my love, but he was an expensive young man, and knew it. I never liked him,' added Amelia flatly. 'Could never understand what you saw in him.'

Louisa sighed. 'He was very good-looking and amusing. But neither can I, now. At the time, though. . .'

'You were young and romantic, my love, and you have let that experience put you off marriage altogether.'

'Not off marriage, Aunt, but off the men who have since offered! I will not settle for a convenient match. I must want it with the whole of my being. Heart, mind and soul.'

'Don't forget body.' Amelia watched her niece blush and smiled unrepentantly. 'You should bring judgement and common sense to bear, as well as inclination and emotion. You can afford to be selective,' she granted, 'but do, I beg of you, refrain from being too difficult to please. I can imagine no worse fate than to become a lonely old woman with no family to depend upon.'

'I shall have plenty of nephews and nieces to cheer my old age. I shall make a splendid great-aunt!'

'You may joke now, Louisa, but——'

Louisa cut her aunt off. 'Do let us drop this unrewarding subject! You're doing it a bit too brown, you know. How shall we spend tomorrow, before the reception?'

'You, I collect, are riding out on Prince Hal.'

'Before breakfast, yes. But afterwards?'

Louisa could tell her aunt was reluctant to drop a subject near to her heart. Aunt Nazeby's dearest wish was to see her comfortably settled. The Dowager's face mirrored her internal struggle before she gave a resigned shrug and her expression drifted into a smile.

The last of the covers had been removed, the dessert set upon the polished table and the servants dismissed before she spoke again. 'Pershaw tells me he has managed to hire a splended coach for our stay which will hold four comfortably and six at a pinch. I will have the bays put to and we shall drive about Paris in order to leave cards with all our friends and acquaintances. Perhaps we may make a call or two. Once people know we are in residence they will call and the invitations will begin to arrive.'

'Yes, we must do the pretty, despite our attendance at the embassy later, when I suppose we shall meet them all. And,' added Louisa, 'if you will agree to lend me your bays, dear Aunt, I shall ask Pershaw to see if he can find me a light carriage to drive. The weather is fine and I cannot abide being shut in a closed conveyance for long!'

'I shall trust my horses to your care with pleasure, my love. I have every confidence in your ability as a whip. If Pershaw is able to find a suitable vehicle you may most certainly borrow them.'

With this assurance Louisa felt herself relax. Next to riding on horseback, she found her greatest pleasure in driving. And she had a new city to explore.

The morning dawned fair and cool while promising a warm day. Dressed in her newest riding habit, of a dark maroon corded material decorated with gold frogging, Louisa adjusted the white stock at her neck and set the becoming top hat more firmly on her light-brown curls. The ends of a matching gauze veil, swathed around the crown, hung in soft folds about her shoulders. After a final, critical glance in the tall mirror she pulled on her gloves, picked up her crop and went down to find Pershaw, who would be waiting in the yard of the stables and coach houses serving a group of residences of which theirs was one. This was approached from the street through a high arch, and from the house through the gardens.

Pershaw had ridden one of the Dowager's lesser horses from England, leading the carriage horses and Louisa's Prince Hal, while his boy assistant used post ponies. So he would be tolerably well mounted and not reliant upon some hired hack when he accompanied her.

When she had bought him, Prince Hal had been considered by many to be too strong for her. But Pershaw had recommended the purchase and she'd known she could trust his judgement. The wiseacres had soon been proved wrong. She enjoyed an instinctive rapport with the animals; they seemed to know she loved them and gave her their affection and obedience in return. A shared enthusiasm for horses had sealed the bond between the elderly groom and his erstwhile pupil.

That morning Hal blew his greeting, nudged her shoulder affectionately, pushed his nose beneath her arm, nipping at her habit, telling her how pleased he was to see her again.

Louisa slapped his gleaming black neck, fondled his muzzle and pushed him off with a laugh, feeding him the expected sugar.

'Yes, Hal, I'm glad to see you, too, old fellow.'

Pershaw threw her up. Hal danced a little to show he felt lively and then they moved off, Pershaw setting a sedate pace through the streets.

Louisa lost no time in mentioning her intention to hire a carriage. 'My aunt has given me permission to drive her bays, Pershaw. I shall be obliged if you will find a carriage for me. One similar to the phaeton I drive at home would suit.'

'I will see to it later today, Miss Louisa. There should be little difficulty.'

They turned into a broad, wide, rather muddy avenue, the leaves of the elm trees rustling overhead in the morning breeze.

'What is this place?' Louisa asked, looking about her with undisguised pleasure.

'They call this the Champs Elysées,' Pershaw replied. 'I am reliably informed that the road was laid out in 1670 by Le Nôtre, the man who created the royal gardens. The places of entertainment on either side have been added more recently.'

As they progressed Louisa eyed what she could see

of the pleasure gardens curiously. 'Are these places like Vauxhall or Battersea Gardens?'

'Very possibly, miss. They are mostly intended for the amusement of the lower orders, I believe.'

'In other words, no lady would be seen there?'

'Just so, miss.'

'A pity. But there must be one the *ton* visits!'

'I have heard mention of the Tivoli gardens, miss.'

'I must enquire,' smiled Louisa. The atmosphere in Paris was quite different from that in London. London represented home, and she loved it. But Paris released from the grip of revolution spelt romance, adventure, a liveliness in excess of even that found during the Season in London. Even the streets smelt different.

They shortly approached a massive structure, impressive despite still being incomplete. She eyed it speculatively.

'This must be Napoleon's triumphal arch.'

'Yes, miss.'

'Will it ever be finished, do you think?'

'I couldn't say, miss.'

Pershaw never overstepped the bounds of his position despite their very real friendship, based on mutual respect. Information he would provide, within his power, but he seldom ventured an opinion other than one connected with his job. Louisa had not expected other than a non-committal reply to a question she considered rhetorical. They continued on in companionable silence.

Having traversed another broad avenue, named after Napoleon's *Grand Armée*, they entered the Bois de Boulogne. It soon became clear to Louisa that this must be Paris's equivalent of Hyde Park.

A few keen horsemen were already out riding, most of them officers in uniform. In addition a number of grooms were to be seen, exercising their masters' animals. Louisa drew a happy breath.

This was the time of day she enjoyed most. She could indulge in a gallop while the rest of the town still lay abed. Later on, were the Bois anything like the Park, the bridle-paths would be crowded with the fashionable parading on horseback or in carriages, intent on seeing and being seen rather than on exercise. She would join them, with Aunt Nazeby, later on. But for the moment she had this part of the Bois virtually to herself. A long, empty stretch of perfect bridleway lay ahead.

'Come, Pershaw!' she cried, setting the eager Hal into a gallop. 'To the far end!'

Hal's hooves thundered over the dry ground. Louisa knew that Pershaw's slower animal would soon be left behind. But as she flew along, her veil streaming out behind her, she became aware of another set of hooves thudding close behind, threatening to overtake.

She did not know who it was—not Pershaw, of that she could be certain—and she had no time to look over her shoulder to find out. Pershaw had not called a warning, so no danger threatened. Whoever it was had therefore thrown down a challenge she was not about to ignore. Exhilaration gripped her as she urged Prince Hal to even greater efforts and triumphantly reached the end of the ride slightly ahead of her pursuer.

She drew rein and wheeled her sweating horse to face her challenger, who reined in his huge grey with consummate skill.

Lord Hugh Deverill doffed his beaver hat, bending from the waist in elaborate greeting.

CHAPTER THREE

LOUISA'S heart, which had been pumping with exertion, missed a beat. Why the mere sight of Hugh Deverill should cause her such confusion she failed to understand. No man had had the power to do so since the year of her come-out. Grey eyes met greeny hazel and held.

'Good morning, Miss Finsham.'

On this occasion his smile did reach his eyes. The lines radiating from them, together with the softened curve of his intriguing mouth, improved the amiability of his looks considerably.

'That is a prime animal you have there,' he went on admiringly. 'May I congratulate you on your horsemanship? I have seldom enjoyed a gallop more.'

Louisa acknowledged his greeting coolly, ignoring the preposterous curl of warmth forming inside her at sight of him, while wondering whether his appearance was due to coincidence or the fact that he had overheard her order to Pershaw yesterday and had sought the meeting deliberately. 'You are too kind, my lord.'

His heavy brows rose and his smile took on a wry, engaging twist. 'I but state a fact, Miss Finsham.' He patted his horse's neck. The animal tossed its aristocratic head, setting its harness jingling and its dark mane flying, blew in appreciation of the gesture but sidled edgily away from Prince Hal, who was dancing about, his energy unabated despite his run. 'Kismet can

49

catch most other horses,' went on his lordship somewhat ruefully. 'I expected to overtake you easily.'

At that moment Pershaw cantered up. He threw
Louisa an enquiring glance while keeping a respectful
distance. Louisa reassured him with a slight nod.

'You should be congratulating Lady Nazeby's head
groom, Lord Hugh. Pershaw here——' she indicated
her old friend with her crop '—selected Prince Hal for
me. I did but agree with his choice.'

Hugh Deverill glanced across and gave the groom a
friendly acknowledgement. 'You undoubtedly have an
excellent eye for a horse, Pershaw. But this fellow was
surely an unlikely choice of mount for a lady?'

'But then,' inserted Louisa quickly, 'Pershaw taught
me to ride. He knew my capabilities. Others warned
me that I'd break my neck, but so far their prediction
has not been fulfilled.'

Deverill threw back his head and laughed. 'You
confound me, Miss Finsham! By what I witnessed this
morning such an eventuality is most unlikely. Pershaw
has my hearty congratulations on choosing a mount
which matches your own spirit so exactly!'

The smile he now turned upon her appeared warm
and almost caressing. Louisa wondered whether she
had been forgiven her excursion to Waterloo. She
decided it could do no harm to return his good humour.
He certainly deserved a set-down but that could come
later. Being in high spirits herself after her exercise,
she positively beamed back.

For a split-second the sight of her radiant face
seemed to shock him into immobility. In that moment
something almost tangible seemed to flow between
them. Then, 'Shall we ride on?' he murmured, and

added quickly, 'Perhaps you will accept my escort back to your *hôtel*?'

'With pleasure, my lord.' She gestured Pershaw to follow as the two horses fell in skittishly side by side. Both were high-spirited animals, hers a gelding, his an entire, not a showy animal but well-found. 'If we can persuade our mounts to tolerate each other's company!' she added on a laugh.

He chuckled. 'They'll soon settle down. I'll warrant that before many days have passed they will be the best of friends.'

That could only mean he intended to ride with her again. A flutter of excitement stirred Louisa's senses. She was finding Hugh Deverill an attractive creature when he relaxed—and when he stopped criticising, she thought, still harbouring slight resentment. But on the other hand they did appear to share a liking for horseback riding. His presence would provide added zest to her morning excursions.

'Is the horse yours, my lord, or hired?' she ventured to enquire.

'Mine, though but recently purchased. He is ex-cavalry, a splendid animal.'

'His former owner is dead?' asked Louisa flatly.

Deverill glanced at her quickly. 'I fear so. An officer of the Greys who died of his wounds.'

'War,' observed Louisa grimly, 'is horrible. I wonder at you, in particular, considering the purchase of such an animal. He is bound to remind you of something you would rather not refine over.'

He studied her brooding face and his own expression lightened further. 'The sale will help his dependants,' he said gently. 'I paid a good price.'

Louisa stared at him for a moment and then nodded her understanding. 'Thus relieving the tragedy a little for a few people,' she acknowledged.

They rode on in silence for a while, Louisa harbouring melancholy thoughts of Amelia's son, who had ridden to his death in a cavalry charge. The silence had not been strained. Rather, it had seemed companionable. Nevertheless, she felt it time to speak again.

'Do you ride early every morning, my lord?'

Hugh brought his own wandering thoughts back to answer her.

'Most mornings, when I have no duty to prevent it.'

Her eyes shone bright with unshed tears. Had he misjudged her? Or had her visit to Waterloo proved salutary? Deverill adjusted his ideas, decided that he might have been too harsh. She held an elusive attraction for him that he could neither explain nor deny. Even caught in the throes of seasickness she had exuded some quality he found quite entrancing. He would have pursued the acquaintance immediately but for that unfortunate exchange at Calais. And, he admitted to himself wryly, for the fact that he knew Lady Nazeby's niece to be an heiress. He wanted no entanglement that could cast him in the role of fortune-hunter.

But he had set out to meet her this morning unable to resist the temptation offered by that overheard order to the groom. Now he was glad he had for her attitude seemed to have changed since Calais and the memory was fading. He could seek her company with a clearer conscience, if not a quieter mind. He smiled again, unable to resist the delight he found in her company.

'And you?'

Louisa's defences began to crumble before the battery of so much charm. When he tried he was able to turn it on to quite ruinous effect. He must have something about him to attract such a reputation for seduction, she supposed, and as far as she knew it was neither fortune nor rank, for younger sons, even of dukes—especially impoverished dukes, as Chadford was reputed to be—were considered of little account. Yet according to Amelia he had not lacked chances to wed a fortune. And according to rumour he did not lack for mistresses.

'Yes,' she admitted, fiddling quite unnecessarily with Hal's harness in order to avoid having to look at him and lose her countenance completely. 'Unless I have been up to all hours the previous night,' she added, a trifle breathless despite the sedate pace of their progress.

'Ah! Balls do tend to continue into the early hours, do they not? The social round here can be exhausting— several receptions, soirées and parties are held every night, not to mention the balls. Lady Stewart is to hold one on the sixteenth. I have little doubt you will receive an invitation once she knows you are here.'

'You already have yours?'

'Attached to the British Embassy as I am, I am the recipient of invitations to almost every function and am obliged to attend most, for in addition to discharging my duties to the English community I am required to cement relations with the French and other foreign leaders here.'

'Oh, lud!' exclaimed Louisa. 'That should prevent you enjoying yourself.'

He laughed. 'Not at all! It is something I seem to be

good at! I don't in the least mind. But evening parties are not the only entertainments to be found in Paris.'

Louisa had recovered her poise enough to meet his eyes, her own dancing. 'There are more delights?' she breathed in mock-awe.

'Oh, many more!' His tone had become light and bantering, matching hers. 'It is a pity you arrived too late to see the Allied review of the sixty-five thousand troops stationed around the capital. I am certain you would have enjoyed the spectacle.'

'It must have been some sight! Tell me about it, pray.'

He smiled a little and prepared to oblige. 'It was indeed an impressive sight. Most of the troops looked exceptionally smart and the Duke's manoeuvres were accomplished extremely smoothly, to the admiration of all!'

'I could wish the troops' behaviour in Paris matched their parade-ground discipline!'

'Lord Wellington's command is superior in that as in every other way. He will brook no laxity on the part of his commanders. The British troops are well-disciplined at all times.'

'So I am given to understand.'

Hugh nodded. 'You would have enjoyed the cavalry,' he continued, his tone becoming enthusiastic. 'I have never before seen such handsome horses. Our own Guards—those who survived that disastrous charge,' he added on a more sombre note, 'were magnificent, as you would expect, as were the Royal Horse artillery. All taken together it was a splendid show, a grand occasion. The Emperor of Russia and the Duke of Wellington took the salute. Everyone was there.'

'I am sure it must have been. War may be dreadful but a military parade always stirs the emotions. One cannot help but be proud of one's army.'

'Very true. And parades have the virtue of being harmless entertainment.'

'Indeed they do! How people can drive out to watch them in action——' She pulled herself up. Noting Hugh's quizzical look, she quickly changed the subject, having no wish to revive the question of her visit to the battlefield. 'How is the Duke?' she asked. 'I have not seen him this age, since he was in London last year, receiving his share of the adulation during the visit of the Allied Sovereigns.'

'He is well. The most important and influential man in Paris, of course. And enjoying the adoration and company of the fair sex. But you will be able to judge the Duke's condition for yourself this evening. He will be at our reception, you may be sure. He goes everywhere.'

Louisa suspected she could detect a degree of censure in his voice, which surprised her, given his own reputation. With her background she was bound to have her own reservations about the Duke of Wellington's friendships with women but had not expected Deverill to share them.

'You disapprove of him?' she enquired, voicing her surprise.

'Not at all, my dear Miss Finsham. Why should I? As with me, it is his duty to be present.'

'Of course,' agreed Louisa, wondering at the endearment, surprised to discover that she did not resent it.

'But—in other ways, perhaps?' she ventured. 'There have been so many rumours circulating about him in London and here. Did not Lady Shelley ride with him at the review we have been speaking of?'

'She did. Many remarked on the fact.'

His tone was non-committal. Louisa probed further.

'I had heard that Lady Frances Wedderburn-Webster was his latest flirt.'

'She was reputedly so, in Brussels.' Hugh gave a short laugh which lacked humour. 'But this is scandal-mongers' tattle, and I would prefer not to indulge in it further,' he declared.

Louisa could not resist a dig. 'Very wise, my lord. After all, he is not the only man who attracts the attention of the gossips.'

Hugh looked at her sharply, suspicious of her bland tone. To her satisfaction she saw a tinge of red appear on his broad cheekbones.

'Not all rumour is true,' he pointed out stiffly.

'Indeed, happily it is not.' Was he implying that the rumours concerning him were untrue? She did not dare pursue the subject, but how she wished she could! 'As you have reminded me, it is unwise to indulge in scandalous discussion,' she said instead. 'Especially for a diplomat.'

'A poor one, I fear, Miss Finsham,' he responded rather grimly.

'Oh, I don't know. I have heard that you travelled to America and did much to negotiate the peace with our former colony. That must have required considerable skill.'

The tone of her voice denied the admiration implicit in her words. She saw his colour deepen.

'More tittle-tattle, ma'am. No man can do more than his best, however threadbare that may be.'

'But you gained the admiration of Lord Castlereagh,' she persisted archly, some devil of mischief driving her on.

'I perceive, Miss Finsham, that I have offended you in some way. If that is so, I apologise. May we not drop this unprofitable subject and ride in amity?'

Louisa drew a sharp breath. She refused to fence with words any longer. The air must be cleared between them. 'Why should we, my lord? You seem to bear me some grudge for showing an interest in the battlefield at Waterloo. Is it wrong to be proud of our army's victory?'

He sighed. His broad shoulders drooped slightly under the dark green riding-coat, then straightened again. 'No, Miss Finsham. If I appeared to criticise I regret my lapse. I, too, rejoice in the Allied victory, and admire the Duke for what he achieved with such an infamous—to use his own term—army at his command. Had he had more of his experienced Peninsula divisions to rely upon the outcome might not have been such a near run thing. It was a dearly bought victory. The Duke himself regrets the loss of so many fine men. He spent some days in Brussels after the victory mourning them.'

'Of course he must, as do we all.' In particular Robert, the late Earl of Thurrock, she thought, her expression brooding. She had known and admired him, without knowing him to be her aunt's son. Her own cousin.

'It was Lord Wellington's defensive skills which won the day, holding on until the Prussians arrived.' Hugh steadied his horse and emitted another short laugh. 'Had old Marshal Blücher not been determined to keep his word to the Duke and insisted on marching on to Waterloo after his army's defeat at Ligny, Bonaparte's plan would have worked. He set out to divide and conquer. He expected the old man to do what Allied commanders had always done in the past—retreat towards their communications and thus save their own army at the expense of another.'

'But Blücher was made of sterner, more honourable stuff! If only that lesson had been learned earlier!'

'Indeed. Miss Finsham, I congratulate you. I did not expect you to understand the import of his actions so readily. And this morning I discover that you, too, find the business of war disagreeable.' He hesitated a moment, collecting his thoughts before going on. 'I have always failed to understand the morbid curiosity which takes so many people on a visit to the battlefield. I hear that making up a party for the purpose is currently the main source of amusement in Brussels. To walk about and pick up anything to be found—any residue of battle—even, perhaps, a soiled letter.'

The question was implicit, but there. Louisa remembered his remark at Calais and winced. So that was what he had alluded to. She stared straight ahead as she answered.

'I think it a minority who indulge in such macabre souvenir-hunting. Has it never occurred to you, Lord Hugh, that some people may be going because they lost a loved one there? That they are making a kind of pilgrimage?'

He looked suddenly stricken and turned to challenge her gaze. 'You?'

She shook her head, meeting his eyes candidly. 'No. But my aunt lost someone she was fond of. I accompanied her.'

He reined in sharply and she did likewise. He stared at her, a kind of horrified desperation on his face. 'How can I ever apologise enough? Please forgive me, dear Miss Finsham.'

She nodded, and a small smile curved the corners of her wide mouth. Greeny hazel eyes sparkled into his. He thought there were tears there.

The endearment was back in front of her name and she was glad. She had need to steady her voice before she spoke. 'You are forgiven, my lord. Your motive, I collect, was honourable.'

'And is why I have attempted to use any skill I may possess in the diplomatic field in the pursuit of peace.'

'A worthy aim which I fully endorse.'

'So, we are friends, dear Miss Finsham?'

'Friends, Lord Hugh.'

The declaration gave her spirits a decided lift. He had received his set-down—mild, as it had turned out, but she'd succeeded in discomfiting him for a few moments—and now the rift was healed. After a moment's silence she spoke again, a note of regret in her voice. 'I fear I must return to the Hôtel des Fleurs soon, or my aunt will wonder what has become of me.' She turned a mischievous smile on him. 'So, my lord, shall we race for the gates? A guinea on it!'

He accepted the challenge immediately. 'Kismet is already straining at his bit! A guinea it shall be!'

The horses raced like the fine steeds they were. Neck and neck they thundered along, the few other riders scattering to let them through. Prince Hal began to lose ground and Louisa urged him to greater effort. But, though Hal went faster than he had ever gone before, still the grey edged ahead and Louisa knew his rider would not hold him in to allow her to win. She was flattered by his lordship's obvious appreciation of her abilities and surprised by his care for her sensibilities.

Kismet won by half a length. Panting, laughing, Louisa eased Prince Hal into a walk and the two blowing, sweating animals moved through the gates and into the avenue side by side. Pershaw was gaining on them quickly, and would soon take his place a few lengths behind.

'Thank you, my lord!' Louisa's happy voice rang out despite her lack of breath. 'I have not enjoyed myself as much this age! I find it difficult to find a worthy opponent. Pershaw's mount is not fast enough, and most gentlemen think it necessary to hold their horses to allow me to win. Thank you for not doing so. I owe you a guinea. You shall receive your due this evening!'

His grey eyes, which seemed more blue than they had yesterday, actually twinkled. 'I could not impede the spirit of either horse or rider, dear Miss Finsham. A race, like a battle, should be fought to win. Any other course betrays either a lack of enthusiasm or an ulterior motive in the loser.'

'What possible ulterior motive could a gentleman have for allowing me to win?' demanded Louisa. 'I had always thought it a matter of chivalry!'

He grinned. 'They may think it the best way to fix your interest.'

Louisa's snort made Prince Hal's ears flatten. 'Then more fool they! But you did not think it to be so, my lord?'

Flirtation was a game she had practised for many years, using it to hold off her admirers. Much of the conversation that morning would have been considered too outspoken for a properly brought up young lady to indulge in with a gentleman and had held little of coquetry on her part. But Louisa was no longer a young miss and in any case had always spoken her mind. Rashly, she was asking him whether he wished to fix her interest. Despite the flirtatious manner in which her question had been posed she was now inviting a set-down. But the devil in her wanted to make this man uncomfortable again.

But he didn't look in the least uncomfortable. 'I had not made up my mind,' he returned blandly.

Made up his mind to what? Insufferable creature! Now he had *her* mortified at having exposed herself so!

But he ignored her heightened colour and, as they passed the embryo Arc de Triomphe and moved into the Champs Elysées, began to point out the various places of amusement lining its muddied, leafy path.

The carriage Pershaw had chosen proved adequate in every way. After a morning spent roaming the quarter of Paris where the *haut ton* resided leaving their cards, and afterwards having partaken of a light luncheon, Louisa and the Dowager joined the throng of fashionable carriages parading along the Champs Elysées at the end nearest to the Place de la Concorde. This, apparently, was where those in the first circle promenaded as an alternative to the Bois de Boulogne. Between the road and the river rose the Grand Palais and the Petit Palais. On the far side of the Place, where a regiment of soldiers was being drilled, could be glimpsed the Jardin des Tuileries, and beyond that the royal Palace of the Louvre. The Palais Royal must be visible in the distance somewhere, but she could not make it out.

'Paris has a vast number of palaces within its boundaries,' Louisa remarked as she nodded and smiled to an old acquaintance.

'I should like to see Versailles,' murmured the Dowager. 'Oh, look, there is the Countess Lieven! She is smiling at us! I wonder whether she will attend the reception tonight? And, I do declare, there is Amy Thurrock, parading the boy for all to see! I suppose she wishes to impress her consequence as widow of one and mother of another English earl!'

Louisa craned her neck to catch a glimpse of Amelia's grandson. She was acquainted with his mother, of course, but had never met the boy, since he was too young to move in Society. At first she could see very little, for the coachman and footman on the approaching carriage's box obscured her view, and Pershaw and Dench on their box were in the way too. But as the two carriages met she obtained a clearer view.

The Dowager Countess of Thurrock acknowledged the Dowager Countess of Nazeby and her companion with an artificial smile and a slight inclination of her head. Louisa returned the greeting politely before turning her attention to the new Earl.

He resembled his father, she thought, from what she could remember. Robert had been a little darker, but the boy had his open countenance. His blue eyes took in everything going on about him. Both mother and son were, of course, wearing mourning; Amy looked pale and ethereal in her black, the young Earl sombre and rather subdued.

Amelia had Pershaw halt the carriage and Amy could not do otherwise than order her coachman to draw up. The footmen sprang down to hold the horses.

'My dear Amy!' cried Amelia with false warmth. 'How delightful to see you! We shall give ourselves the pleasure of calling upon you shortly! And you, my lord!' she addressed the good-looking boy cheerfully. 'James, my dear boy! So you are the Earl now!'

'I wish Father had not been killed,' responded James. His voice shook. 'I would rather *never* have inherited than that Papa should have died!' he added fiercely.

'We all share in your grief,' Amelia assured him, her own voice far from steady. 'To think he came through the Peninsula campaign only to die now! War is cruel.'

'But I must shoulder my responsibilities bravely,' asserted young James, no doubt repeating a lesson relentlessly instilled. 'How do you do, ma'am?' he added rather tardily, lifting his hat and making a grave bow.

'Well enough, I thank 'ee.' Amelia indicated Louisa with a wave of her hand. 'My lord, may I present Miss Finsham, my very dear niece? I do not believe you have previously met.'

Louisa smiled at Amelia's grandson, a slight mistiness before her eyes. What an excellent creature he was! Showing such sensibility at so young an age! She loved him already. But she could see that he needed protection from his mother's less agreeable nature. Amy Thurrock was prodding him in the ribs.

'Don't stare, boy! Make your bow as you've been taught!'

Colour rushed into the lad's face. He had been gazing as though mesmerised at the lovely, fashionable woman giving him such a warm smile. 'P-pleased to make your ac-acquaintance, Miss Finsham,' he stuttered.

'My lord,' murmured Louisa. 'I am honoured to make yours.' She flashed him a reassuring smile. 'Do you ride horseback?'

'Of course!' He had recovered his composure quickly and now sounded rather indignant that she should feel the need to ask.

'Then perhaps I may see you in the Bois de Boulogne one morning. I often ride there before breakfast.'

'Really, Miss Finsham?'

His enthusiasm was plain. Louisa decided to push her luck.

'My groom and I could call for you one day, if that would suit?'

'He has his own grooms!' cried his mother indignantly. 'If he wishes to ride he will be accompanied by his tutor and a groom from his own household.'

'But, Mama, there can be no need to trouble——'

Amy cut him off firmly. 'They are paid to be troubled! If you wish to ride you will do so with them in attendance. But,' she added, shafting an insincere smile at Louisa, 'I am sure your offer was well-meant, Miss Finsham, and I thank you for taking an interest in a fatherless boy.'

'I was used to ride with Papa when he was home,' gulped James, near to tears but swallowing them down manfully. 'I shall look out for you, ma'am.'

'And I you.'

Further civilities having been exchanged, the two carriages moved on, for they were causing a blockage.

'So,' said Amelia. 'What do you, think?'

'He is a fine boy,' said Louisa sincerely, 'and stands up to his mother well, but he needs help. I trust we shall become friends.'

That evening Louisa chose her dress with especial care. In due course she would order new gowns from one of the distinguished French mantua-makers who plied their trade in Paris but meanwhile she had plenty of elegant English gowns to choose from.

'Which one, Betty?' she wondered, eyeing the selection laid out on the bed. A profusion of white crêpe and muslin, some sprigged, of yellow gauze, and silks of palest pink, forget-me-not blue, leaf-green, primrose, ivory, lilac, and a light brown rather like milky tea, met her eyes.

'The green suits you, Miss Louisa.'

'I know—but I think it must be the white crêpe for my first appearance. The bugle beads are all securely attached, I trust?'

'Of course, Miss Louisa.' Rather indignantly, Betty picked up the garment and spread it for her mistress's inspection. The pearl-like white beads decorating the tiny bodice shone satisfactorily in the late afternoon sunlight. 'I ironed the satin petticoat only today, and the ribbon trimmings are fresh as the day the dress was made.'

'Yes.' Louisa fingered the satin and the tiny pink and blue flowers nestling among the ruched ribbon encircling the low neckline and the hem, the only touch of colour the mantua-maker had allowed. 'I have had it only a short time and worn it very little. It will do splendidly. Is the hot water ready?'

'It should be here any moment. I don't know what those lazy Frenchies are about!'

Whereas only yesterday Betty had gone in fear of losing her position, now she was treating the French servants with superior scorn. At that moment the pitcher of steaming water arrived and Betty was able to receive it with a sniff and an 'About time, too!' which the young maidservant probably did not understand, thought Louisa, amused.

An hour later, with the last of the sun casting a rosy glow over her, Louisa slipped the dress over her chemise and inspected the result in the ormolu-framed cheval mirror.

Betty had excelled herself in arranging her hair, threading her brown curls with beads and ribbons to admiration. The scandalously low-necked bodice, permissible in a woman of her more advanced years, emphasised her feminine shape, the little puffed sleeves the slenderness of her arms. The skirt hung in gentle folds from the fashionable, slightly lower waistline to an elaborately decorated hem easing into a train.

Louisa twisted this way and that, assuring herself that all was as it should be. She could do nothing about her colouring, which lacked the pale fairness fashion demanded, though her complexion remained clear enough *and* without the use of Gowland's Lotion. Against the whiteness of her gown it had taken on an ivory hue. But she had accepted this limitation on her fashionable appearance many years ago and in truth had suffered little from its consequences. Satisfied at last, she draped a fine scarf over her arm, smoothed down the long trailing ends of the satin bow flowing from beneath her bust and picked up her feathered fan and tiny silk reticule. A final glance in the mirror assured her that she was fit to make her first entrance into Parisian Society.

They were by no means the first to arrive. Judging by the attendance, Sir Charles and Lady Stuart were well-liked and offered fine hospitality. They greeted the Dowager and herself warmly.

Lord Hugh Deverill, Louisa noted, was engaged in serious conversation with a group of gentlemen at the far end of the glittering salon. Though no Corinthian unable to move for the skin-tightness of his garments, he appeared to advantage in evening dress. She could not help but notice him, for he stood out as a fine figure of a man among so many less well-endowed in stature. One in particular, whom she later discovered to be Prince Talleyrand, had a club foot, which did not improve his awkward, heavy, shapeless appearance. Even from a distance she took a dislike to his ugly features and his unpleasant laugh. She pitied Lord Hugh for having to converse with such men.

Her attention was soon distracted by the greetings of friends and by introductions to those she had not met before. The Dowager found a chair on which to sit and coze amicably with ladies of her own age, leaving Louisa to mix as she would.

Soon Louisa's voice could be heard exchanging lively conversation with a group of younger guests, among whom were a blue-coated dragoon captain, a couple of red-coated officers of the line regiments and a hussar distinguished by his golden tassels and fine boots. Uniforms representing most of the allied armies were scattered about the salon, their buttons and metal accoutrements scintillating in the light from myriad candles set in chandeliers and sconces, their brilliant colours mingling with the delicate shades of the ladies' gowns. Every glittering detail was reflected in the huge mirrors lining the walls.

Although almost surrounded by admirers, she was not surprised, shortly afterwards, to hear a deep voice she instantly recognised speak at her shoulder. She had known he would seek her out.

'Miss Finsham. My apologies for not being free to greet you on your arrival. I am happy you are able to be here.'

Louisa swung round to receive his formal bow. She curtsied in response, smiling her pleasure at seeing him again.

'Do not apologise, my lord! I have been well-entertained!'

He produced a wry smile. 'So I have observed.'

For some mysterious reason her court had melted away. That Hugh Deverill could have such an effect upon perfectly self-assured young men had not previously occurred to her. And had he been watching her? Flattering if he had. She flashed him a brilliant smile.

'Here, my lord! I do not forget my debts!'

She opened her reticule and dug in its depths, bringing out a golden guinea. He accepted the coin with a grave bow belied by the laughter in eyes which sought hers.

'I will afford you the chance to recoup your losses soon, dear Miss Finsham.'

Again that promise to ride with her! Louisa's heart

began to flutter—a feat it seemed determined to perform every time she met Hugh Deverill.

Just behind him stood an older man, almost as tall as himself, possessed of a good figure and a pleasant countenance, accompanied by an elegant woman of about Amelia's age. Louisa had met neither of them before.

Hugh turned to include them in the conversation. 'May I present Monsieur Alexandre d'Arblay and his wife, Madame d'Arblay, Miss Finsham?' Everyone made their devoirs. 'Monsieur d'Arblay was chief of staff to the Maquis de Lafayette,' Deverill went on, 'and is a liberal constitutionalist helping to put France on its feet again. His wife you may know best as Miss Fanny Burney, the famous novelist. I thought you would be interested to meet her.'

'Of course!' exclaimed Louisa with pleasure. 'Dear ma'am, I have read all your books with such delight! My aunt, the Dowager Countess of Nazeby, subscribed to *Camilla*! It is indeed an honour to meet you.'

'You flatter me, Miss Finsham.'

'If you will excuse us, I fear Monsieur d'Arblay and I must return to our discussion with Prince Talleyrand and the others. But,' Hugh added, looking straight into Louisa's eyes, 'I shall look forward to speaking with you again later.'

The men departed and Louisa soon discovered how Fanny Burney had met her husband while he was living in exile at Juniper Hall, in Surrey.

'He had been dispossessed of all his lands and fortune and was very depressed,' explained Madame d'Arblay. 'I met him when I went to stay with my sister, who lived near by. Quite a colony of exiles lived at Juniper Hall. Have you met Madame de Staël yet?'

'No, *madame*. We arrived but yesterday.'

'She does not appear to be here tonight, which is strange. But you will no doubt attend her salon before long. She is a fellow authoress, a great debater, and wields great influence.'

Louisa laughed. 'I shall look forward to meeting her!'

Madame d'Arblay chuckled. 'She is quite formidable, I assure you! And men adore her, despite her unfortunate looks.'

'But not Monsieur d'Arblay, I suspect!'

'No, indeed, although he admires her greatly. Thank God my husband was able to return to France under Napoleon, for he endured his exile with great chafing of the spirit. Now he feels he can truly serve his country once again.'

'And you do not mind making your home in France, ma'am?'

Fanny d'Arblay smiled. 'I am no exile. I am able to visit England whenever I wish. Besides, home to me is where my husband is.'

Louisa wondered for a moment whether she could ever be happy living in some foreign land, whomever it was with. But she had little time to ponder the question, for a stir at the door interrupted her thoughts.

'The Duke has come at last,' murmured Madame d'Arblay. 'It is his habit to arrive late. See how the ladies cluster around him!' She laughed slightly. 'He is besieged wherever he goes.'

'His was a famous victory,' murmured Louisa noncommittally. 'He is coming this way.'

'Since Waterloo he is become the most important

personage of the day. I have the honour of knowing him quite well, and admire him enormously.'

'Despite his liking for the ladies?'

'Even the best of men can behave foolishly when flattered by a woman. Unfortunately he is susceptible to the fair sex.'

'It is his wife I pity.'

'And I. But she is quite unsuited to the position he now holds. He proposed as a young man, you know. The marriage has proved to be a sad mistake.'

'But he is wed, and the flirtations in which he indulges cannot, surely, be excused by a man who protests to behave with honour!'

'His conscience is his own, my dear. I only know that I find him a most agreeable friend.'

It would have been inexcusable to pursue the matter further. Louisa silently watched the famous man's progress.

He had entered quietly with a dark woman on his arm.

'La Grassini,' murmured Madame d'Arblay helpfully under her breath. 'The Emperor's erstwhile mistress. She has found favour with the Duke, too.'

'And the lady now claiming his other arm is Frances, Lady Shelley, I see. I have not met her this age.'

'She would not be far behind! He has been paying her marked attention lately.'

'But where is Lady Frances Wedderburn-Webster?' wondered Louisa.

'In retirement. The creature is expecting to be confined at any moment,' murmured Louisa's companion somewhat tartly.

As he approached them, the Duke greeted both

women as old friends, immediately effecting introductions to the ladies on his arms.

'Madame d'Arblay!' he went on effusively. 'You appear in splendid health! And Miss Finsham. Oh, yes. My dear young lady, at last to have the pleasure of your company here! Your appearance is positively enchanting tonight. It does a man good simply to look at you.'

Doing it a bit too brown, thought Louisa. He was in his mid-forties, no longer young, but not old, either. And as for his heavy-handed compliments—she supposed she should be used to them by now. She kept a smile on her face and greeted the great man charmingly. After all, as Madame d'Arblay had found, there was much to admire about Arthur Wellesley even if his hair was thinnning and his nose seemed to protrude more noticeably than ever. Most women found him attractive. She did not happen to be one of them.

She was about to make a curtsy and send him on his way when she caught a glimpse of Deverill, standing behind the Duke, his expression forbidding.

His eyes seemed to be boring into her. Did he think her about to succumb to the allure of power? How dared he look at her like that?

Her gaze returned to Wellington's face. He still smiled at her, clearly desiring to prolong their exchange despite the two women already hanging on his arms. An idea sprang into her head. She would show Hugh Deverill exactly how much his displeasure meant to her! She laughed, albeit rather shrilly.

'My lord, I do not think I have yet paid tribute to your victorious generalship!' Quite deliberately, she stepped towards him. 'How else may I show my appreciation of your great victory but with a kiss?'

CHAPTER FOUR

LOUISA reached out, took his face between her hands and kissed him on both cheeks in the approved French style.

The Duke, not at all embarrassed, gave one of his neighing laughs and said, 'You are not the first to offer me such a charming salute, Miss Finsham.'

'Your Grace,' responded Louisa, curtsying again, wishing heartily that she had not indulged her pique with Hugh Deverill in such a manner. Not understanding her friend's action but sensing her acute embarrassment, Madame d'Arblay intervened.

'We all thank God that the Legislature demanded Napoleon's abdication and negotiated peace so that Paris itself did not have to be conquered by force of arms, your Grace. The city escaped without need of battle.'

Wellington smiled. 'I too am glad we did not have to fight in the streets of Paris, Madame d'Arblay. Blücher's men merely harried Bonaparte's troops to its gates.'

'Those of us who reside here have no fault to find with the British soldiery,' went on Fanny d'Arblay earnestly, 'but we could wish that other victorious armies of occupation would behave with more restraint. They trample the cornfields and ransack the homes of those less fortunate than ourselves.'

Wellington frowned, his face grave. 'Blücher is a

famous old fellow but seems unable to stop his troops
from plundering. Have you met him?'

Both ladies admitted that they had not yet had the
privilege of meeting the Prussian marshal.

'He's over there.' The Duke indicated an elderly man
with a large moustache who was engaged in some
uproarious joke with his companions. 'Allow me to
effect the introductions.'

She could scarcely refuse. As Louisa joined the
throng of ladies now surrounding the hero of Waterloo
and followed him across the room, she noted that Lord
Hugh Deverill had disappeared.

Hugh found himself more disturbed than he was prepared to admit by the scene he had just witnessed.
Louisa knew the Duke—why should she not speak with
him? She must greet him, or be accused of lack of
conduct. What concerned him was her reaction to
catching his own eye as he watched the great man. Why
had she behaved in such an extraordinary manner?

He caught a glimpse of her across the salon. She had
been drawn into the Duke's immediate circle and he
did not like it. Gossip would be bound to follow. She
had already invited it. But the consequences of that
rash action of hers might die a quick natural death if
she could be persuaded to drop out of the Duke's set.

He took no conscious decision, but it was not long
before he had excused himself from the small crowd of
guests gathered around him and made his way to her
side.

Louisa could never afterwards decide quite how he had
done it. She discovered Hugh Deverill at her elbow

and tried to ignore him but, with a skill she assumed to be the result of long practice, he had soon detached her from the Duke's court and steered her out of the salon.

He had smiled, murmured, 'Come with me, I have something to show you,' and she had obeyed.

She was still wondering why when they reached the comparative calm of the hall. People were strolling about and servants passed to and fro but there was no crush here.

'Well, my lord,' she demanded, assuming a coolness she did not feel, for she knew she had behaved outrageously, and conscience and embarrassment were assaulting her, 'what is it you wish me to see?'

His hand touched her elbow, turning her towards open double doors. 'The ballroom,' he told her. 'It is magnificent, as are many of the other rooms. This was a palace, after all. And I think the library would interest you.'

'You intend to give me a personally conducted tour? I am honoured, my lord.'

'No need to be.' He grinned, all his charm directed towards lifting her from her present mood. ''Twas merely an excuse to avail myself of your company. But I believe you will appreciate what you see.'

Louisa was not proof against his persuasive manner. She smiled back. 'In that case, let us proceed!'

'May I offer you my arm?'

'Thank you, my lord.'

The tour began. Louisa was certainly impressed by the size of the rooms and the splendour of the decorations and furniture, but far more affected by the extensive knowledge and intimate manner of her companion. Finally, he led her into the library.

The room was empty and although the door stood open, for convention's sake, they were essentially alone. She had forgotten the Duke and all that had gone before in the pleasure of Hugh's company. She gave an exclamation, dropped his arm, and started forward.

'What a wonderful collection of books!' she cried, turning impulsively to demand of her escort. 'Are they all in French?'

'By no means! There are many here belonging to the embassy. You like reading, dear Miss Finsham?'

'Above everything!'

'I fear there are few novels in this collection.'

'That does not signify,' said Louisa. 'My aunt teases me about the learned books I read!'

He chuckled. 'Independent in all matters, including your choice of reading, I collect, my dear Miss Finsham! I can see no reason why you should not borrow from here, if any of the books interest you.'

'Really?' Louisa's eagerness and gratitude shone from her eyes. He actually seemed to approve, whereas most men, while not critical, were condescending in their attitude. 'Thank you. Mayhap I can come one day and inspect them?'

He smiled. 'Indeed you may. I will mention it to Sir Charles.'

Louisa ran her finger along the spines of the nearest volumes and turned back to him. 'But now, my lord, grateful as I am and much as I appreciate your company, I feel I should return to the salon. My aunt will be wondering what has become of me.'

His face immediately sobered. 'Will you return to the Duke's company?' he asked.

Louisa's eyes opened wide. Memory returned. 'Why should I not?'

He appeared to hesitate, but then proceeded somewhat apologetically to say, 'I would account it the height of foolishness. You would become the object of gossip.'

She had already laid herself open to that, and knew it. But what business was that of Hugh Deverill's? How dared he lecture her? Had he shown her over the embassy in order to create an opportunity to do so? Disappointment gave her voice an added edge.

'Were I to avoid every gentleman the gossips tease I should feel free to address very few!' she returned smartly.

'True again, my dear Miss Finsham. But in his position the Duke would be wise to show more discretion. The tattle-mongers scarcely need to utter a word.'

'Nonsense! He merely enjoys the company of attractive women!'

She knew she was defending the Duke against all her true instincts. Hugh Deverill had that effect upon her. He stood looking at her, and the look in his eyes made her long to be at peace with him. Yet she could not bring herself to admit to an error of judgement. She had enjoyed independence for too long to be dictated to over such a matter now. She drew a breath.

'And because you do not approve my conduct I must in future ignore a great man? Is that the truth of it?'

He shook his head in denial. 'I have only your reputation at heart, Miss Finsham.'

'My reputation is of consequence to no one but myself, my lord! And now, if you will excuse me, I will return to my aunt!'

She flounced round and left the library before he could see the tears in her eyes.

Independence, thought Hugh, could be charming. He admired it. Yet it could also lead to uncomfortable consequences. With the best intentions in the world he had managed to alienate her.

He did not take exercise in the Bois the next morning; or if he did it was not within sight of her. James did not appear, either. Despite the advent of several young gentlemen with whom she had become acquainted the previous evening, all vying with each other to ride by her side, Louisa returned to the Hôtel des Fleurs feeling unusually depressed.

The previous evening had proved a disaster. The Duke, she realised, thoroughly enjoyed the adoration to which he was subjected. But if the *ton* hoped to discomfit her by their gossip, Louisa determined that they should not succeed. At least to all appearances.

They were, after all, in Paris, where no one but the English would dream of making a great work out of so innocent a salute. She would quote St Ambrose's dictum. Point out that he had advised that when in Rome one should live in the Roman style, and so she could surely allow herself a small excursion into the ways of the Parisians!

A perverse streak in Louisa's nature had driven her to join the sycophantic throng in the face of Hugh Deverill's obvious displeasure. When, later in the evening, he had sought her out, she had so enjoyed his company until he had tried to warn her off involvement with the Duke. She hadn't needed warning, and his interference still rankled.

Her reaction, on returning to the salon, had been to behave in a lively manner, flirting with the Duke and his ADCs and with officers of other nationalities, too. Her laugh had rung out while all the time, inside, all she'd felt was confusion. Just because Hugh Deverill had taken her to task she'd found herself behaving in a fashion quite at odds with her normal demeanour, and she didn't exactly know why. She was usually lively, yes. She often flirted mildly, too. But last night some inner turmoil had driven her on to an extreme of behaviour she now sincerely regretted.

The result had been to ensure her a bevy of admirers wherever she went and life was too full of reviews, balls, receptions, soirées and visits to the theatre for her to refine over anything for long. She managed to push Hugh Deverill to the back of her mind and ignore his intrusion there. Well, almost.

The invitations poured in. July drifted into August. Hugh Deverill never again appeared in the Bois to ride with her, but thrusting him from her mind completely proved difficult, for he was at every function she attended, hovering in the background and, she was quite certain, watching her every move.

To her delight young James appeared in the Bois one morning, accompanied by his tutor, a gentleman named William Coynd, the youngest son of a landed family forced to put his Oxford education to good use in the earning of a living. He had no expectations and would be condemned to tutoring all his life unless he could wed a fortune. He was a personable young man and Louisa found him agreeable.

Her friendship with James grew apace. He had a

passion for horses so, despite the disparity in their ages, they had plenty of interest in common.

'You ride awfully well, Miss Finsham,' he remarked after a particularly fine gallop.

His pony had struggled gamely to keep up with Prince Hal. Since it had not been called a race, Louisa had held Hal back so that they could remain side by side.

'So do you, my lord. Do you not find this time of day quite splended for riding? I so enjoy the early morning.'

'Mama did not wish me to come,' confessed James, 'but I persuaded her to allow it. I shall be glad when I am old enough to please myself without having to ask her permission for everything I do.'

'I am sure she has your best interests at heart,' murmured Louisa, mentally crossing her fingers for what she suspected to be a lie.

'Papa had resigned his commission, you know. He had to return to the colours, of course, when the call came. I wish he had not died. He was very brave.'

His voice wavered and the tears were not far away but he manfully thrust them back. 'I miss him most terribly,' he confessed. Louisa wished she could stretch out a hand to comfort him but the size of James's pony rendered that impossible.

She offered what solace she could. 'I knew him, a little. We met on several occasions when he was on leave from the Peninsula, and during last autumn. I thought him a fine gentleman.'

'Did you?' James's face lit up. 'Where did you meet? What did he say?'

He wanted to talk about his father, and Louisa obliged, as far as she was able. If she exaggerated the extent of her acquaintance with the dead Earl, she told herself she was justified by the pleasure her reminiscing brought his son.

'I shall ride every morning,' announced James as they parted that first day. And he did.

Others continued to attend her. The hussar, Major Hewitson, became a constant companion. Mr Coynd, the tutor, soon proved himself another admirer, keeping as close as he could to Louisa and joining in the lively conversations. She detected some rivalry between him and the major but could not bring herself to set him down. He was, after all, the grandson of a peer, however impoverished and forced to occupy a menial position.

They were sometimes joined by the Duke himself, often accompanied by Lady Shelley, proudly riding one of the Duke's horses, sometimes even Copenhagen.

'I am so honoured!' she exclaimed on one such occasion, patting the chestnut's neck. 'Do you attend the review tomorrow? I am to accompany dear Wellington again, riding this creature.'

'Yes, I shall be there. You are a splendid horse-woman, ma'am,' said Louisa. 'No doubt he appreciates that.'

'Well, so are others, I'm sure, including yourself, Miss Finsham. I am certain you could manage Copenhagen as well as I!'

'But I have my own Prince Hal,' returned Louisa, and the conversation languished.

Amelia watched her niece, worried by the change in her. After eight years of holding down an exemplary position at the pinnacle of Society she had thought Louisa beyond such frenetic and immodest behaviour.

'Really, Louisa,' she chided at last, 'I cannot imagine what has got into you recently! You are like to become the talk of the town if you do not stop rattling about and encouraging the Duke—who ought to be old enough to know better—and all those young men as you do!'

'The officers know it is all a tease, Aunt. And you call attending the salons of the *ton*—of Lady Castlereagh and Madame de Staël, among others— "rattling about"?'

'Not precisely, but. . .' Amelia sighed and trailed off.

Louisa immediately suffered a pang of guilt. 'Do you not enjoy accompanying me, dear Aunt? I had not thought how tedious you might find such occasions!'

'My love, it is not the tedium I object to, for I have my gossips to keep me amused, but your lack of decorum. You have set the old tabbies gossiping behind their fans!'

'Am I really behaving so very badly, Aunt? I do not mean to. There must be something infectious in the atmosphere here, for I declare all the ladies behave just as I do!'

'Just because others make spectacles of themselves over our national hero there is no call for you to do the same! I had thought you more sensible, Louisa. And they do not all venture out in the early morning as you do, to ride with the Duke and all those young men!'

'What harm can there be in that? I am always accompanied by Pershaw or another groom. Lady Shelley is often present.' She ignored Amelia's scornful snort at that information, adding quietly, 'And I have achieved our aim of making friends with Jamie. I believe I have his confidence.'

'That at least is something to be grateful for. Forgive me for ringing a peal over you, my love, but I have only your best interests at heart.'

'Of course you do, Aunt, but I think you refine too much over a little tardy giddiness on my part. The war is finally over. Having surrendered to the navy off Rochefort, Napoleon is now on his way to exile in St Helena, so I hear, and we are in Paris celebrating a great victory!'

'I dare say you are right. In any case, you are no green girl; you have been out too long for me to govern your behaviour now. But do give heed to what I say.'

Louisa could accept such strictures from her aunt. She went over to Kiss Lady Nazeby fondly. 'I will, Aunt,' she promised.

The ladies had been waiting for their first morning callers to arrive. As Louisa finished assuring her aunt that she would indeed consider mending her ways— indeed, she shocked herself at times with her flirtatious behaviour and was beginning to wish she had had the sense to take Hugh Deverill's warning in the spirit in which it had been intended, having become increasinly certain that he had not meant to offend her—Chausson announced the Countess of Thurrock.

Amy entered with a flounce of self-importance, her cheeks aglow and her pale blue eyes bright with suppressed excitement.

Once greetings had been exchanged—Amelia and Louisa hiding their surprise, for James's mother did not often grace their rooms with her presence—their visitor produced some newspapers to flourish before their eyes.

'Have you seen them?' she demanded.

'Seen what?' enquired Amelia carefully. She exchanged an anxious look with Louisa which their guest fortunately failed to notice in her excitement. Could Miss Finsham's excesses have reached the pages of the Press?

'What is being said in the *St James's Chronicle*, of course!'

'You have received copies from London?' put in Louisa, her curiosity piqued. Not to mention her apprehension. But of course whatever had been written could not possibly concern her! 'No, we have not seen them. What do they say?'

'Oh, they make a great play on the letter W. "Fashionable Alliteration", the author calls it, but goes on to record a report supposedly prevalent in the first circle here that the Duke—although it does not name him, of course, but refers to a "distinguished commander"—is captive to the charms of a certain lady. Lady Frances Wedderburn-Webster, of course! It surmises that the affair will end in criminal conversation! And it claims that the husband—the obnoxious Captain James W-W, you know—is suing the fortunate lover for fifty thousand pounds' damages! What do you think of that?'

'Rumours have been surrounding the Duke this age,' shrugged Amelia. 'She was here then and went on to Brussels when Bonaparte returned. But she was not the only one. Lady Shelley was there, too, riding beside him at his reviews, as she does now.'

'But the rumours surround Lady Frances

Wedderburn-Webster, not Frances, Lady Shelley. Captain W-W's wife is the one likely to find herself divorced!'

'And the Duke may now be using Lady Shelley as a smokescreen,' mused Louisa.

'Not to mention yourself, Miss Finsham.' Amy Thurrock smiled in malicious triumph. 'You have been much in his company recently. What is your opinion of this scandal?'

'I have nothing to say to it, ma'am. I was not there and cannot judge.'

She was rescued from further personal questioning by the advent of several other ladies of their acquaintance. Louisa remained silent while the company enjoyed some enlivening *on dits* over the current scandal and the possibilities of damages and crim. con.

At length, 'He cannot possibly make every young woman he admires his mistress,' stated Amelia firmly. 'He enjoys the company of young people, both gentlemen and ladies. I believe his interest to be purely avuncular.'

'Would you agree with that, Miss Finsham?' asked Amy, all wide-eyed innocence.

'Certainly, my lady,' replied Louisa with all the aplomb she could muster. 'Think how fond he becomes of his ADCs! And Lady Frances was already heavily pregnant at the time of the supposed adultery. No one denies the Duke had mistresses in India and the Peninsula. But I am persuaded that this is not so unusual in an active gentleman of his disposition so often, of necessity, stationed away from home.'

'Really, Miss Finsham!' Outrage informed the voice of an elderly tabby as she clutched at her breast as though on the point of swooning. 'How shocking! A young lady of your breeding to speak so plainly of things about which you should know nothing!'

'Fustian!' exclaimed Louisa roundly. 'How could I fail to know? Were I a simpering miss at her come-out you might be excused your shock. But even you, Miss Cunningham, have spoken openly before me and at five and twenty I believe I am as entitled as you to know something of such matters!'

The tabby's gasp and Amy's titter were lost in the arrival of another visitor.

Having drawn the company's attention by means of an ostentatious cough, 'Lord Ew Deverill,' announced Chausson in sonorous tones.

Louisa's heart stopped for an endless moment. Hugh Deverill, here? He had made no duty calls on them until now, apart from one made early on when she had been visiting the modiste. She had often wondered since whether he had chosen that precise time specifically in order to avoid her. It would not surprise her in the least if he had. Apart from polite murmurs of greeting when contact was unavoidable, they had scarcely addressed a word to each other since that first, disastrous evening.

Now, having resumed its beat, her heart leapt and jumped at sight of the tall, elegant figure bending over the Dowager's hand and making his general, polished devoirs to the other ladies.

He approached Louisa last. For too long he had watched from a distance, reluctant to interfere again. Now, it seemed, he could render her a service. He bowed over her hand.

Louisa was aware that her hand trembled in his warm

clasp, that the brush of his lips across her knuckles—an unnecessary contact, for he had not kissed any other hand and the gesture indicated an intimacy they did not share—sent a shiver down her spine.

He sat in a chair close beside her, which had unfortunately been vacant. His near presence made her extremely uncomfortable.

He crossed his long legs, adopting an easy, elegant posture, prepared to listen politely to the ladies' chatter for the prescribed twenty minutes of his visit.

They, however, could not feel free to continue with their pleasurable speculations with a gentleman present. Apart, that was, from the Countess of Thurrock who, rising to take her leave, could not resist taking a parting shot at Louisa.

'My son appears to enjoy riding with you in the Bois, Miss Finsham. I am so thankful no scandal attaches to *your* name, or I would be unable to sanction his expeditions. Of course, Lady Frances, being so close to her confinement, has retired to the Wedderburn-Webster estate. Just as well,' she ended significantly, 'for I could not allow him to join a party which included *that* lady.' She turned the battery of her wide, ingenuous eyes on Hugh. 'Have you see these copies of the *St James's Chronicle*, Lord Hugh?'

He lifted negligent brows as he rose gracefully to acknowledge her parting curtsy. 'Copies are regularly delivered to the embassy, my lady.'

'Then you must have seen the ones I have here. How long it has taken for them to reach me!'

'Just so. Ours only arrived this morning. No doubt adverse winds in the Channel account for some of the delay. But as to the articles to which I am certain you refer, they do but repeat gossip which has been current for some time. I collect that it can cause no further anoyance to the parties concerned. I would advise an action for libel against the proprietors of the paper. Were it me I would consider actions for slander, too.'

Why did Louisa get the firmest impression that Hugh Deverill had presented himself that morning to show his solidarity with her, knowing that she had laid herself open to the spite of the gossips? Had his early profession of friendship meant more than mere words, after all? Had the warmth she had sensed survived the intervening coolness between them?

All her confused emotions, of resentment and guilt, excitement and apprehension, were swallowed up in her pleasure at his championship. And the look of consternation on Amy's suddenly flushed face made her ready to forgive him anything.

Once the Dowager Countess of Thurrock had departed, no doubt to spread her gossip in other establishments despite Hugh's veiled threat, the remaining ladies felt constrained to change the subject, with Hugh Deverill present. There was plenty to occupy their tongues, quite apart from the Duke's scandalous affairs.

Louisa, grateful for his presence and wishing to restore goodwill between them, took courage and addressed her somewhat silent companion.

'I have not had the pleasure of meeting you while riding in the Bois recently,' she murmured.

He scrutinised her face, his own breaking into a rueful smile.

'You are always surrounded by others, Miss Finsham. What chance could a dull dog like me expect of gaining your attention while you are entertained by illustrious dukes, youthful earls, gallant hussars and all their attendants?'

Louisa's eyes widened in a mildly flirtatious manner designed to hide the sudden thumping of her heart. Could it be that he was jealous? The idea had a most peculiar effect on her ability to breathe.

'Come, sir,' she chided gaily, glad that her state of inexplicable inner turmoil was not reflected in her voice, 'if you appear dull it is entirely your own fault! Now were you to exert yourself to show greater pleasure in the company about you——'

Her roasting could not be mistaken for anything else. His answering smile was wry.

'You have noticed my tendency to impatience with idle chatter, I collect!'

'And with idle flirtation, I believe.' Greeny hazel and grey-blue eyes met squarely. The grey-blue held a watchful, slightly questioning expression which unsettled her anew. 'But, you know,' she went on mischievously, enjoying the exchange despite her wayward emotions, 'one must give the Great Man his due in adoration. He is undoubtedly the saviour of Europe.'

'You know I do not argue with you there, dear Miss Finsham.' The smile in his eyes deepened in response to her obvious mockery. 'I would even go so far as to say of the world, since Bonaparte's ambitions knew no bounds.'

'And so, you see, we must all pay court! And some will no doubt fall victim to his consquence and power, if not his personal charm.'

'But not you, I collect, Miss Finsham,' he commented quietly.

When had the conversation turned serious? A sudden suspicion made her bite her lip. Had he overheard her answering Lady Thurrock, just before Chausson announced him? Was that why his attitude had changed? Yet that could not explain his presence here in the first place.

'He is always most courteous and kind. But even were I tempted to engage in a more intimate relationship I should not be able to forget the Duchess Kitty. And I should undoubtedly be quite ruined,' she added in mock-tragic tones.

'What is that you say, Louisa? Why should you be ruined?'

Lady Nazeby's sharply agitated tones cut across their exchange and Louisa realised she had allowed her voice to rise in her enjoyment of an entertaining if improper conversation. She beamed reassuringly.

'I shall not, dear Aunt. I was funning.'

'Well, I'm very glad to hear it! But you should not say such a thing even in jest, my love! You are tempting fate! And to say it to a gentleman! Really, Lord Hugh, you should not encourage my niece in her rackety ways!'

'My lady, my admiration for your niece is in part due to her refusal to bow entirely to Society's ideas of correct behaviour. The strait-jacket imposed upon young ladies of spirit must be irksome in the extreme. Yet I do not believe Miss Finsham would ever stray beyond the limits of true propriety.' Rising, he bowed to his hostess. 'Regrettably I must take my leave or I shall outstay my welcome. Your servant, ladies.'

His eyes did not meet hers, for which Louisa was

vastly thankful. She knew she would be unable to hide the utter confusion his words had provoked.

And then, before Amelia could ring for Chausson, the major-domo had flung open the door.

'Is Grace, ze Duke of Villainton and Madame Grassini.'

Seldom had Louisa felt so ready to sink. She was not the fluttery, fainting kind and had never pretended to be so, but at that moment she would have given much for a sniff of her aunt's hartshorn.

Wellington and Deverill exchanged greetings in passing with the utmost civility, Lord Hugh bowed to the songstress with impeccable formality, and then the Duke and the opera star were making their devoirs with practised ease. Everyone knew that Wellington had been enraptured by La Grassini's singing and by her person ever since he had first heard her perform in Paris the previous year.

At close quarters Louisa found La Grassini's features disappointing. On the stage, of course, she was too distant for fair criticism. But even here she had managed to make a theatrical entrance.

She began to chatter in her heavily accented French, which she interspersed with Italian when she could not think of the word she wanted. Louisa found the gravest difficulty in understanding what the woman said. She suspected the others of being similarly at sea.

Polite, pleasant as ever, the Duke, in his grey frock-coat and high boots, soon put a stop to her chatter and himself demanded the attention of all the ladies present, those whose residence it was and those who had already greatly overstayed their correct twenty-minute welcome.

Madame Grassini, he interpreted, had wished to call upon the Dowager Countess to pay her respects and he had escorted her. Louisa listened apparently attentively to the conversation flowing about her, her mind occupied elsewhere.

The Duke appeared worried beneath a veneer of normality. She suspected him to be more concerned over the reports circulating than he would openly admit. It was fortunate for him that, being in such a delicate condition, Lady Frances Wedderburn-Webster had been unable to appear in Society recently, leaving him free to concentrate his attentions upon La Grassini. His friendship with Lady Shelley and her husband—and with herself as well, more recently—had been designed to obscure any former indiscretions.

But he was a ladies' man and that was that. It did not make him any the less a great general. He had defeated Napoleon. And, like everyone else, she could not help liking as well as admiring him.

Just as she liked Hugh Deverill. His mistress had not followed him to Paris. Rumour said Lady Kingslea had been kept at home by an ailing husband. Would he marry the widow if Lord Kingslea died? Louisa found that proposition even less appealing than his present relationship with the woman.

They had been invited to a supper party at Lord Castlereagh's the following day, a signal honour. The prospect did not, however, prevent Louisa from taking her usual morning exercise.

Inside the gates she found James Grade, Earl of Thurrock, Viscount Thurston, awaiting her, mounted upon a large chestnut gelding. The youngster sat his new mount well, thought Louisa as she drew Prince Hal to a halt beside the boy, who was bristling with pride.

He did not forget his manners and greeted her with an exquisite formality, which brought a small tilt to the corners of her mouth, before allowing his excitement to spill over.

'What do you think of him, Louisa? Isn't he a splendid animal?' he demanded.

Louisa inspected the horse with knowledgeable and admiring eyes before saying, 'Splendid indeed. Pershaw!' She turned to the groom with a smile. 'Am I not correct in agreeing with Lord Thurrock?'

Thus consulted, Pershaw dismounted and stepped forward to run his experienced hands from the chestnut's powerful crest along its strong neck, on down its muscled shoulder to its knee before picking up the leg to inspect the neat round hoof, making soothing noises to reassure the horse all the while. Then his hand ran over the flank and hind quarter, down the thigh to the hock, fetlock and another hoof. He eyed the horse critically as he circled it to perform the same inspection on its other side.

'Walk him round if you please, my lord.'

Full of confidence mixed with expectation, Jamie did as asked. 'Well?' he demanded as he drew up before the groom.

'Excellent piece of horseflesh, my lord,' Pershaw pronounced at last, giving a last soothing stroke to the horse's delicate head. Its ears twitched and it whickered softly in appreciation of the fondling. As though aware of receiving admiration, it lifted its head, setting the creamy mane rippling. 'Deep-chested, sound in wind and limb. Possibly,' Pershaw added diffidently, 'a little too strong for your lordship as yet?'

'Oh, no,' said Jamie confidently. 'I can handle Conker. He's obedient, and I'm very strong.'

'Where did you buy him?' asked Louisa, thinking that such an animal must have cost a small fortune and wondering at Amy's allowing the expense.

'I didn't, he's from the stables at home. Father promised him to me the moment I reached thirteen, which I did, last week.'

'Congratulations,' murmured Louisa. Yes, she'd known that—Amelia had been sad not to be able to attend the celebrations. Supposing his mother had bothered to organise any.

'So I had Percy——' he grinned conspiratorially at his groom '—send for him.'

He was fast finding the courage to exert his natural authority. Louisa wondered whether his mother had raised any objection. He answered her without knowing it.

'Of course, Mama would rather I continued to ride the pony, but I'm almost a man now, and I told her so. So she shrugged and said she supposed I could break my neck if I wanted to, but not to blame her.' He grinned suddenly, a wide, boyish smile that went straight to Louisa's heart. 'Not that I'd be able to, of course, if I were dead.'

'Don't talk such nonsense,' she admonished with mock-severity. 'How would you like to race Prince Hal to the end of this ride?'

His young face lit up with enthusiasm. 'Do you mean it, Louisa?'

Of course!' At that moment her attention was drawn

to a lone rider approaching on a massive grey. So he had taken her hint and intended riding with her again! 'And look, here comes Lord Hugh Deverill on Kismet. I will introduce you and we will invite him to race with us.'

Thank God, she thought, the Duke had not put in an appearance that morning. She and Lord Thurrock were riding side by side, with Major Hewitson and Mr Coynd a few paces behind, the grooms bringing up the rear.

Louisa drew rein as Deverill approached, wishing that his appearance did not always so affect her breathing. It was quite ridiculous; she was past the age to go into vapours over a man.

He lifted his hat and inclined his body in greeting, punctiliously polite. 'Good morning, Miss Finsham.'

'Why, Lord Hugh!' The sun had risen and was slanting across him through the trees, gilding the ends of his black hair. The little burst of joy in her heart at sight of him could not be denied, and she allowed herself to indulge it for a moment before she went on in what she hoped was the merely friendly tone she would use with any acquaintance. 'I do not believe you have met his lordship, James Grade, Earl of Thurrock. Jamie, may I present Lord Hugh Deverill?'

Their devoirs made, Jamie eyed the man with interest. He appeared to like what he saw, for he smiled his eager, boyish smile. 'I have heard of you, sir. My mother has spoken of you.'

'Nothing to my detriment, I trust?'

James flushed and looked uncomfortable. Louisa wondered exactly what Amy had been saying in front of the child.

'Oh, no, sir!' he assured an amused Deverill. 'Well,'

he added honestly, 'not more than she usually says about everyone! I believe she admires you, sir.'

'You are acquainted with Major Hewitson of the Hussars, my lord, but you may not have met Mr Coynd, Lord Thurrock's tutor,' put in Louisa hurriedly, seeing the wry twitch of Lord Hugh's lips at this information. Amy's admiration was not necessarily something to be desired. She had observed him exercising his excellent manners to the full in an attempt to be polite on numerous occasions, and after yesterday's set-down she wondered how much longer Lady Thurrock would continue to speak well of Lord Hugh Deverill!

But Deverill's attention had already been diverted. After acknowledging the stiff greeting of Hewitson, he turned to the other man with raised eyebrows. 'William Coynd!' he exclaimed. 'Can it be you?'

'Indeed, my lord.' Coynd appeared rather less than eager to acknowledge the acquaintance. 'It is many years since we last met.'

'Coynd came up during my last year at Oxford,' explained Deverill easily.

'Lord Thurrock has a new mount, and we were just about to prove its speed in a race,' Louisa explained. 'Will you join us, my lord?'

'With pleasure, ma'am.'

'Major, will you not take part as well?' invited Louisa. Coynd's horse would not be up to the competition, but she was feeling kindly disposed towards him. 'You too, Mr Coynd. Come, sirs! Lay your bets! Pershaw shall start us!'

Both the Hussar and the tutor agreed, though with little enthusiasm, their expressions disapproving of such a display of unfeminine behaviour in a young lady. She should be content to ride sedately through the Bois, exchanging gentle and charming conversation with her escorts, not placing bets on the result of her own hoydenish intention to race in public!

On this occasion, thought Louisa with secret elation, Lord Hugh seemed rather more approving than critical, and the smile he sent her as they attempted to bring the horses into line for the start discomposed her so much that for a critical instant she lost control of Prince Hal who, excited and eager for the gallop, took the opportunity to leap forward. The other animals took off after him and Pershaw was left staring after them, his improvised starter's flag—his handkerchief—fluttering uselessly in his hand.

CHAPTER FIVE

THE whoops and shouts, the sound of thundering
hooves behind, told Louisa that the race was on. Her
sense of guilt at having set off before the rest of the
field soon died in the excitement of the competition,
for Jamie's Conker and Deverill's Kismet were soon
drawing level and Hal, responding to the challenge,
was galloping as though his life depended upon it.

However, Conker was younger, his chest deep,
Kismet stronger, with more endurance. By the time the
steaming horses reached the designated finish Conker
led Kismet by a head, Hal's nose was on a level with
Deverill's knee. Hewitson pounded in from two lengths
behind and poor Coynd, on one of Lady Thurrock's
lesser hacks, trailed in a miserable last.

'I cannot remember when I have enjoyed myself
more!' cried Louisa, her face flushed with exertion and
excitement, her eyes sparkling with the joy of living.
'Jamie, you have a capital creature there! Mind you, he
had a lighter burden to carry! Otherwise I do believe
Kismet might have won! What say you, my lord?'

'Lord Thurrock won fair and square. My only doubt,
ma'am,' said Hugh Deverill, his attempt at a grave air
unable to disguise the grin he could not suppress, 'is
over your own lamentable attempt to gain an advantage
at the start.'

Louisa knew he was roasting her and laughed, but

Coynd, coming up at that moment, took the reprimand seriously.

'Look here, Deverill,' he began belligerently, 'I'll not have you casting doubts on the lady's honour! I may deprecate her desire to race like a man, but I cannot believe she would cheat. Her horse was too strong for her, she couldn't hold it.'

'Oh, I am absolutely certain you have the right of it, Coynd. I did not believe for a moment that the lady had intended to cheat, and if I gave that impression I am all contrition.'

'Don't be so addle-witted, Mr Coynd,' snapped Louisa, although Deverill's air of assumed humility made her want to laugh. 'Of course Lord Hugh did not imply anything of the kind! You may depend upon it, he was funning! And Hal is not too strong for me. I lost concentration for a moment, that was all.'

'Miss Finsham is above suspicion,' murmured Hugh.

Coynd suddenly turned away, but not before Louisa had caught sight of the high flush suffusing his cheeks. He had not taken her remark kindly. She could sympathise, and regretted her sharpness.

'Come, gentlemen,' she said lightly, trying to make amends, 'it does not signify. The race is done, and Lord Thurrock is undoubtedly the winner despite my irregular start. Let us settle our debts. Jamie, here is my guinea.'

Since that first race with Deverill Louisa had always carried a coin or two in her pocket against such a time as this. As she handed him his winnings, James beamed. 'I didn't think you cheated, Louisa, I saw what happened—you were looking at Lord Hugh when your horse decided to go. I didn't try to stop Conker from following, and none of the others held back.'

Louisa willed the flush this revealing comment provoked to recede. 'You rode him splendidly, Jamie. Your father was right, he suits you well.'

She and the young Earl had been on first-name terms almost from the beginning of their acquaintance. The deference due to his rank was offset by Louisa's additional years and they had quickly adopted each other as friends.

'Well,' said Jamie, his honesty forcing the confession, 'Conker's very obedient, otherwise he would be too strong. But we get along like anything and he tries to please me.'

'That is by far the best relationship to have with your animal, my lord,' observed Hugh, handing over his dues with a smile. 'Make a friend of your horse and it'll do anything for you.'

Hewitson paid up handsomely and with rather less good grace Coynd discharged his debt to his pupil. The party began to ride easily along another bridleway. She found Coynd and Hewitson crowding her, while Jamie and Lord Hugh rode ahead.

'I do admire your spirit, Miss Finsham,' offered the major with a stiff smile. Everything he did was stiff, Louisa thought; he seemed unable to relax. Perhaps it was the uniform. Though other Hussars managed to behave in an easy manner, so it couldn't be entirely that. 'I wonder Lord Wellington does not invite you to review the troops with him,' he went on, unconsciously adding to the irrational annoyance Louisa already felt towards him.

'I have no desire for that honour, sir,' she returned,

stiff herself at an implication she would rather not pursue. 'I have no intention of becoming an object of ridicule. So far as I am concerned, His Grace must content himself with the company of his official ADCs.'

'I am glad to hear it,' put in Coynd severely. 'Such a public display would not become a lady.'

'Oh, I would not entirely agree there,' returned Louisa perversely. 'Lady Shelley is an excellent horse-woman and behaves with perfect propriety when she accompanies him at his revues. *She* cannot be considered an object of ridicule. And without such a diversion, I am persuaded that the occasions must become tedious in the extreme to someone of His Grace's character.'

Take that how you like, she thought tartly.

Far from being critical of such an opinion, however, the gentlemen vied with each other to agree with her, even Major Hewitson admitting such parades to be irksome to those taking part.

Suddenly tired of their implied criticisms of her behaviour and their less well-concealed eagerness to obtain her good opinion and engage her interest, Louisa spurred Hal forward, edging him between the two riders ahead, who readily parted to allow her to join them. Until now she had enjoyed the company of the major and the Earl's excellent tutor, who was well-educated, entertaining and polite. But today both men seemed dull, and had contrived to irritate her beyond measure.

She addressed Deverill, still riding easily and companionably, apparently oblivious of the exchanges taking place behind. 'Do you attend Lord Castlereagh's supper party later, Lord Hugh?'

'I do. Both you and Lady Nazeby are also invited, I believe.'

'Indeed, my lord, and look forward to the occasion with eagerness.'

'You will find yourself in an exclusive but mixed company. His Lordship must invite anyone of consequence who is in Paris, as well as those French ministers the Allies nominated to govern the country under King Louis XVIII.'

'Excellent! I have not yet had an opportunity to enter into converse with Talleyrand or Fouché, and although I have seen them at evening functions such occasions are always such a sad squeeze one cannot hope to speak with everyone present. I trust their characters are more agreeable than their appearances would suggest.'

Deverill chuckled. 'I will leave you to judge that for yourself. I dare not venture an opinion on such a delicate matter!'

'They're hideous,' stated young Jamie with conviction. 'Everyone says so.'

'"Everyone" being your mother, I collect,' murmured Louisa.

'And Mr Coynd,' averred Jamie stoutly.

'I should not,' advised Hugh mildly, 'voice that opinion in strange company, my lord, or you may cause an international incident!'

'I am never in strange company, so I can't,' muttered Jamie morosely. 'I'm not old enough. It's awful to be young.'

'Not a bit of it,' differed Deverill briskly. 'Though to enjoy your youth properly you should live in the country, not in a town. I remember spending days roaming the estate at home, sometimes on horseback, sometimes on foot, speaking to the tenants, fishing in the stream, helping to bring in the harvest. . .'

The nostalgia in his voice brought Louisa's eyes to his face, to discover its hard planes softened by memory. He loved his home; of that there could be little doubt. Here was a man with a heritage rooted in the land. What a pity he had not been born the eldest son, able to indulge his love of it.

'But,' he was saying now, 'you have this park and a wonderful city to explore. Does Mr Coynd not take you to see the sights, the museums and art galleries? Have you never ridden out to Malmaison or Versailles?'

Jamie pulled a face. 'We've been to a few places in Paris. But they're most awfully dull.'

'Then he is not explaining them to you properly. Perhaps, one day, you will allow me to escort you on a tour of the city?'

'That would be absolutely splendid, my lord! Could Miss Finsham come, too?'

Hugh Deverill slanted a quizzical smile in her direction. 'I would account it a great honour were she to consent to accompany us.'

Louisa felt the blush rising and fought to contain it. 'I should be delighted to engage for such an expedition, my lord.'

She thought William Coynd might resent the interference, but forbore to comment. The prospect was too attractive to be dimmed by the casting of any doubt.

'Then I will arrange it.'

'Mama will not mind *you* taking me,' put in Jamie eagerly. 'She greatly approves of you, my lord.'

'I am flattered. Meantime, may I have the honour of escorting you to Lord Castlereagh's, Miss Finsham?'

He was offering his protection again. Louisa almost refused it, for she certainly needed no such thing!

But then the appeal of appearing in Society on the arm of such an eminently eligible escort overcame her rebellious spirit. 'Thank you, my lord,' she accepted meekly.

The smile he turned on her in reply reduced her to breathless silence.

Lord Castlereagh, the Foreign Secretary, was of course Hugh Deverill's ultimate superior. Only Sir Charles Stuart, the ambassador, stood above him, and both men had been invited to the supper.

Lord Hugh entered the salon with Louisa on one arm and Amelia on the other. Both ladies, he acknowledged, did him credit, but it was Louisa who, from the first moment of seeing her awaiting his arrival in their drawing-room, had claimed his stunned attention.

She wore an undergown of fine bud-green silk covered by a soft, hazy gauze, giving an overall effect similar to the shining grey-green of the underside of a willow leaf. Trimmed with satin ribbons in shades of bronze and brown, it suited her to admiration. As she moved the silk clung to every curve of her shapely figure, temptingly caressed the long line of her limbs. The low neckline revealed the tops of soft, creamy breasts. A string of pearls encircled her slender throat, taking their lustre from her glowing skin. Several shades of ribbon had been ingeniously threaded in her hair, asking to be pulled out so that he could run his fingers through the abundant curls. Some heady perfume wafted about her person, sending Hugh's already heightened senses into a spin. He found it difficult to keep his breathing even.

He had thought her perfect before, in that white creation she had worn to Lady Stuart's reception. That had been designed *décolleté* enough to leave little of her lovely figure to the imagination. This dress had a higher neckline and concealed rather more of her breasts but its effect was the same. And to him her looks surpassed even their previous excellence. His imagination ran riot over what that bodice concealed. He had to confess himself enchanted.

She stirred his senses so much it had become painful. In his imagination he could still feel the softness of her in his arms as he carried her across that heaving deck. And, he realised helplessly and rather angrily, he had lost all desire to bed with any other woman since that moment. The much publicised affair with Maria Kingslea had never in fact taken place anywhere but in her imagination. Her husband was his friend, her pursuit of himself an embarrassment. He heaved a small, unconscious sigh. Setting Maria down kindly was proving somewhat difficult. Soon, he would have to be brutal in his rejection.

But he must not forget that Louisa was unmarried. If he broke all the rules of acceptable behaviour and paid her marked attention it could lead to his being trapped into matrimony, a state he had long since resigned himself to eschew, regarding marriage as impractical since he did not command the means to keep an establishment worthy of the name.

To enter into a wedlock with Louisa would be asking to be branded a fortune-hunter, a breed he despised.

So why had he laid himself open to attack from the scandal-mongers and matchmakers by entering Castlereagh's salon with her on his arm? The plain answer was because he had not been able to help himself.

Quite apart from her undoubted attraction for him he found her intriguing. He could not make her out. She did not approve of the Duke's infidelities and he would lay odds that she did not fancy herself in love with the fellow, as so many of the women who flocked about that powerful figure did. Why she had allowed herself to be flattered into joining the Duke's court was part of her mystery, though he could see why the Duke encouraged her. All the women he favoured were either clever, like Madame de Staël, or beautiful, like Lady Shelley, but mostly both. Louisa was both. But since her arrival in Paris her behaviour had been too flighty to accord with the decorum required in an unmarried woman of her years. Talk had been rife. And because of that he had discovered that she carried no previous reputation for indiscretion. Just a lively, independent spirit. Which was, perhaps, why she had not wed years ago. . .

He glanced down at her animated, quite lovely face and could see no guile there. He did not know what to think, except that he should tread warily and keep a tight rein on his senses, for her capable hand in its silken mitten was burning a hole through the cloth covering his arm. And, despite everything, in the teeth of all his excellent intentions, he felt protective of her, just as he had on board the packet, when she had been a complete stranger. Then, he had not known who she was. Pleasant dalliance had beckoned enticingly. Now, every fibre of his being was shouting, Beware!

She would never arrive anywhere unnoticed, for she possessed style. Her natural elegance, her vivacity and unconventional looks attracted attention the moment she entered a room. He could hear the buzz that went round at their appearance together. She had made a conquest. He had made a conquest. Whichever it was the gossips were whispering he found he no longer cared. If being the butt of speculation was the price of spending an evening in her exquisite company it was a cost he was prepared to pay.

'Where would you like to sit, Aunt?'

Louisa's low, musical voice floated into his consciousness and he realised he had become so absorbed in his thoughts that he was in danger of neglecting his duty as escort.

'Oh, I do not mind, my love. But look, there is Clarissa Marchant! I have not spoken with her this age! I believe I will go and sit with her!'

Having comfortably settled Lady Nazeby in congenial company, Hugh again offered Louisa his arm and they circulated among the other guests. Her usual train of admirers soon gathered, but never for a moment did she allow them to break the intimacy between herself and her escort, keeping them at a distance with charm and diplomacy.

Hugh marvelled. Not that he would have allowed any one of her swains to detach the beauteous creature from his arm, but her social skills were abundant, a word here, a smile there, a witty rejoinder always at her command. How was it, he wondered again, that she had not been snapped up many seasons ago? What had her father been thinking of? Or Lady Nazeby, for that matter, since she had stood as substitute mother for so many years? Between them they should have contrived to have her settled long before this. No gentleman could wish for a more accomplished wife. Should any gentleman wish to become leg-shackled. Which he most certainly did not.

Louisa had heard that earlier sigh and now noticed a slight tensing of the hard muscle under her hand. She found the particular attention he was paying her exceedingly pleasant and wanted nothing to disturb their present amity. Yet she could not ignore that signal of withdrawal. He was not entirely relaxed. Perhaps he was regretting his offer to escort her. After all, she had made herself the object of gossip over the last weeks and, although her friends knew her too well to criticise openly, others less kindly disposed did not scruple to do so. And Hugh Deverill had a position to uphold.

So, at the first opportunity she removed her hand. He cast her a quick, enquiring glance which brought the ready furrows to his brow, though only for an instant. They quickly smoothed out as he gave her an amiable smile.

'We should seek our seats in the music-room,' he suggested neutrally. 'I believe Madame Grassini is to honour us with a song.'

'That will be delightful. I had not realised how attractive a contralto voice could be until I heard her sing at the opera the other evening.'

'The Duke,' observed Hugh mildly as they strolled through to join others assembling for the concert, 'has found a seat in the front row, with Lady Shelley and

Madame de Staël. Where would you like to sit, Miss Finsham?'

'Oh, anywhere. I would suggest that we join Lady Nazeby and Lady Marchant, but I see they have found seats with several of their gossips.'

'I see vacant chairs in the row in front of her.'

Louisa had acknowledged Wellington upon his arrival but indulged in no further converse with him. To regain Hugh Deverill's good opinion had, for some reason, become of some importance. She therefore accepted his polite ushering of her to a seat out of harm's way near Amelia with a certain wry amusement.

Everyone enjoyed Giuseppina Grassini's superb performance, though Louisa found the Duke's unconcealed enchantment distasteful. Poor Duchess Kitty, she thought. To have one's husband paying court so openly to another woman must be dreadful. And to be forced to suffer the scandal of the Wedderburn-Webster affair and rumours of his other indiscretions as well. She feared she would never be able to trust any man enough to marry him. A sadness settled over her features. She would like to be wed, would like a family, but could any joy children might bring compensate for the pain of a husband's infidelity?

Hugh noticed the gloom settle over her features. Was it the song she found melancholy, or the fact that Wellington was so enraptured with the songstress? A longing smote him to see rapture on *her* face. Rapture for him. He closed his eyes, attempting to control his libido, to shut out the disturbing presence at his side. The attempt proved a dismal failure.

The music was just a harmonious background for Louisa's distracted thoughts. She could not concentrate on it with Hugh Deverill's thigh bare inches from her own. What was wrong with her? She had never been so affected before! Even being held in Radburn's arms, whom she had loved, had not made her tremble and caused the blood to rush around her veins so wildly that she had to shake out her fan and flirt it rapidly to cool herself.

'Are you too hot, my love?' whispered Amelia, leaning forward and speaking rather too loudly, thus earning herself hostile glances and a hiss or two. When La Grassini was singing, no one dared to chatter, as they did while lesser mortals performed.

Louisa shook her head and grew even more heated as Lord Hugh's glance rested on her again.

The endless concert finished at last and Louisa rose to her feet with relief.

'Delightful,' enthused Amelia as Hugh escorted them through to the supper-room. 'I can forgive that woman anything! She has such a divine voice!'

'Indeed she has, my lady,' agreed Hugh politely, conscious only of the divine creature on his arm.

Tables had been scattered about the room and were already laden with delicious food. Other dishes had been placed on trestles to one side, from which Lord Castlereagh's guests could serve themselves to additional delicacies should they so desire. Despite this, a battalion of servants stood ready to keep the covers full and to serve the wine.

With a degree of necessary determination, Lord Hugh ushered them towards a table already occupied by several people.

He bowed to those already assembled and then addressed a splendid figure sitting at the head. 'Your

Excellency, my lords, may we have the privilege of joining you?'

All immediately rose to their feet and Lord Hugh introduced the ladies first to the splendid figure of Prince Metternich, the Austrian chancellor. His appearance completely eclipsed that of either the ill-formed Talleyrand or the ferret-faced Fouché, who had both managed to convince the Allies that, although they had in the past served Napoleon, they should nevertheless be included in the new French government.

Metternich bowed elegantly over the ladies' hands. 'Delighted, Lady Nazeby. *Enchanté*, Miss Finsham.'

His exquisite manners quite disarmed Louisa although she mistrusted the way he looked at her. His expertise in the *boudoir* had become one of the *on dits* of Paris and Louisa had no intention of falling victim to his supposed charms. She acknowledged the introduction with becoming reserve. Even to annoy Hugh Deverill she could not risk giving this flirtatious nobleman the slightest encouragement.

Not that she wished to annoy Lord Hugh that evening. He was behaving with the utmost courtesy and had not glowered at her once, reserving a diplomatically muted glance of disapproval for the over-effusive Austrian prince.

They were then presented to Prince Talleyrand and Joseph Fouché, the regicide chief of police, recently elevated to the dukedom of Otranto. The latter man was a thin, sallow creature, and Louisa did not trust him at all.

'I believe you are already acquainted with Monsieur

and Madame d'Arblay,' went on Hugh smoothly, and
Louisa greeted the couple with genuine pleasure.

'Dearest Louisa, I fear you will find the conversation
here very dull. When these gentlemen get together they
can speak of nothing but politics,' observed Fanny as
the men filled their plates with a variety of cold meats,
pâté and tartlets. The two had quickly come to first-
name terms after their initial meeting. Louisa greatly
valued the friendship of the older woman, who had
undertaken to improve Louisa's French.

'You find it boring?' asked Louisa in surprise. She
herself found the political situation quite fascinating.

'Oh, no, not personally. My husband is concerned,
and so, naturally, I take an interest.'

'I do not anticipate finding it dull,' smiled Louisa. 'I
rather wish women were allowed to enter into politics.
Or almost any profession,' she added wryly. 'I find the
social round intensely confining, but what else is there
for me to do? You found an outlet for your energies in
the writing of novels. I wish I had the talent to do the
same.'

'My chief happiness has come from raising a family,'
remarked Fanny, and added, 'Why have you not wed,
Louisa?'

The enquiry had been made so gently that Louisa
could not take offence. She shrugged. 'I escaped the
bonds of an arranged marriage in the first flush of my
youth, thanks to my father's happy indifference to my
fate, and since coming of age I have failed to find a
gentleman I felt I could trust with my future happiness.
I prefer independence to becoming the slave of a man
I do not love.'

'Too particular by half,' snorted Amelia, overhearing. 'Try to put some sense into her head, will you, dear Madame d'Arblay?'

Fanny smiled. 'I do not think Louisa requires any lessons in sense, ma'am. I myself did not marry until late in life, and then only because I became greatly attached to Monsieur d'Arblay.'

'An excellent creature, I'm sure, but a foreigner! Don't you marry a foreigner, Louisa.'

'I cannot positively undertake not to, dear Aunt, but I will do my best to please you in my choice when I make it,' laughed Louisa, diverted by her aunt's forthright speech. 'But do remember, Aunt, you are sitting among foreigners here.'

'They are talking in French,' shrugged Amelia, though looking a little contrite, 'and are paying no attention to what we may say.'

'But understand and speak English excellently, ma'am,' pointed out Fanny with a smile.

As if at some pre-arranged signal, Monsieur d'Arblay glanced towards his wife, who took him to task. 'It would be polite to conduct your conversation in English, Monsieur d'Arblay. Miss Finsham can understand a little French, but the Countess has only a slight knowledge of your language.'

'Don't trouble about me,' began Amelia, but the gentlemen's attention had been drawn and Lord Hugh immediately reverted to English.

'Our apologies, ladies! Gentlemen! We are boring the ladies with our conversation.'

'Not necessarily,' protested Louisa quickly. 'How can we know whether we are bored, when we cannot understand? Pray continue your conversation, but in English, if you please!'

Metternich laughed and immediately offered his profuse apologies. 'To me,' he explained, 'language is seldom a barrier! I am at home in German, French, English, Russian and Italian.'

'I wish,' sighed Louisa, 'that I could say the same!'

'You have an ear for languages,' offered Madame d'Arblay with a knowing inclination of her head. 'You are improving your French at great speed.'

'Are you interested in languages, Miss Finsham?' asked Lord Hugh, his face breaking into the magnetic smile that set Louisa's pulse beating, for some reason she refused to admit. 'If so, I could offer my services to teach you a little German and Italian.'

'You appear fluent in French, my lord. Do you then have the same command of the other languages?' Louisa had wondered what hidden talents he possessed to fit him for such a responsible position in the Foreign Office, and was beginning to find out.

The smile broadened. How much more attractive it was than Metternich's smooth, practised charm.

'I trust so, Miss Finsham. Together with a smattering of Russian but lately acquired, and enough Dutch to make myself understood.'

'That must be useful when speaking with the Prince of Orange,' chuckled Louisa, smiling across to where the gentleman in question sat at a table graced by the presence of Wellington and his court. 'He appears to be recovering from the injuries he sustained at Waterloo.'

'Indeed, I believe he is.' Lord Hugh's lips twitched. 'And the Prince speaks good English. I fear my Dutch is wasted on him.'

'If only we all spoke the same language!'

'Indeed, Miss Finsham,' said Metternich, 'that might contribute to the united and peaceful Europe I would like to see.'

'As would we all, Your Excellency.'

The new voice was that of their host, doing his duty by circulating among his guests. What a contrast, thought Louisa, between the brilliant, accomplished Austrian, the truth of whose words, so 'twas said, was always in doubt and who loved to gain his ends by trickery, and the courtly, handsome Englishman, whose word was his bond, whose morals were impeccable, and who was incapable of deceit. Both of them had opposed the Revolution and its subversive violence and, in their different ways, both had succeeded.

Lord Castlereagh did not remain in conversation with them for long, moving on with charming courtesy to speak with other guests. After his departure the conversation at the table continued in English, ranging over the entire field of European politics. Louisa noted that Lord Hugh spoke knowledgeably but never took sides, and could only admire his skill in guiding the talk into amicable paths. And she came to understand why the Allies had insisted on Talleyrand's and Fouchés being put into office.

They were both clever, devious men. Talleyrand had fled France on the fall of the monarchy, returning after the death of Robespierre to become Minister for Foreign Affairs under the Directory and, subsequently, under Napoleon. As chief of police Fouché, a survivor if ever there was one, had an unenviable reputation. But, by virtue of his network of spies and a ruthless police system he had a firm grip on a population which, above all, needed to be returned to law and order.

Both had their own interests firmly at heart and were ready to serve any master who offered them power. So long as they toed the Allied line, their positions were assured. The Allied powers knew that both men would be assiduous in their efforts to govern France and could be relied upon to protect the restored Bourbon dynasty from further revolt. Their own futures depended upon its survival.

Thoroughly stimulated by the discussion, Louisa found herself joining in from time to time, challenging an opinion here, offering her own there. Fanny d'Arblay did, so why should not she? Amelia had long since lost interest and excused herself, moving to join more congenial company.

Eventually the party broke up and Lord Hugh made ready to escort the ladies home.

'Ma'am,' he said, addressing the Dowager, 'I failed in my duty to amuse you during the evening. I trust you did not feel too neglected. I must ask you to forgive my regrettable manners.'

'Nonsense,' rejoined Amelia robustly. 'I was not bored, I just could not listen to that dreadful murderer Fouché and the grotesque Talleyrand a moment longer!'

Lord Hugh smiled, not for one moment taken in by this protestation. 'Then I must apologise for introducing you to them. But I collect your niece was not so nice over the company she kept. I believe, Miss Finsham, you enjoyed the discussion.'

He inclined his head in her direction and offered her his arm. Louisa took it, her earlier discomfort at such close contact much reduced by the elation of her spirits.

'Indeed, my lord, I must thank you for the chance to

listen and learn! I found the evening most stimulating. How I wish I were a man! I would become a politician, I declare!'

'I,' said Lord Hugh quietly, 'am exceedingly glad you are not a man.'

They had reached their carriage and a footman was assisting Amelia to climb in. Grateful that her aunt had not heard this last provocative remark and that it was too dark, despite the flambeaux, for anyone to see her blushes, Louisa flirted her fan, although the evening was cool. Now, of course, she was alarmingly aware of the firm muscles beneath her fingers. But she replied with spirit.

'You, my lord, can have no idea of the frustrations we females endure! I have received a good education, languages apart, which is a pity since I seem to have a gift for them, only you see my governess was English and could not teach me more than she knew—but to what purpose? According to you gentlemen all I am fit for is to run a household and bear your children! I,' she added defiantly, when she had recovered her breath, 'should like above everything to do something different, but I am not allowed!'

'Many women who marry and bear children also wield great influence,' he responded quietly. 'Madame de Staël is a case in point.'

'But her husband was Dutch Ambassador!'

'And Countess Lieven, although of German extraction, reports everything she sees and hears to Tsar Alexander's foreign office.'

'And *she* is married to the Russian Ambassador in London! Those women are the fortunate exceptions, my lord, you must see that!'

'Perhaps. But if you truly desire to find some worth-
while activity inside or outside of marriage, you, Miss
Finsham, will do so, of that I am convinced. But now
the carriage awaits. We are delaying your aunt's departure. Allow me to help you to mount the step.'

CHAPTER SIX

'I *vow* I have never known it so hot,' grumbled Amelia, fanning herself vigorously. 'I declare, had we been in England, we would have left London for Minchingham by now!'

'Do you wish to return, Aunt?'

Louisa kept her voice neutral with an effort. Quite the last thing she wanted at that moment was to depart from Paris, however hot and uncomfortable it had become.

'And leave Jamie here at the mercy of that woman? No, my love,' said Amelia in a resigned voice, 'I shall remain here as long as Amy Thurrock does. And I collect she will not wish to miss Lady Stewart's ball on the sixteenth or the Duke's banquet two days later or all the other exciting events of this victorious summer.'

Smiling, Louisa admitted, 'Neither should I! I am glad you are decided to stay. If the open curricle would not be too uncomfortable for you, would you like me to drive you out of Paris after breakfast? I missed my ride this morning because of the storm, but it is over now and the countryside should be fresh after the rain. Mayhap,' she added on sudden inspiration, 'Lady Thurrock would allow Jamie to accompany us! There would be room to squeeze him between us.'

'I wonder——'

'It's worth a try! Shall we not send a note, asking her?'

'It would certainly be preferable to riding about the airless streets of the city in a closed carriage leaving cards and making calls!'

Soon a footman was speeding round to the nearby Thurrock establishment with the invitation. To both ladies' delight he returned with an affirmative answer. But Mr Coynd and a groom were to ride escort to the smart rig Pershaw had found for Louisa to drive. Dench would travel on the step behind them.

The outing proved a great success. Louisa revelled in the feel of the two spirited horses responding effort-lessly to her every command and sprang the bays the moment they had passed through the village of Montmartre. Jamie made no attempt to conceal his admiration of her skill with the ribbons. Mr Coynd rode faithfully behind, his gaze fixed on the slender figure handling the matched pair with such ease.

Since acquiring the use of the curricle Louisa had often driven herself about Paris on errands and visits, with Betty and Dench in attendance, but this was the first occasion on which she had ventured into the surrounding countryside. Doing so without a suitable escort would be unwise, for one could meet up with a group of ill-disciplined soldiers or, worse, armed mal-contents. So William Coynd and Jamie's groom, Percy, both armed, were not unwelcome additions to the party.

The ladies had brought a cold collation, a light nuncheon aimed largely at Jamie's youthful appetite. After driving for an hour they came across a most pleasant spot where meadows and trees bordered a narrow stream, with not a soldier of any description in sight. Louisa slowed her cattle.

'What do you think, Aunt?'

'An excellent spot! Such a beautiful view, and with room to draw the carriage off the road, too.'

Louisa nodded and drew up. Dench jumped down to lead the horses off the carriageway. Coynd leapt from his horse, threw the reins to Percy and hurried forward to hand the ladies from the curricle.

While Percy and Dench dealt with the horses, watering them in the stream before tethering them and leaving them to crop the grass, Louisa sent Coynd for the hamper and proceeded to unpack it.

The servants took their food to a little distance and sat apart to eat. Mr Coynd partook of his meal with them, of course, and once more proved himself an entertaining companion. But since the morning of his meeting with Lord Hugh Louisa had discovered in herself a growing aversion to his manner. He presumed upon their acquaintance, attempting to turn it into a warmer relationship than she for one was prepared to accept. The Dowager, however, concentrating upon pleasing her grandson, appeared not to notice his tutor's encroaching ways.

'May I take the ribbons? Please, Louisa!' pleaded Jamie eagerly as they set off for home.

'Have you driven before?' asked Louisa cautiously.

'I can drive a pony trap, and Papa was used to let me drive his curricle and pair about the estate—he was teaching me,' replied the boy. 'He said it was never too young to learn. And I'm thirteen now!'

'Then you may,' said Louisa, handing over the reins and whip with a smile. 'But do not forget we may meet with other traffic on a public highway.'

'I'll drive carefully,' promised his lordship with a wide grin.

He drove exceptionally well considering his years and lack of experience, and Louisa was not slow to tell him so. 'You will be a fine whip one day, a most complete hand.'

Jamie flushed with pleasure. Amelia beamed with pride.

'Papa was a non-pareil,' he announced proudly. 'But,' he went on, his face suddenly sunk in gloom, 'Mama will not hear of my having a carriage of my own yet.'

'Then you should apply to your grandmama,' advised Amelia briskly. 'She is a trustee, is she not? I am certain she will do her best to persuade her.'

'Thank you, ma'am!' cried Jamie, his face lighting up again. 'A splendid idea! I will!'

'But for now you had better give me back the ribbons,' Louisa suggested. 'We are nearing the city.'

Reluctantly, Jamie did as bidden. 'If I had my own carriage I could go to Waterloo,' he observed. 'Mama won't hear of that, either.'

'She has not visited the place herself?' asked Amelia curiously.

'No. She swoons at the very thought of seeing a battlefield. But I would like to see the place where my father died.'

'Understandable enough,' murmured Amelia, swallowing. 'But I can assure you there would be little to see. In this matter I believe your mother to be wise. It is best to remember him as you saw him last.'

'Riding away in his regimentals,' sighed Jamie. 'He looked so splendid and gallant.'

'I am certain he did. I can just picture him.'

Amelia was having difficulty in keeping her voice steady and her tears at bay. Louisa broke back into the conversation, attempting both to rescue her aunt from embarrassment and to lighten the atmosphere.

'Your papa would not wish you to be sad, Jamie. He died bravely, doing his duty. That is what every man of conscience would wish to do. To meet his death in such a gallant rearguard action would have pleased him. How much bettter to die so than to be killed in an accident, or to die in bed of a fever.'

'Why did he have to die at all?' muttered Jamie rebelliously.

'That, Jamie dear, is not for us to question,' murmured Amelia. Louisa was relieved to see that her aunt had regained her composure.

They were nearing Jamie's residence when, with a strange mixture of feelings, Louisa caught sight of a familiar figure striding purposefully towards them. He was both a reminder and an escape from the memory of Brussels, for meeting him must change the tenor of the conversation.

'Look!' exclaimed Jamie, showing that his attention had not been entirely sunk in thoughts of his father. 'There's Lord Hugh!'

'So it is,' murmured Louisa a trifle breathlessly, and drew her cattle to an expert halt.

Lord Hugh had already seen them and lifted his hat, bowing and smiling to the three in the curricle and nodding pleasantly to Coynd on his horse behind.

Seeing Louisa so happily ensconced in the sporting curricle, managing Lady Nazeby's pair with consummate elegance and ease, Hugh wondered at his own current lack of enterprise in that direction. At home in the country no one enjoyed the pleasure of handling the ribbons more than he. In Hampshire he was considered a fine whip, almost a non-pareil. He had not commanded the means to cut a dash when in Town and over the years had found he could travel the crowded streets of a city so much more conveniently on foot or horseback. That being so he had not troubled to acquire an outfit. He was in Paris on business, not pleasure.

All the same, a burning desire to take Miss Louisa Finsham for a drive consumed him. Preferably into the depths of the country and unaccompanied. But the Bois would do.

Amelia, returning the greeting, became suddenly aware of her niece's agitation. Glancing at Lord Hugh, she noted his bemused gaze fixed upon Louisa's face, which had taken on a decidedly pink tinge. Amelia's smile widened. Could she at last hold out some hopes that her wayward niece had met a man who could overcome her mistrust of marriage? Amelia liked Hugh Deverill, and thought he would make a suitable if not a splendid match. Although, of course, he was likely to spend much of his life in foreign parts, a circumstance of which she could not approve.

'Miss Finsham drove us out into the country,' offered Jamie eagerly. 'She is a splendid whip, and we had a top-rate run; she allowed me to handle the ribbons! Her ladyship's cattle are absolutely prime goers!'

'I am glad to hear it, and to see that you are safely returned! I must apologise for not yet keeping my promise to escort you both on an outing, my lord, but I have been greatly occupied with official business these last days. However, I had not forgot. We will make an excursion soon.'

They were causing a blockage in the road, so could not stand for long. Once the adieus had been made, Louisa gave her horses the office to start, the groom released their heads and leapt back on his seat and Lord Hugh continued on his way, musing on the possibility of suggesting that Miss Finsham allow him to drive her in the Bois. The project presented considerable difficulty. He had no liking for the idea of hiring a turn-out of indifferent quality. Miss Finsham deserved nothing but the best he could offer. At that moment he could offer nothing. He could set about purchasing a first-rate outfit and although that would no longer put him at Point Nonplus he saw little reason for thus expending his hard-earned wealth, since it would merely satisfy a whim, not a real need. The simplest solution would be for her to allow him to drive her curricle. He doubted whether the independent Miss Finsham would even consider such a proposition, even were he imprudent enough to suggest it. He could send home. . .but to bring his curricle and pair across would take altogether too long. Cursing his own lack of foresight, he strode on. But he had not anticipated paying court to a lady. . .if he *was* paying court to Miss Louisa Finsham.

His stride faltered. Was he? And if so, to what purpose?

Lord Hugh had not offered to escort them to Lady Stewart's ball. A lapse which afforded Louisa an alarming degree of disappointment. Which led to an unwelcome bout of heart-searching.

She did not choose to ride the following morning, the morning of the ball. She could not have said precisely why, but she was sunk deep in the dismals. It must be the muggy weather, she decided, since it was definitely not due to Lord Hugh's omission of the previous afternoon. He clearly did not wish to make his interest so clear that his intentions would be questioned. Which was as it should be.

Unless the weather turned cooler Lady Stewart's ballroom would be unendurable that evening. Although looking forward to the occasion, Louisa dreaded the crush, the stifling atmosphere compounded of smoking candles and overheated bodies which was bound to prevail since it always did on such occasions.

Her aunt had decided to remain in her room until later, so Louisa breakfasted alone in the small parlour. She had scarcely finished her coffee when Chausson announced a visitor for her.

'Mr Coynd?' queried Louisa in surprise. 'Whatever can he want? I hope nothing has happened to Jamie! Where is he?'

'I have showed heem into ze morning-room, *mademoiselle*.'

Louisa hurried through, anxiety clouding her brow. It must be Jamie; the tutor could have no other reason for calling on her.

She entered the room, carefully leaving the door open behind her to placate the proprieties, to find Mr Coynd pacing impatiently. She had seldom seen him other than on a horse, and was surprised to see how jerky was his stride. He turned upon her entrance and executed an elaborate bow.

'Miss Finsham!' His voice sounded strangely hoarse.

Louisa curtsied. 'Good morning, Mr Coynd!' She walked to a chair and seated herself, indicating that her visitor should do the same. 'You wished to speak with me? Is it about Jamie?'

'Lord Thurrock?' He looked startled as he perched on the edge of a nearby sofa. He was not ill-looking, considered Louisa, being smoothly handsome, but he lacked the address of someone like Lord Hugh. Perhaps that was due to being forced into a semi-menial position. 'No, it is not about James, Miss Finsham.' He paused a moment and suddenly burst out, 'Miss Louisa!' His voice and manner became ardent. 'You must know that I hold you in the greatest regard, Louisa. You have become the dearest object of my heart!' He flung himself on one knee in front of his startled hostess and placed a dramatic hand on his brocaded waistcoat, somewhere about the region of his heart.

'Mr Coynd! Please!' exclaimed Louisa, recovering her voice and keeping it steady with some difficulty. She had had many proposals in her time, but none as embarrassing as this one threatened to become. 'Please go no further, sir, and get up, do!'

'No, my dearest Louisa! Not until I have your answer!' he declared, ignoring the first part of her injunction. 'I beg you to make me the happiest of men by bestowing your hand in marriage upon my unworthy self!'

He reached out to capture the said hand but Louisa managed to snatch it away in time.

Despite the less favourable feelings she had entertained for him these last days Louisa had still found him generally agreeable and did not want to set him down too severely. Neither did she wish to refuse him without leaving him his dignity.

'My family is ancient and its reputation without reproach,' he was going on earnestly. 'I know I have no fortune to inherit, but I am not entirely without means——'

'And I have plenty for both of us,' murmured Louisa, beginning to see the point of his surprising proposal. He could have no idea that her husband, if she took one, would gain control merely of her income, not of her fortune, which was the subject of a complicated legal settlement. 'Unfortunately, sir, I have no desire to marry, either you or anyone else. And now, if you will excuse me——' She began to rise.

But he remained at her feet, impeding her movement. 'My dearest Louisa! You cannot be so cruel! A refusal will break my heart!'

'I think not, sir, merely dent your pride a little, for I am persuaded you cannot love me and I am certain I do not love you. I am sensible of the honour you have done me in offering for my hand, but I do not believe I have ever given you cause to hope that your suit could be successful. And I was not aware of granting you permission to address me by my first name,' she added, unable to ignore his familiarity.

Coynd struggled to his feet, now every bit as stiff in his manner as Major Hewitson. 'No,' he said bitterly. 'You were all gracious friendship until Lord Hugh Deverill appeared on the scene!'

'Lord Hugh?' Louisa took the opportunity to rise to her own feet and fixed him with a repressive eye. 'His presence could make no difference to my opinion of you. You are Lord Thurrock's tutor. As such, you were and are entitled to my courtesy. But nothing more.'

'I may be a mere tutor to you, Miss Finsham, but my blood is as good as yours! I am grandson to an earl!'

'Blood, my dear sir, has nothing to say to it. I do not wish to marry you, that is all. I bid you good day.' She reached for the bell-pull. 'Chausson will see you out.'

The butler must have been hovering, probably listening, thought Louisa wryly, for he entered the room almost before she had rung.

'Show the gentleman out if you please, Chausson.'

Chausson bowed with grave dignity. 'Zees way, *monsieur.*'

'I shall not give up hope,' said Coynd, bowing.

Louisa was surprised by his dignity in defeat and felt rather sorry for him. She inclined her head. 'That is your privilege, sir, but I must warn you, your hope is misplaced,' she told him, as gently as she could.

Relief at his departure left her trembling. What an unpleasant interview with which to begin the day! At least she would not have to face him at the ball tonight. He was not in a financial position to move much in first circles, despite the right to which his blood entitled him. For which she was truly sorry, for his sake. But Hugh Deverill was a younger son and *he* had managed to advance his fortunes in a most creditable way.

No, she could not feel too sorry for Mr Coynd. But his presence would put a damper on her future outings with Jamie. She would just have to treat the tutor with cool reserve and hope he did not again overstep the bounds of propriety.

* * *

Louisa entered the Stewarts' residence arm in arm with her aunt. Amelia was resplendent in a gown of blue figured sarcenet with matching feathered turban. This Sir Charles Stewart, their host for the evening—confusing, she thought, to have two gentlemen of that name in Paris, although their surnames were spelt differently—was Lord Castlereagh's half-brother. He and his wife, popular and gracious hosts, waited to receive them. In the ballroom myriad candles in the chandeliers and wall-sconces lit the brilliant scene, several long mirrors on the walls reflecting men garbed either in colourful uniforms or in civilian finery: exquisite waistcoats under superfine coats worn with white breeches and stockings. Most escorted ladies in pastel muslins with flowers, ribbons and feathers in their hair. The scene was worthy of a painting, she thought, absorbing its exotic beauty with appreciation.

She herself had chosen a high-waisted gown in cream silk trimmed with primrose and violet, the skirt falling gracefully to the floor at the front, with a train behind, which could be raised by strings for dancing. An overskirt of filmy gauze floated about her like a sunlit cloud. Betty had fashioned a matching head-dress of ribbons and feathers which she knew became her. Her greeny hazel eyes roved the ballroom, searching for sight of the tall, imposing figure on whose arm she had once anticipated entering the room.

She soon picked him out. Like most other men he was bending over a beautiful woman. He moved and looked round, as though aware of her scrutiny. His face lit up and he made as though to come across to greet her.

But Louisa had recognised the woman he was with

and the shock made her gasp. She had not known that
Lady Kingslea had arrived in Paris. Louisa turned
abruptly, unable to keep her countenance, to find
Major Hewitson at her side. Just in time, she covered
her mortification with a brilliant smile.

He bowed, flushing slightly at the unexpected
warmth of her greeting. 'May I claim the honour of the
first pair of dances, Miss Finsham? You did promise
them yesterday morning——'

'Indeed, Major, so I did!' She handed him her dance
card, annoyed to notice that her hand trembled slightly.
Idiotish creature! To let the presence of Deverill's
mistress overset her. She had known precisely what he
was. But, she acknowledged, had allowed herself to be
bamboozled into forgetting! She would not forget
again.

Amelia departed for the card tables, where she
would spend her evening with other dowagers and
chaperons. A small crowd of admirers gathered round
Louisa, all anxious to mark her card. When Hugh
Deverill joined them and, with natural authority and
address, inserted himself ahead of the lesser mortals
clustered about her, she allowed him to take her card
without protest. She could scarcely make a scene here,
but the look she directed at him would have withered
anyone else. He lifted an enquiring brow, but otherwise
ignored her frosty demeanour, putting his initials
against a couple of dances and returning the card to her
trembling fingers without comment, except to bow and
remark, 'I shall look forward to standing up with you
in due course, Miss Finsham.'

'Devilish uncivil of him,' grumbled the man he had
displaced, a young captain of the ninety-fifth, dashing

in his green uniform. 'Deuce take it, I was about to claim the supper dance!'

Louisa hadn't noticed which dances Hugh Deverill had marked. Now she regarded the card with dismay. He had claimed the pair before supper. Not only would she be forced to dance a waltz with him, but also to endure the entire supper break in his company!

Major Hewitson, so heavily moustached it was difficult to make out more than a well-shaped lower lip and high cheekbones, danced surprisingly well, his apparent stiffness being all in his manner, not in the athletic limbs of a top-of-the-trees cavalryman. As they moved up the set Louisa began to relax, determined to enjoy herself, to put the thought of Hugh Deverill from her mind until the supper dance forced her to remember him.

Hewitson was not a great conversationalist, and he performed the movements of the dance mostly in silence, while Louisa chattered and smiled merrily to hide the distress in her heart. They came together and parted again at the dictates of the steps until they reached the top of the set, then joined hands to gallop down the middle to take their places at the other end. Panting, eyes brilliant, Louisa suddenly realised that Hewitson's blue gaze was fixed on her face with an expression of open admiration she had not seen there before. Her liveliness, her brilliant smiles, must be encouraging him more than she intended, she surmised, and realised that even in her first flush of indignation against Hugh Deverill she had not behaved with such boisterous, wanton disregard for conduct.

The thought sobered her. For the remainder of the two dances she moderated her behaviour. But the

major had received enough encouragement to overcome his natural shyness with the ladies.

As he returned her to her seat he asked where Lady
Nazeby might be found. 'I should like to seek an
interview with her,' he explained.

Louisa frowned. 'To what purpose, Major?'

'Is that not obvious, my dearest Miss Finsham? I
wish to seek her permission to pay my addresses to her
niece.'

Appalled, Louisa gazed up into his ardent eyes. Not
two proposals in one day! ''Twill do you no good,
Major,' she told him as calmly as she could. 'Lady
Nazeby's permission would be worthless. She is neither
my guardian nor in truth my chaperon, since I am past
the age when I need either, though she is kindness itself
in accompanying me on such occasions as this to offer
the protection of her presence.'

Undaunted, 'Then to whom should I apply, Miss
Finsham?' he persisted.

'No one, sir. The only person to whom you could
usefully apply would be me, and I must inform you
now that you would be well-advised to refrain from
doing so. I like you, Major Hewitson, but as a friend. I
would not welcome your addresses.'

He looked so embarrassed and crestfallen that
Louisa took pity.

'Do not refine over me, sir,' she advised gently. 'I
am not worthy of your regard. I fear I have flirted with
you most unforgivably tonight and am well-chastened
by the result. If I have given cause for hurt, I beg you
will feel able to forgive me.'

She stood up gazing into the Hussar's eyes, seeking
reassurance that he had not been too overset by her

refusal to entertain his suit. To the man watching from across the room it appeared as an intimate exchange beyond that of mere friendship. She had been flirting with the young cavalry officer throughout their dances, and now she appeared to be pleading for more of the fellow's attention. How, he wondered tersely, could the man possibly deny her anything she asked? He was surprised by the pain tearing through him at the thought. He wished he had not sought to engage her for the supper dances. She would clearly rather have spent her time with Hewitson. But, deuce take it, why should he allow the gallant major free rein? She couldn't truly entertain a *tendre* for the man. He had observed no previous sign of any such emotion in her and he'd seen them together often enough. No. When his chance came he would seize it and wipe memory of the other fellow from her mind.

At her apology the major cleared his throat and appeared more embarrassed than ever. 'I must ask you to forgive me for misreading your feelings, Miss Finsham. As for mine, they remain the same. But I shall not bother you further by expressing sentiments which must cause you distress.'

'And we may remain friends?'

'If that is your wish.'

She gave him her most warm smile. 'It is, Major. I value friendships above everything. I have no wish to marry.'

Mollified by this last statement, he made his bow and left. Louisa had little time to ponder on this latest turn of events, for she was immediately claimed for the next set, which was already forming. But although she smiled and danced energetically with a succession of partners she was careful not to incite further expressions of tender regard by a continuation of her immoderate behaviour. She had just had it forcefully brought home that to react in such a way because a certain gentleman had chosen to return to his mistress produced unfortunate consequences which affected others besides herself. And what did it matter to her if Hugh Deverill's mistress was in Paris? He was nothing to her.

A protestation which grew more loweringly unrealistic as the evening wore on.

Arriving late as usual and not, to Louisa's eye, looking his usual buoyant self, the Duke of Wellington soon presented himself before her.

'Dear me,' he remarked upon being informed that her card was already full. 'Yes, yes. But I cannot forgo the pleasure of a dance with you, my dear Miss Finsham.' Saying which, he boldly struck out the initials of one of his junior officers, substituted his own and handed back the card with a smile. 'You appear to be without the company of your aunt this evening, Miss Finsham. Will you not join my party?' He indicated the group of dashing ADCs and beautiful young women, who seemed to grow in numbers every week, gathered at one end of the ballroom.

Louisa, having quietly extricated herself from his court over the last week or so without, she hoped, giving cause for offence, did not wish to fall into that trap again. Her unaccountable reaction to Hugh Deverill seemed to have precipitated her into one indiscretion after another, and it had to stop.

She acknowledged the invitation with a grateful smile while seeking tactful words to refuse it. 'You are most kind, my lord, but I am quite comfortable here, I thank you. My aunt is but in the next room, enjoying a hand of cards. And here,' she added thankfully, 'is my next partner come to claim me!'

The Duke had no call to abide by the strict rules which governed her own behaviour at a ball. For him to dance more than twice with one of his young matrons did not cause a scandal, at least not one of the kind that could ruin a young lady's reputation, get her talked about and spoil her chances of making a good match. Lady Shelley appeared to be his favourite partner and Louisa had to admit she was as good a dancer as horsewoman. But for all his attempt at high spirits Louisa thought he often looked preoccupied that evening. More disturbing articles had appeared in the *St James's Chronicle*. She felt sorry for Wellington. For the hero of Waterloo it must be particularly distasteful to have the Press snapping at his heels like angry terriers, she thought, but, to the publishers, the more revered and famous their victim, the better they were served.

Between her worried anticipation of the coming supper dance and her indignation over the Duke's plight—he might not be above reproach, but he didn't deserve such vindictive persecution—Louisa accepted her partners, danced, made polite conversation, went through the motions like an automaton, but all the time she was acutely aware of Hugh Deverill's presence.

He had not joined any particular party, moving about the ballroom between dances, exchanging greetings and conversation with different people as he went. Doing the pretty as a diplomat, she thought with scorn. Though why she should scorn him for simply doing his duty she refused to consider. So far he had not danced twice with anyone, even Lady Kingslea, who did not lack for other partners. Louisa had to admit her to be an attractive creature, tiny, vivacious and fashionably fair. She seemed to have come with Lady Sidford. Louisa wondered why Lord Hugh had not joined their party.

There came a dance, though, the one before that for which he had engaged her, when both he and Lady Kingslea appeared to be absent from the ballroom. Her eyes searched the throng anxiously, willing one of them to be present. But neither was.

Were they together? In the conservatory, perhaps, or taking the air on the terrace? The intimate scenes presented by Louisa's imagination caused her to stumble and lose her place in the dance.

She apologised to her stout, sweating partner, a minor Russian prince, who gallantly brushed it aside. 'Understandable,' he said in his almost impeccable English. 'Many of the bourgeois present have no talent for the art of the dance. No wonder they make you lose your place.'

'Really, sir,' responded Louisa, jerked from her preoccupation by his condescending tone, 'I have never sought to blame another's performance for my own shortcomings. In my experience many of the rich cits dance extremely well, while some members of the aristocracy do so extremely badly.'

'Your kind heart does you credit, Miss Finsham,' puffed the Prince with even greater condescension, essaying a bow, the elegance of which was badly impeded by his corset.

Louisa decided that even good manners could be

taken too far and was glad when the movements of the dance saved her from having to reply. But because of this diversion she missed their return. When she next saw him Lord Hugh was leaning against the wall, arms crossed, watching her. She immediately felt a flush of heat invade her body. For an instant she glared back, then quickly looked away, but not before she had noticed his expression. The candles in a nearby sconce threw flickering shadows across his face, making it inscrutable, apart from the fact that his mouth was set in a tight, disapproving line.

He had the effrontery to disapprove of *her*!

She tossed her head defiantly, and felt her curls bounce, dislodging a feather already come rather loose from the effects of her energetic dancing. The moment the music stopped she excused herself to the Prince and made for the ladies' retiring-room. Lady Stewart's maid was in attendance and soon repaired the damage. Louisa lingered as long as she felt able, reluctant to return to the ballroom, hoping that by the time she did both dances would be over.

But as she approached she heard the strains of a Viennese waltz strike up. Hesitating on the threshold, wanting to disappear again but not quite having the determination, she became aware that Lord Hugh had been watching out for her and was at her side.

He bowed. 'I am flattered that you did not entirely renege on our dances, Miss Finsham. If you are fatigued, perhaps you would rather seek the fresh air of the terrace?'

Dear God! She'd rather endure to dance with him than spend even a few moments alone on the darkened terrace in his company! If he took advantage——

'Thank you, my lord, but I am not in the least fatigued,' she retorted sharply. 'I was forced to retire to restore my toilet.'

He glanced at her immaculate head, let his eyes linger on a face pink with indignation and maybe something else, and a small smile softened his lips. 'Then let us make the most of this waltz.'

He held out an imperious hand. Louisa placed hers in it and felt his other hand at her waist. Automatically, hers reached up to rest on his muscled arm. She had no time to savour the alarming effect this close contact had upon her before she was swept into the dance by a partner who was clearly expert in the art of the waltz.

CHAPTER SEVEN

THE experience was like nothing she had known before. It lasted far too long, yet not long enough.

She could spend the rest of her life in Hugh Deverill's arms, she realised dazedly as he whirled her around in the swift steps of the dance. It was where she belonged. Some part of her had recognised it the moment he had picked her up and carried her across the deck of the packet boat, but she had stubbornly refused to give the idea credence. Now, she could no longer deny it. Not that she had to like feeling the way she did, for she profoundly disapproved of his seducing other men's wives.

That evening she had watched him proving himself a polished, accomplished member of the *ton*, dancing with more grace than his appearance might suggest, conversing easily with one partner after another. Now she was experiencing his undoubted social skills at first hand. He would have taken Almack's by storm had he deigned to seek admission there. But he had kept his talents well hidden from London Society. She wondered why.

Her steps fitted his perfectly. All too soon the orchestra speeded its tempo to bring the dance to a breathless end. As it did so Hugh tightened his hold, drew her towards him until their bodies touched, and swept her into a series of dizzying twirls. When they stopped she had to cling on for a moment until the room ceased spinning. And her vertigo could only partly be attributed to the exigencies of the dance. It had almost as much to do with the potent effect of her partner's close proximity.

She regained her balance to discover both his hands at her waist, steadying her. He was too near, his presence overwhelming. She drew a deep breath, only to become aware of the scent of him, not unpleasantly sweaty like that of the Prince, but clean and fresh, tinged with the faintest hint of sandalwood.

He, of course, was neither dizzy nor out of breath nor unduly affected by her nearness. He was, however, gazing down at her with something in his eyes which disappeared the moment she looked up. His mouth curved into a twisted smile.

'It seems we suit each other in the dance at least. Our steps match well.'

'But in very little else, I vow!'

'Do not be so sure, my dear Miss Finsham.' His eyes slid from the confused expression in hers, rested a moment on the tell-tale pulse fluttering like a trapped bird at the base of her throat, paused briefly to drink in the beauty of her breasts as they rose and fell in agitation. Then they lifted to rest on her parted lips. 'It seems to me that we suit in at least one other way.'

His hands tightened on her waist. His gaze remained on her mouth, his meaning obvious, but his thick black lashes veiled the expression in his eyes.

Louisa gasped at this forthright declaration and stepped back. He dropped his hands immediately. 'We are becoming a spectacle, sir!' she informed him sharply, realising that almost everyone else had left the floor, many already making their way out of the ballroom in search of supper. Nevertheless, too many curious glances were being thrown their way. 'I am already become an object of gossip, and I will thank you not to aid the scandal-mongers in their task!' she finished tautly.

He bowed. When he spoke his voice had become remote, icy, sending a chill through her. 'Indeed, Miss Finsham. I have been at some pains to aid you in countering their tattle, and for that reason refrained from offering my escort this evening. To appear once on my arm should have been enough to silence it, to appear twice might well have given it a new direction. But your own behaviour so far tonight can hardly be said to have assisted your cause.'

Louisa, who had been somewhat mollified by the first part of his statement, was incensed by the remainder. 'You surely flatter yourself, my lord, to suggest that your patronage should offer me protection from the gossips! And how dare you criticise my behaviour? Although in truth you have done little else since we met!'

'I had not meant to appear critical, merely to offer you advice.'

'Oh! You. . .you hypocrite! You can stand there condemning me when your mistress. . .'

She suddenly trailed off as an amused smile lightened his face, belying the suddenly intent look in his eyes.

'Never tell me you are jealous, my love?'

'Of course not!' But she was! It was not righteous indignation she had felt at the sight of Lady Kingslea, but another, much more oversetting emotion. And how dared he call her his love? 'I simply despise men who cuckold others!' she snapped.

Again he bowed, all gravity now. 'That is your privilege, Miss Finsham. Shall we proceed through to supper?'

Louisa did not feel she could eat a thing and did not want to remain in his odious company. But people were still looking at them, suspecting a quarrel by their manner, although their voices had been kept low. She did not wish to make matters worse. So she nodded.

He offered his arm. And, because she did not want to make a spectacle of their differences, she took it.

'I had thought,' he said quietly as they paced together towards supper, 'that we had become friends. Maria Kingslea is not in Paris at my invitation.'

'She's not?' muttered Louisa uncertainly.

'No.'

'Oh.'

She considered this for a moment, surprised that he should have volunteered the information.

'Then why is she here?' she demanded.

He shrugged and looked down at her, saw the uncertainty reflected in her face and smiled deprecatingly. 'To try to persuade me into becoming her lover.' She did not possess conventional beauty but striking looks which were infinitely more attractive, he thought as he continued to drown in her wide, greeny hazel gaze. The tiny green flecks around her iris enchanted him.

'Your lover? But I thought. . .'

'You were not alone. Maria saw to that. But my visits to the Kingslea establishment were made to see my old friend, her husband. She took some convincing, but I believe that she has now finally accepted the futility of her campaign.'

Louisa dragged her eyes from his to where Maria Kingslea was flirting with a portly Prussian count. Following her gaze, Hugh felt a surge of relief. Maria's immediate pursuit of another man showed how little she had really cared for him.

Why he felt it necessary to explain himself to Louisa Hugh could not fully understand. But the contempt in her eyes had been too discomfiting. He valued her good opinion.

The supper-room was crowded. He found seats in a secluded corner, from which Louisa could watch proceedings from behind the protecting screen of a huge potted fern, and, leaving her fanning herself to stir the air from a nearby open window, went off in search of food, for the dishes had been laid entirely on side-tables in the French buffet style.

He returned unexpectedly quickly given the dense-ness of the crush, bearing, with commendable dexterity and steady hands, two plates laden with delicacies plus two glasses of wine.

'I thought you might enjoy this claret better than lemonade,' he remarked with a smile as he balanced his booty on the narrow ledge of the pedestal holding the potted plant, 'and I also assumed that you would not wish your wine watered.'

'Thank you, my lord. You guessed well. I have long passed the age of being obliged to consume lemonade, and have a fairly strong head. I find the wine here delicious. The addition of water ruins it.'

'Precisely.'

His absence had given Louisa time to gather her wits and to realise that her censure, and her extreme reaction, had been unwarranted. She had behaved foolishly, and deserved Lord Hugh's displeasure. But although she did not enjoy being at odds with him it would be difficult to apologise. Yet if she did not she would put in jeopardy the tentative friendship which had begun to spring up between them. On the other hand, with her new knowledge of her own vulnerability, could she afford to renew and even deepen it? She would be asking to suffer hurt again.

But he had taken the trouble to put her misapprehension right and appeared ready to be on terms again. Logic and intrinsic honesty forced her to conclude that she must do the same, although no amount of honesty could force her to admit openly to jealousy. So she must word her apology carefully. And not allow him to guess how much his nearness disturbed her.

Once he was seated, therefore, and she had enjoyed a sustaining mouthful of wine and enjoyed a first taste of a delicious pigeon patty, she began, her voice pitched as low as was consistent with his being able to hear her.

'I have to confess, my lord, that I do not accept criticism easily. It is a fault in me which I know renders me most unsuitable as a wife.' His raised eyebrows gave her pause for an agonising moment. She should not have mentioned marriage, even by implication. Colouring hotly, she rushed on. 'Since we met you have found many reasons to criticise me, my lord, and my response has been, I fear, to behave in a manner to thoroughly deserve it. I loathe infidelity and hate flirts—of either sex—who use their powers to humiliate and demean. If I have appeared on occasion to be one, then I beg you to believe that I am truly sorry. I do not seek to engage a gentleman's interest simply to inflate my own vanity.' Her speech ended, she bit into the patty with a determination designed to disguise her discomfiture.

'Then I must apologise most sincerely, for, as I have already said, I did not wish to offend you. If I drove you to an extreme of behaviour by my ill-advised words I am truly sorry.'

Louisa swallowed convulsively and felt the food go down in an uncomfortable lump. She smiled. 'After such a handsome apology, what can I do but pronounce you forgiven?'

'And yet,' he mused, a slight smile curving his lips, 'consciously or unconsciously, your natural manner and spirits do engage the interest of almost every gentleman you meet.'

Not her looks, thought Louisa ruefully. She picked up her glass and tried to wash down the lump of food with a generous mouthful of wine.

'I cannot conceive of what you might mean, my lord.'

'No?' His tone was not unfriendly, merely quizzical. 'Tell me, dear Miss Finsham, how many proposals of marriage have you turned down since your come-out?'

Colour flooded Louisa's face again as she remembered the two she'd received only that day. 'I cannot remember,' she muttered awkwardly. 'But I have never led any gentleman to hope for an acceptance should he make a declaration!'

Only David, Lord Radburn, she thought in distress. She had given him every encouragement, but she had been the one to suffer the pain of rejection, not he.

'Have you not?'

'No, sir!'

He sounded mildly sceptical. It seemed important to convince him. 'Would you say, my lord, that my dealings with Mr Coynd should have lead him to expect a positive answer to a declaration?'

That had shaken him! He stared at her in confused amazement before his gaze narrowed.

'William Coynd has proposed marriage to you?'

'Aye, sir. This very morning!'

He eyed her steadily. 'I confess to feeling surprise. Nothing in your behaviour that I have witnessed, admittedly in limited circumstances, had led me to believe that you favoured him above Major Hewitson or any other gentleman for that matter. Yet your general air of lively friendship may make many men feel——' He shrugged, allowing the gesture to complete the thought for him. 'I suppose he may have interpreted your interest in riding with young Lord Thurrock as a particular interest in him,' he mused, 'although I doubt it. . .he needs a fortune. . .and can be quite unscrupulous when it suits him.'

'I can assure you, my lord, that my desire to ride with the young Earl had nothing to do with the presence of Mr Coynd! On the contrary, he accompanied his lordship only on the Dowager Countess's insistence, although I confess I found him agreeable company at first.'

'And therefore treated him in your usual delightful manner. But you have not found him so agreeable latterly?'

'Since your meeting with him in the Bois he has tended to behave in an over-familiar manner.'

'I see.' He drained his glass. He had not eaten much. 'I fear you have become victim of an old jealousy, Miss Finsham, for which I apologise. I might have guessed my presence would cause him to move speedily to secure his fortune.'

'You believe it was my fortune he desired, sir, and not my person?'

He smiled suddenly, a sweet, placatory smile which rendered her rather breathless. 'Knowing him, I fear so, my dear, though I am certain he would not despise your person. And you must be aware that your fortune may have inspired many of the proposals you have received, since you protest you gave the gentlemen no conscious encouragement.'

Louisa coloured again. She had thought herself beyond being put to the blush by anything a gentleman said, but this man seemed to have that kind of effect on her. 'I am, sir,' she retorted tartly. 'I have long suspected that my fortune accounted for the large number of suitors who have sought my hand despite every discouragement I have offered. I can think of no other reason for it.' A certain pride made her go on. 'Although I do not believe Major Hewitson to be in need of funds. He is reputedly vastly rich, so my person may not be entirely devoid of value in certain gentlemen's eyes.'

'I never suggested it was. On the contrary, I myself find it quite entrancing.' His leisurely gaze conducted an assessment of her charms, raising her temperature further. Finally his thick brows lifted, furrowing his forehead. He met her embarrassed, furious eyes, the expression in his own amused. 'So Major Hewitson was encouraged to ask for your hand, was he?'

He had seen her flirting with poor Major Hewitson earlier. Had she remembered that in time she would not have mentioned the Hussar's proposal! But she

had, and could scarcely blame Lord Hugh for his
reception of the news. But his attitude made her fume.

'Not precisely.' Louisa crumbled a morsel of bread
between her fingers, rolling it into a small hard wad in
lieu of grinding *him* into little pieces. 'But he requested
permission to apply to my aunt on the subject.'

'And what answer did you give?'

He sounded lazily amused. But his fingers had
tightened about the stem of his glass and his grey-blue
eyes had become watchful.

'I told him that such an application would not serve,
for my aunt has no say in the matter.'

'He should apply to you?'

'Yes.' Louisa faced him challengingly. 'I am in the
fortunate position of being able to make my own
decision over whom I marry. I also informed him that I
had no intention of bestowing my hand on any gentleman at the present moment.'

'Do you not wish to wed?' he asked softly.

His gentle tone disarmed her. Her anger dissipated
as swiftly as it had risen. She shrugged slender bare
shoulders outlined by the low neckline and little puff
sleeves of her gown. But her chin lifted in an unconsciously defiant gesture. 'Only if I can find an agreeable
gentleman who does not covet my fortune and threaten
to lose it by gaming or dissipate it by expensive living.
Or both.' There was no call to inform his of the exact
status of her dower. She never advertised it. Any man
she would consider suitable as a husband would not
care.

'And you have not met such a one?'

'No.'

She would not elaborate further or tell him of her

youthful heartbreak. That would serve no purpose but to make her more vulnerable. Besides, David Radburn was in the past, and had been a mistake. She reached for her glass again. The wine was making her excessively hot. Having taken another sip, she used her fan energetically to cool her flushed face.

'I am sorry. You do not deserve to waste into an old maid.'

She looked at him, startled by both his words and his tone.

'I would rather that, my lord, than make a bad marriage. If only I were a man! I could take up a profession and feel of some use in the world.'

'So you have indicated before. But then the world would have lost the gracious presence of a beautiful woman and, mayhap, a distinguished hostess.'

'Really, sir! You are roasting me!' But that had not been his intention. She could see it in his eyes. She rushed on, heedless of the sudden thumping of her heart. 'As it is, I shall probably retire to the country and concentrate on farming and breeding horses on my aunt's estate. I already know all Pershaw can teach me. Aunt Nazeby can leave the estate as she wills, and has promised it to me.'

'So you have expectations, in addition to your present fortune.'

'Yes, but no one knows of my aunt's intention! They believe Minchingham will revert to the Nazeby estate. I beg you will not speak of it!'

She had said too much. Could she trust him with the knowledge? His gaze had become serious and held some element she could not quite fathom. Was it simply admiration? Compassion? Or appraisal?

'I will not. I am honoured that you felt you could entrust your secret to me,' he averred quietly.

But she hadn't felt that at all. The atmosphere between them had suddenly become so easy that she had spoken without thought! But all the same, looking into his steady eyes, knowing how many diplomatic secrets he must be obliged to keep, she knew she could trust him.

Hugh stood up. Louisa glanced at him enquiringly, fanning herself against the heated atmosphere. People and noise filled the supper-room and yet they had seemed to be quite alone behind their fern. Now he was preparing to abandon their isolation. Disappointment shot through her like a pain.

'You are feeling the heat,' he observed.

'It is the wine,' said Louisa, wishing to blame anything but his presence for her flushed appearance. 'I should have had it watered after all.'

He regarded her quizzically for a moment. Then his rough-hewn yet utterly compelling mouth curved into a smile, proving again how much more attractive were his rugged features than the foppish good looks of Mr Coynd or the classically sculpted face of Major Hewitson! 'Whatever the cause, allow me to escort you to the terrace for a breath of fresh air,' he suggested. 'It should be pleasant in the garden after the atmosphere in here. Will you need a shawl?'

Her disappointment turning speedily to anticipation, Louisa rose with alacrity, clutching her fan and tiny reticule. Somehow the thought of walking on the terrace with him had lost its terror. The prospect beckoned invitingly. And if people wished to gossip, let them!

'I shall do perfectly well as I am,' she assured him. 'The evening is so warm I cannot possibly catch a chill!'

'Exactly my sentiments.' He offered his arm. 'Shall we proceed?'

How wonderful it was to be in amity with him again. Louisa placed her fingers on the offered arm and as she did so a thrill of pleasure ran through her.

Passing among the other guests to reach the door, they were accosted by several friends and acquaintances, all of whom, Louisa was certain, were speculating as to the exact degree of intimacy between herself and her escort. Hugh appeared to have put aside his scrupulous desire not to arouse more gossip by being seen to show an interest in her. She had never considered that particular matter to be of any consequence. His partiality for her could be considered entirely proper. The Duke's, if any, could not.

He was to be seen, still surrounded by his bevy of youthful admirers, though looking rather less cheerful than normal. Her dance with him was still to come. Prince Metternich's, too. The ball was little more than halfway through.

The terrace ran right across the back of the house, accessible from several rooms. Hugh appeared to know his way, leading her down the curving staircase and through the library to a tall door standing open to the night.

A rocket shot skywards as they emerged, set off from one of the pleasure gardens lining the Champs Elysées.

'A poor show,' said Hugh disparagingly. 'Only wait until the display to be held in the Tivoli gardens next week. Shall you go?'

'I believe so.'

'Then,' he said softly, 'you must allow me to escort you.'

Louisa looked up into his shadowed face and smiled. 'That would indeed be a kindness, sir.'

A few flambeaus had been provided to cast light on the terrace and several candle-lanterns hung from trees further off. But essentially the gardens were lit by the soft rays of a full moon. People strolled in and out of the shadows, appearing and disappearing, the night air carrying their voices to the couple still standing on the terrace.

'There is a pond with a fountain beyond that greenery,' advised Hugh. 'Should you like to see it?'

Such an invitation would shock any chaperon, thought Louisa, amused. She had no idea where Amelia was; she had not seen her in the supper-room, so she was probably still engaged with her cards. There was no one to say her nay. Not that her aunt could have stopped her, but her disapproving presence would have cast a shadow over the escapade.

'Very much,' she acknowledged demurely.

Her hand remained on his arm as they trod the path towards the pond. Emerging from the shelter of the narrow band of shrubs, Louisa gave a small gasp of delight. Statuary gleamed in the moonlight and the trickling sound of water flowing from the fountain filled her senses with soothing magic.

'Charming, is it not?' murmured Hugh.

They had circled the pond when the moon disappeared behind a cloud, leaving them in almost total darkness. Hugh drew her aside, into the shelter of a large shrub. Without a word he took her in his arms and lowered his lips to hers.

David had kissed her, once. She had found it pleasant enough, but scarcely earth-shattering. Why had she
ever imagined herself in love with him? she wondered
as her heart began to pound and her limbs to liquefy so
that she was obliged to hang on to the lapels of Hugh's
coat for support.

As he felt her response, what had begun as a tender,
exploratory tasting of her lips deepened into fierce
demand. Despite her inexperience Louisa found her
lips clinging to his, felt strange spears of delicious
sensation invading her body.

This was what instinct had been telling her it would
be like in the arms of a man she loved. Joy surged
through her, renewing her strength so that she was able
to loose her hold on his coat and lift her hands to his
nape, where her fingers could tangle satisfyingly in the
vibrant silkiness of his hair.

They shouldn't be doing this, yet she had expected
no less when she'd accepted his invitation to walk in
the gardens with him. She loved him. The temptation
had been too great.

But then, dashingly, she remembered that he did not
love her. He was no stranger to this kind of dalliance.
It meant nothing to him. And the moon emerged from
behind the cloud and voices could be heard, drawing
nearer.

She used her hands to push at his shoulders. For a
moment longer he savoured her lips before he let them
go; but he kept her within the circle of his arms.

Shaken to the core, Louisa leant her forehead against
his shoulder, recovering her composure. His breathing
was ragged and his heart beating like a drum inside his
chest. So he had been moved, too. That was something

to cling to, although she had been led to believe that men quite easily were—moved.

She thought she felt the light touch of his lips upon her hair. 'Louisa,' he murmured.

It was the first time he had called her by her given name. The sound of it on his lips thrilled her through, but she could not allow him to guess.

'You forget yourself, my lord,' she accused, her voice low and far from steady as she extricated herself from his embrace. The soft voices were coming ever nearer, though the people they belonged to were out of sight behind intervening shrubs.

'Oh, no, my dear, that I do not,' Hugh kept his voice down and drew her deeper into the shadow of the bushes. She had to follow or risk detection. 'I have wanted to kiss you since we first met crossing the Channel. But if I have offended you by doing so I pray you will forgive me.'

The errant moon had appeared again. Its rays penetrated the sheltering branches enough for her to see his face, and its expression was grave. Yet the light in his eyes gave a hint of the suppressed elation he must be feeling at her ready surrender to his practised seduction.

Decorum and self-esteem told her to protest that he had. But the words of condemnation would not come.

'No,' she admitted instead, 'you did not offend me. When I agreed to walk out here with you I expected nothing less.'

The soft gleam of her smile caused him to catch his breath.

'Then you have felt it too! This attraction which pulls us together whether we will or no!' He reached out and captured her hands. His voice deepened. 'What shall we do about it, Louisa?'

'Do about it? Why, my lord, what do you suggest?'

'Hugh,' he murmured. 'You must call me Hugh, at least when we are not in company. As to what we do— I confess I have no inclination to wed. And—thus far I have never attempted to steal any woman's virginity.'

'Then it seems, my lord, that you can suggest nothing to the point.'

His grip tightened on her hands. 'Hugh,' he insisted. 'Say it, my dearest girl. I long to hear it on your lips.'

'Hugh.' His name came out cold and hard. Her saying it like that could not provide him with the same pleasure his speaking hers so tenderly had given her, but she could not help that. His words had killed all the lovely warmth his embrace had kindled. He had been playing with her. And she, fool that she was, had allowed him to. Now pride did come to her rescue. 'I am grateful to you for the experience—Hugh. I have reached an age when I feel at liberty to indulge my curiosity about such matters, to allow my desires a little rein. . .up to a point. I found your kiss pleasant enough.' A man of his experience would surely know that—it would do no good to deny her reaction. 'I should not in the least mind repeating it. But of course I could not allow any deeper intimacy.'

'Until after you were wed.'

The words had been said in a flat voice, but Louisa at once suspected them. She had to make her position quite clear.

'Naturally.'

'You told me you had no intention to marry, at least at the moment.'

'So I did! And I meant it!' But oh, how quickly she would change her mind were *he* to propose! she thought sadly.

'I see.'

'And now perhaps you will be so kind as to escort me back to the ballroom. The dancing must soon begin again.'

'Not so fast!' His voice and manner had lost their tension. A smile seemed to have entered his eyes. 'I will resist the temptation to make you an offer if you will promise to reject it should I weaken. Having agreed that neither of us desires matrimony we may surely remain friends. And I, too, found the experiment of a few moments ago exceedingly agreeable. Since I gather you have no objection, I shall repeat it whenever opportunity presents itself.'

Before she had time to collect her wits she was back in his arms, his lips claiming hers. For a moment she resisted, wished those voices would come even nearer, but they did not. On the contrary, they had passed by and were fading into the distance. But then she forgot all about resistance, all about others in the garden.

His lips were too persuasive. Not demanding, not passionate, not possessive but caressingly, teasingly tender. This was the Hugh she loved. The one to whom she could so easily fall victim.

Had he asked her to become his mistress then she would have agreed. Afterwards, she was to ask herself how she could possibly have lost all regard for reputation and propriety. But at that moment she knew she would gladly abandon the whole world if she could only remain in Hugh Deverill's arms.

CHAPTER EIGHT

HOWEVER, he did not ask. He finished the thoroughly
unsettling kiss, released her and ceremoniously offered
his arm.

'You wished to return to the ballroom. No doubt
your next partner is anxiously awaiting your
appearance.'

Louisa felt almost too fragile to walk. How dared he
assault her senses in that practised, calculated manner?
His voice had been coolly teasing—but she noticed his
breathing had suffered and his hand trembled slightly.
So although he tried to hide it under a careless manner
he had not been unaffected by that embrace any more
than the other. He had just exercised better control
over his reactions.

Determined to hide her own mortifying weakness,
Louisa took his proffered arm, willing her hand to
remain steady and her legs to carry her. The first
devastating effect of his kiss was passing, though, and
she managed to stroll back to the library door quite
steadily, assuming an insouciance of manner she was
far from feeling.

In the dimness of the terrace, deserted now, he
stopped again to take her hands and place lingering
kisses on each palm, resurrecting all the wretchedly
delicious shooting, melting sensations she had felt
before. Yet she hadn't the resolution to stop him. For

the moment the sheer, enervating pleasure of the caress held her in thrall.

'Can you find your own way back from here?' he asked quietly. 'It would be sensible for us to return to the ballroom separately. Otherwise the gossips will have a field-day.'

Louisa nodded abruptly. She had not spoken a word on the way back, afraid her voice would betray her. Now all she wanted was to escape the disturbing, magnetic presence of this man, to recover her poise before being forced to dance again.

He, of course, was proving once more how adept he was at conducting this kind of intrigue. Whatever he protested about his affair with Maria Kingslea being nothing more than rumour, they had both been absent at the same time, returning separately to the ballroom. Now he was sending her back on her own. Yet she had only herself to blame for her predicament. She had invited his caresses. Which made it all the more lowering to realise how little the interlude had meant to him.

He remained behind on the terrace when she turned and almost ran in. Still in a flutter, she made her way up to the ladies' retiring-room. Since no strains of music reached her ears the after-supper dancing could not yet have begun. She had time.

'Why, Louisa, my love! There you are!' Lady Nazeby turned from one of the ornately gilded mirrors to greet her niece. 'I had wondered where you could be.'

Several other ladies looked round at this and Louisa found herself flushing guiltily. But a glance beyond her aunt into the mirror told her she had nothing to fear from her appearance. Her hair and costume were still in perfect order. Hugh's hands had not wandered. Had done no more than hold her tightly against him. His lips had wreaked only invisible devastation.

'It was so hot. I merely sought a breath of fresh air,' she informed her aunt rather breathlessly. Her lack of breath could be explained by her having climbed the stairs too quickly.

'Alone?'

Surely Aunt Nazeby must realise she did not wish to answer such a question! Ignoring the curious looks, Louisa retorted with the truth. 'No. Lord Hugh escorted me.'

'Oh,' said Amelia blandly. 'I do believe Deverill to be quite the most agreeable and considerate gentleman here. He even took the trouble to seek me out in the card-room earlier, in order to pay his respects.'

'Earlier?' repeated Louisa faintly.

'Yes, shortly before the supper dance. He said he was taking you in, and wanted to make certain I did not disapprove. As though I would!' she added airily.

Relieved to the point of jubilation, castigating herself for another excursion into the realms of unjustifiable distrust, Louisa concentrated on the unnecessary task of rearranging the neckline of her dress. Closer inspection in the mirror showed her lips to be swollen to a new ripeness. So some of the devastation he had wrought did show. As she dabbed her skin with eau-de-Cologne she prayed no one else would notice.

'I must hurry,' she said. 'The orchestra is tuning up. They will be standing up for the next set soon, and my partner will be waiting.'

'You have every dance taken, I'll be bound,' smiled Amelia happily. 'You always do, my love.'

Her aunt, thought Louisa, seemed inordinately smug about something. She wondered what.

The remainder of the evening seemed endless. Louisa had developed a headache and at one point decided to leave early, but finding her aunt happily immersed in her card game hadn't the heart to tear the older woman away. Hugh Deverill sat at a nearby table deeply engrossed in a hand of whist. He did no more than glance up and acknowledge her with a slight nod and she looked quickly away. She supposed he considered he had done his duty by dancing until supper and now he intended to enjoy himself.

She returned to the ballroom reluctantly, to be claimed by a succession of partners, including General Alva, the Duke's Spanish ADC, Sir Charles Stuart the ambassador, Prince Metternich and Wellington himself. She should be feeling flattered by so much elevated attention, she knew, but somehow her success brought little satisfaction. If she could not dance with Hugh she did not want to dance with anyone. He had quite spoilt her evening. Maria Kingslea, she noted, was concentrating her undoubted charms on the Prussian count and had already stood up with that foreign nobleman at least four times.

Of Hugh there continued to be no sign in the ballroom, but she knew where he was. Not that the knowledge did her a bit of good. Unable to follow him with her eyes, she found herself doing so in her imagination instead. It really was most inconvenient to be so affected by a man. She could only hope that her stupid infatuation would soon die.

'Did you enjoy yourself, my love?' demanded Amelia in the darkness of the carriage on the way home. 'I thought it a splendid occasion. And I won handsomely at the card table.'

'You were always lucky at cards,' smiled Louisa, evading her aunt's question.

'Skilled, I would say,' protested Amelia good-humouredly. 'I cannot understand why you do not play. I am certain that with your brain you would make a handsome profit.'

'But being a woman I am not allowed to have a brain,' teased Louisa. 'Besides, I prefer other forms of amusement, Aunt. And I would risk losing, which I could ill afford.'

'You amaze me, Louisa. So spirited and adventurous in some ways and so cautious in others! You invite scandal by your rash behaviour yet will not risk a few guineas on a hand of cards!'

'I have moderated my behaviour, Aunt Nazeby. Do not ring a peal over me, I beg. I have developed such a headache!'

'You spent too long in the garden,' observed Amelia with an ingenuousness Louisa knew to be deceptive. Lady Nazeby did not miss much concerning her niece.

The carriage passed a flambeau at that moment and Louisa hoped its light would not reveal her discomposure.

'It was so beautiful out there,' she offered defensively.

'And the company delightful, I have no doubt. I wish that young man might speak for you, my love. He has not done so yet?'

Stunned, Louisa could only stare at the pale blob which was all she could see of her aunt's face now the flambeau had been left behind. 'No, Aunt, he has not, and will not.' Her voice sounded lamentably strangled. 'He has no more wish to wed than I have!'

'So you have spoken of it,' murmured Amelia artlessly. 'It is plain to see you have developed a *tendre* for him, and he is far from indifferent to you, my love. You should try to fix his interest. You are unlikely to find a more suitable candidate for a husband.'

'Oh, do not tease me so, Aunt! I have developed no such thing! I have said many times that I do not wish to marry. And my head aches so!'

'I wonder why? Oh, very well, my love,' she agreed, at Louisa's exasperated snort, 'but do not blame me when you are old and lonely——'

'Aunt!'

'Forgive me, my love.'

Subdued at last, Amelia subsided into silence. The rattle of the iron wheels on the cobbles, the clip-clop of the horses' hooves were now the only sounds to disturb Louisa's throbbing head. And, to her relief, they too soon stopped as the carriage drew up before their *hôtel* and she was able to alight. Once inside she bade her aunt a hasty but affectionate goodnight and made for the sanctuary of her room.

She could not sleep. Long after Betty had been dismissed she sat by the open window listening to the night noises drifting in. The chirrup of a nesting bird, the neigh of a horse in the nearby stables, the distant grinding of carriage wheels and sound of hooves as some late-night reveller returned home soothed rather than offended her jangled nerves. Her head still throbbed, but not so badly, for she had taken just a little laudanum. But not enough to send her to sleep. Mayhap she should have taken more.

The moon threw its light over the scene, reminding her of those magic moments in Sir Charles and Lady Stewart's garden.

But what was the use of remembering? It only brought pain to overlay the pleasure. She had found a man she would be happy to wed, in the right circumstances. Aunt Nazeby was correct there. But Hugh Deverill was not the marrying kind. And he had believed her when she had protested her reluctance to enter into the state of matrimony.

He was charming, courteous, no idle fop but a conscientious and, some said, brilliant diplomat. And she tended to believe, now, that his reputation for seduction was highly exaggerated. He was all she had ever wished for in a husband.

But he had absolutely no reason to wed. He could take his pleasure, satisfy his needs where he willed, just as other single men did. And many married men, too, she reminded herself sternly. Yet she would be prepared to take the risk if she could wed Hugh Deverill.

She attracted him. There was little doubt on that point, she thought, becoming hot at the remembrance of his kisses, elated yet alarmed, for she could scarcely understand or trust her own astonishing response. But he had firmly closed the door on any idea of marriage between them. Only one course remained open to her. She must recover from this nonsense, avoid proximity, treat him merely as a friend and make quite certain never to give him another opportunity to kiss her.

* * *

Louisa abandoned her early morning ride for the next couple of days, preferring to avoid those who had— and the one who had not—proposed marriage to her. She missed the contact with Jamie and felt rather guilty at allowing her personal feelings to prevent her from keeping an eye on Amelia's grandson. She sent him a message of regret, saying she hoped to resume her morning exercise shortly.

Meanwhile another challenge loomed ahead. She had to face Lord Hugh at the Duke of Wellington's banquet in honour of the Emperor of Russia and the King of Prussia. With any luck at all, in such a large company, she might avoid having to speak to him at all.

She knew she was not looking her sparkling best and therefore took care with her toilet. But nothing could hide the tired lines about her eyes, the result of two almost sleepless nights.

Betty tutted over her mistress's sad looks as she fiddled with frills and ribbons and carefully arranged her curls to best effect. Amelia kept a discreet silence, simply eyeing her niece from time to time in thoughtful contemplation.

Thanks largely to Betty's efforts Louisa presented an elegant and attractive appearance when she arrived at the Duke's residence, a few yards from their own. Amelia had not ordered the carriage out to carry them so short a distance, the ladies preferring to walk, escorted by two stalwart footmen. Seeing the crush of carriages waiting their turn to disgorge their passengers at the Duke's door, Amelia remarked that although it might not be quite genteel to arrive on foot it was certainly more convenient. Holding her train clear and picking her way carefully over the dusty ground, Louisa agreed.

Lady Castlereagh was acting as Wellington's hostess. She and Amelia were old friends. The Duke had a special word for Louisa and they passed on into the reception-room to discover the seating arrangements.

Hugh was already there. He came forward, smiling easily, his hair arranged *à la Titus*, dressed more dashingly than she had seen him before in a splendid blue silk cut-away tailed coat over a cream brocaded, collared waistcoat studded with coloured stones and embroidery. Cream small-clothes descended over his powerful thighs to white silk stockings and polished black pumps. Expensive Brussels lace frothed from his shirt-front. His cravat had been tied with complex and faultless artistry. He must consider this a very special occasion.

The tumultuous reaction the sight of him provoked shocked Louisa. But she had been ready for the meeting and managed to greet him with formal courtesy and without a blush.

'We are to be dinner partners, I find,' he murmured. Seeing the consternation she could not hide, he smiled wryly. 'Do not be alarmed, my dearest Miss Finsham.'

Amelia's attention had fortunately been diverted by the arrival of the Duke of Alva, deputed her partner for the occasion. Wellington's Spanish ADC bowed before the older woman with elaborate courtesy and led her away. Louisa watched her aunt's departure with a sense of having been abandoned in her hour of need.

When Hugh resumed their conversation it was essentially private. 'I promise to serve you with perfect decorum despite the provocation of your delightful presence,' he whispered wickedly.

Louisa had to swallow before she was able to reply. The highly correct Hugh Deverill in flirtatious mood was something she had not seen before and therefore had not expected. Yet his manner did lighten the atmosphere between them. She could treat the entire situation as a joke.

'I am persuaded that there will be others at the table, my lord, which will safely inhibit any liberties you may feel inclined to take,' she returned archly.

But nothing could dampen the effect of sitting beside him for the entire banquet. The thought almost made her swoon. If she did, of course, she would be excused attendance. Many ladies would have resorted to a strategic and interesting faint in the circumstances, but Louisa was made of sterner stuff. Such cowardice would only deprive her of the opportunity to be present at a function to which all the nobility of England and all the leaders of the Allied nations had been invited. She would not allow Hugh Deverill's presence to spoil her evening. Particularly as she had begun to wonder what strings he had pulled to acquire her as his partner for the evening.

He chuckled and the sound made Louisa's toes curl. He knew exactly how she was feeling and relished her discomfort.

'May I be permitted to say how well your gown suits you, my dear Louisa?'

Louisa covered her acute discomfort at his tone and the familiarity with a rush of words. 'I had it designed by a modiste here in Paris.' She touched the bows and embroidery decorating the extremely low neckline and smoothed down the panel at the front of her skirt, which was outlined with ruched ribbon and dotted with finely worked star motifs. 'She suggested that white silk with gold ornamentation would suit this occasion to admiration.'

'Then she is a clever woman, and her judgement exceptionally sound.'

'I shall tell her of your approval, my dear Hugh. I am certain she will be quite in raptures to hear of it.'

His smile held genuine amusement. 'Well taken, my love. But depend upon it, I meant it. I have never seen you looking more desirable.'

He covered her gasp of outrage with a chuckle and presented his arm. 'Come, Miss Finsham. They are forming up to go in.'

There was no avoiding it. Louisa placed her fingers on blue silk and joined the queue awaiting the signal to move through to the banqueting hall.

The Duke always did things in lavish style and this was a particularly grand occasion so no expense had been spared. The covers were already laid as they took their places. Silver sparkled in the sunlight streaming in through several large windows, overpowering the flames of candles set in exquisitely wrought branches placed at intervals along the tables. Beautiful silver epergnes loaded with exotic fruit had been set between them.

Louisa found herself seated next to Walter Scott, Madame d'Arblay's partner for the evening. The ladies greeted each other warmly. Louisa was not much impressed by the other famous author, for his club foot made him awkward, and his gerneral appearance did not inspire admiration. She did, however, admire his writings and she soon forgot his appearance.

'I am honoured to meet you, sir,' she murmured as Fanny introduced them.

Once everyone was seated and grace said, it was the gentlemen's duty to serve their partners.

'What will you have?' asked Hugh politely, turning back to her after having made himself pleasant to a French lady on his other side. 'The trout look good, or perhaps you would prefer a portion of lamb? It looks splendidly young and tender.'

'Thank you,' responded Louisa, 'but if you could reach it I should prefer a little of the salmon cooked in pastry.'

The dish looked delicious, the pastry scales brown and glistening, and Louisa thought that if anything could tempt her suddenly lost appetite that might. Hugh drew it towards him, carefully cut the large fish in half, carved out a portion from the middle and placed it upon her plate, adding a slice of lemon.

Polite acknowledgement of his service seemed the best approach to a difficult situation. 'I admire your skill in keeping the pastry intact,' murmured Louisa. 'My thanks.'

'The skill was all the chef's, I fear. But the fish it surrounds looks capital. I believe I will have the same.' He cut himself a portion. 'I will call for glasses of white Bordeaux wine, if that will suit?'

Louisa having assented, he ordered the wine. When it arrived he bowed to her and both drank, as custom demanded. His eyes still held a devilish glint which betrayed Louisa into a blush and forced her into mindless chatter.

'I do wish,' she said as she pinched salt over her fish, 'that they had salt spoons in this country!'

'Give them time,' grinned Hugh.

But Louisa did not intend to fall victim to that smile or any of the other things about Hugh Deverill which made her heart throb so uncomfortably. Besides, she would never have a better opportunity to speak with the famous author on her other side. She therefore concentrated her attention on Walter Scott and Fanny d'Arblay, leaving Hugh Deverill rather isolated, since the French lady was well engaged with her own dinner partner.

Still far too aware of him beside her, she noted that he did not seem in the least disturbed. Whenever she looked his way he appeared to be absorbed in consuming his own food while watching and listening to all those about him. He could be quite self-contained when he chose. She almost felt piqued because he did not seem overset by her rather pointed neglect.

As each course was served she was forced to return her attention to him, of course, for he had to serve her with her choice of food and order more wine. For her second course she chose jugged pigeon and for the third tried a custard tart flavoured with cheese and found it delicious.

Hugh dipped his napkin in his finger glass to wipe his mouth before dessert. 'Madame Grassini and Madame Catalini are about to sing, I believe,' he remarked.

'Delightful,' murmured Louisa, rinsing her fingers.

Having allowed her to ignore him for most of the evening, he now seemed determined to recapture her attention. 'I see you are now on intimate terms with Madame d'Arblay. I trust your French has improved?'

'Considerably, I thank you, my lord. Madame d'Arblay has been so kind as to say I have an ear for it.'

'I promised to instruct you in the German language,' he went on, switching without warning to French, 'but have so far lacked the opportunity. However, I could call at your establishment for an hour most mornings after breakfast if you still wish to learn.'

Torn, Louisa lowered her eyes. How could she refuse such a tempting offer? Yet she did not relish the idea of being forced to deal more intimately with Hugh Deverill. Though should she accept propriety would demand that they were not left alone together. Her aunt or Betty would always sit with them.

And she did so enjoy extending her knowledge of foreign tongues. Her mind had always devoured learning, to everyone else's dismay. 'It is not ladylike,' her aunt protested whenever she found her niece avidly reading a weighty tome borrowed from some friend's library. 'Besides, you will give yourself brain fever!'

'Nonsense!' Louisa always responded.

At least Hugh Deverill did not seem to think it strange that she should wish to learn. Languages were, of course, a generally accepted exception to the belief regarding a lady's need to absorb knowledge. But still.

Her decision made, she looked up again and gave him her first genuine smile of the evening. He had a quizzical, expectant look on his face which made Louisa wonder whether he thought her delay in answering due to incomprehension on her part. The smile turned mischievous. She would delight in surprising him.

'Thank you, my lord,' she returned in the same language. 'I accept your offer most gladly. Should we meet while riding in the Bois, perhaps you would agree to partake of breakfast with us. We can then begin the lessons immediately afterwards.'

He was grinning with open amusement. 'Capital, Miss Finsham! Your French is now quite excellent. And in so short a time! I can see that you will have little trouble in mastering German, or any other language.'

'But I had the advantage of some small knowledge of French. I have none of German.'

'Then I'll wager I can teach you enough in two months to enable you to converse with Marshal Blücher.'

'I may not remain here for two months.'

'You are thinking of leaving?'

Did he sound dismayed? Louisa thought she must be imagining it. 'We have no firm plans as yet. Lady Nazeby will decide upon the time of our departure. And her decision rests upon—certain considerations beyond her control.'

'I see.' He looked faintly puzzled by her last statement, but to her relief chose not to pursue it. 'Well, should you still be in Paris on the nineteenth day of October, we will put my abilities as a teacher to the test. Agreed?'

'Agreed. But I will not wager on it, for to win I have only to pretend not to be able, or perhaps to neglect, to learn.'

'But you would do neither,' he offered softly. '"Twould be worse than holding your horse in a race.'

'You are right, of course,' Louisa acknowledged ruefully. 'So, ten guineas on it, sir?'

'Done.'

Solemnly, they shook hands, just as the orchestra struck up, signalling that the opera stars were about to sing.

'I shall have to present myself at your breakfast-table in all my dirt if I do as you suggest,' he murmured.

'I do not suppose, sir, that you will inconvenience us in the least. And we can in any case offer you the facility to wash.'

'Then I am happy to accept your generous offer, Louisa.'

No one else could have heard the familiarity. But it made Louisa aware that he had no thought of abandoning his intention to pursue a more intimate connection. Thankfully, she turned her attention to the recital. And for the remainder of the evening he behaved towards her with punctilious correctness. Yet the memory of those more personal exchanges could not be eradicated. Their relationship could never truly return to what it had been before Lady Stewart's ball.

Louisa discovered that she did not want it to.

As he handed her into her carriage, 'I shall not be riding early tomorrow,' Hugh informed her. Her stab of disappointment quickly changed to indignation as he went on, 'I will call for you at three. A drive in the Bois will be pleasant, I believe, and we can then discuss my proposed tutoring in the German Language in more detail.'

'You assume too much, my lord! I may not be free tomorrow afternoon!'

'But you are, are you not?' he demanded, using his quizzing-glass for the first time that Louisa could remember in order to regard her through it. The smile on his lips incensed her further.

'You did not ask, my lord. I may not wish to drive with you!'

'I have arranged to borrow a carriage. It is available for tomorrow only.' And he added, low, 'Please, Louisa?'

'Do not be so ungracious, Louisa!' Her aunt's voice came from the depths of the carriage, where she was already seated. 'You are making unnecessary difficulties. You have no engagement tomorrow you cannot break! No doubt your man—Dutton, isn't it?—will accompany you, Lord Hugh?'

'He will, ma'am.'

Louisa wanted to go. It was his high-handed assumption that she would fall in with his plans that had made her argue. But his low-voiced plea had already softened her resolve, before ever her aunt had swept any grounds for objection aside. Aunt Nazeby, thought Louisa wryly, seemed determined to forward Hugh's suit. She would never be persuaded that his intentions were not serious.

'Very well,' she acquiesced. 'I will expect you at three.'

'Until tomorrow,' he murmured, and lightly brushed her fingers with his lips.

Watching from the drawing-room window, Louisa saw the splendid equipage draw up before the door. A sporting curricle with enormous springs, painted and gilded, the seats luxuriously padded and upholstered in red velvet. Unusually, a small seat had been inserted behind for a groom or footman. Dutton sat impassively as Hugh brought the spirited pair of matched chestnuts to a halt. He had no reason to jump down, for a footman had run out to take their heads.

Hugh lodged his whip, sprang from the vehicle and threw down the reins. Louisa bit her lip. She had not expected either him or his borrowed outfit to look so fine. They would be the centre of attention in the Bois. He was making his interest too plain.

Everyone would think he entertained thoughts of marriage. She would be left in a mortifying position when he withdrew his attentions, as he surely must. . .

But she would be returning to England soon. Perhaps he foresaw that as a natural end to a pleasant flirtation. If so, she would enjoy his friendship while she could.

A servant announced him. He strode into the room, every inch the handsome, virile gentleman, and bent over her gloved hand. No wonder her heart began to flutter!

Louisa controlled her emotions and greeted him coolly. She had dressed in her best apricot carriage dress and wore a chip-straw bonnet tied under her chin with matching ribbons. A large spray of white ostrich feathers curled about the brim.

'Enchanting,' he murmured. 'Thank you for being ready. The carriage is outside.'

'I saw it,' said Louisa, scorning subterfuge. 'It is quite splendid. Where did you discover it?'

He grinned. 'It belongs to Prince Metternich. He was so good as to offer me its use when I spoke of my wish to drive in the Bois.'

'Last evening?' enquired Louisa as they made their way downstairs.

'Just so. The port put him into an excellent mood.'

Louisa had to laugh. 'So it would appear!' They

descended the steps and she halted to examine the carriage at closer quarters. 'I wonder he would allow such an expensive carriage and exceptional pair to be driven by anyone but himself!'

'But then,' grinned Hugh, handing her up, 'I have a persuasive tongue. When I particularly want something I am a difficult man to refuse.'

'Then,' said Louisa quietly as he gathered the reins and gave the horses the office to start, 'I must strengthen my defences.'

He did not answer for a moment, being occupied in negotiating his team round a corner and into a stream of other traffic. As they settled into a steady trot he turned his head to her.

'Do not do that, I beg. I engage not to ask you for more in the way of friendship than you are willing to give. But I should enjoy to ride with you, to drive with you on occasion, and sometimes to be accorded the honour of escorting you and Lady Nazeby to your engagements.'

His flirtatious manner had dropped from him as though it had never been. He had never appeared more serious. Louisa did not know whether to be glad or sorry. She had enjoyed their sparring, she realised. And did he not mean to kiss her again?

'Lud, sir,' she laughed, 'do not take my words too seriously! I should hate to have you revert to the disagreeably critical creature you were!'

His eyes twinkled. 'Was I so very disagreeable?'

'To me you seemed so.'

He negotiated the gate into the Bois with casual ease. He was an excellent whip, Louisa noted with interest.

'You would rather suffer the occasional kiss?' he suggested outrageously.

Louisa considered. She shot him a glance from the corners of dancing eyes. 'Almost,' she admitted.

'Then I shall be constrained to consider my conduct most carefully.'

She gurgled with laughter. 'I am persuaded that you always do, my lord.'

They were on terms again and she was glad. They drove in amicable silence among the throng of other carriages in the Bois, exchanging nods and smiles with acquaintances, stopping occasionally to speak with a person with whom one or both of them enjoyed greater intimacy. The stares of interest they received were embarrassingly obvious.

'We are giving the scandal-mongers much food for their tongues,' remarked Louisa at last. 'Perhaps we should not have done this, Hugh.'

'Do you mind?' His voice held sudden concern.

Louisa pursed her lips. 'Not really. It is flattering for a woman of my age to be seen to be pursued.'

He grimaced, acknowledging the accusation. 'Since you are determined on dwindling into an old tabby I am surprised lack of flattery should concern you.'

'Ah, but I would prefer it to be plain that I choose not to marry. If no gentleman paid me attention Society might begin to whisper that I could not catch a husband.'

'That must be patently untrue.'

'Perhaps. But you are laying yourself open to gossip, Hugh. Your motives will be questioned.'

'My motives are my own affair. I shall not allow gossip to influence my actions. Apart——' he suddenly grinned '—from keeping me within the bounds of perceived propriety.'

A question had been burning Louisa's tongue ever since the previous night. Now she asked it. 'Why did you borrow a curricle to drive me in the Bois, Hugh?'

He glanced at her sideways. 'Because I wanted to.'

'Why?'

His lips twitched. 'Vanity. I wanted to be seen parading with the most stunning lady in Paris.'

'Flummery, sir!'

He viewed her heightened colour with amusement. 'You do not know your own charm, Louisa.'

He had avoided answering her question. She could not pursue the subject further.

'I told you last evening,' he went on calmly. 'I wished to discuss the German lessons I have engaged to give you.'

'Oh. What is there to discuss?'

'Not much. You have paper and pen, of course. I will provide a dictionary and books to read.'

It was an excuse, of a certainty, but she did not challenge it. Instead, for the remainder of the outing she assiduously questioned him on the German language and, to his amusement, insisted on being taught a few words.

'What is a horse?'

'Just as in English there are many words to describe the precise kind animal, but 'a horse' is *ein Pferd*.'

She repeated the words. 'And a tree?'

'*Ein Baum*.'

By the time he deposited her at her door she had acquired a vocabulary of some dozen words. Whether she would remember them until the following morning they both doubted. But the exercise had been fun.

Back in her room Louisa reviewed their conversation. Whatever Hugh had promised, she knew she must keep to her determination not to drift into a situation where he could kiss her. If she did and he took advantage of the chance, she would be lost.

So began a strange interlude for Louisa. She saw Hugh Deverill almost every day, spent intimate hours with him mastering the new language, yet they were never alone. For one thing, Jamie had expressed an interest in joining the lessons, and Louisa leapt upon the idea. Lady Thurrock being amenable, since William Coynd had no knowledge of German and the lessons would be free, he returned to the Hôtel des Fleurs with Louisa and Hugh, breakfasted with them, and left when Hugh did. And Mr Coynd, appearing as reluctant to accompany the boy as Louisa was to have him do so, persuaded his employer that her son would be in excellent hands and there would therefore be no need for him to waste his time at Lady Nazeby's. A groom in attendance would suffice. Since this reasoning was extended to the early morning horseback-riding as well, Louisa was completely relieved of the embarrassing presence of Mr Coynd.

Major Hewitson, Lord Wellington and several other gentlemen continued to join her party, however. She therefore had little difficulty in avoiding any close encounter with Hugh Deverill until the moment came for them to return to the Hôtel des Fleurs. Then Jamie acted as a buffer. During the return ride they spoke in French, for his benefit.

'Mr Coynd is not much good, you see,' the boy
confided. 'And I must be able to speak French if I want
to travel. . .' He trailed off.

'Travel where?' asked Louisa.

'My Grand Tour,' explained Jamie rather hurriedly.
Louisa thought it was not what he had meant to say,
but let it pass.

'Then you had better learn Italian as well.'

Jamie glanced quickly at the speaker. 'Do you know
it, Deverill?'

'Sufficiently well. But two languages are quite
enough for you to begin with. Leave Italian until you
have mastered the others. You have plenty of time.'

Jamie seemed content to accept this advice. 'Yes.
And I could learn Italian best when I reach Italy, I
suppose.'

Hugh smiled. 'If I am able, my lord, I will be glad to
give you a grounding in the language before you set
out.'

In September Lord Byron arrived in Paris, as did the
Lambs. The arrival of Lady Caroline and her husband
caused no little stir.

Neither her husband's nor Byron's presence pre-
vented Lady Caroline from pursuing the Duke by every
means at her disposal.

She began to appear in the Bois, dressed in an eye-
catching purple riding habit. Louisa blushed for her.
The Duke appeared indulgently amused by the young
woman's excessive attentions. Louisa wondered
uncomfortably if her own brief foray into flattery had
amused him as much.

'Did you notice how she was dressed the other

evening?' she asked Hugh on the way back to breakfast one morning. Jamie had sent his regrets, finding himself confined to bed with a cold. 'She appeared half-naked!'

'She wore a scarf,' observed Hugh mildly, his eyes dancing.

Louisa snorted. 'That flimsy thing! I have never seen anything so outrageous as the way she dresses. She invites condemnation!'

'She is an exhibitionist,' grinned Hugh, amused by Louisa's vehemence while wondering whether she could possibly be jealous over the other woman's undoubted success with the Duke and other gentlemen. But he immediately dismissed the thought as unworthy of the woman he had come to know. Deuce take it, she had a large enough court of admirers of her own. 'I feel sorry for William Lamb,' declared Louisa. 'She quite ignores him.'

'Do not many married women cut their husbands from their lives?'

'Perhaps they do,' admitted Louisa, 'but I cannot agree with it. However the marriage was brought about, one has made one's vow before God. That, I think, is why I shall never marry. I could not trust my husband to keep his.'

Hugh eyed her thoughtfully. 'You hold to a most unfashionable philosophy.'

Louisa realised she had been led to reveal more than she had intended. 'Lud, sir,' she said lightly, 'how serious we are become, when I was merely indulging in tabbyish criticism of a notorious woman! But——' she lifted questioning brows '—I have heard little said against her from one quite famous for his critical tongue! Can it be that you overlook Lady Caroline's misdemeanours while challenging others for similar offences?'

'I do not need to exercise myself over Lady Caroline, Louisa. Her behaviour does not in the least concern me.'

CHAPTER NINE

To LOUISA it felt as though something had hit her in the chest. He could only mean that he *did* care what *she* did!

Why should he? Even now? And in the beginning, when it had all started, he had not even known her.

At that moment they reached the house and she was able to avoid answering because it became necessary to dismount and hand the reins to a groom to lead Prince Hal away. Hugh did the same with Kismet and the two horses clip-clopped off to the stables as the humans mounted the steps to the door.

She no longer suffered quite the same degree of agitation in Hugh's presence. Familiarity, she supposed, had worn the edge off her reactions. But unfortunately for her that did not mean she loved him the less. On the contrary, as she explored his mind, her love grew.

'Louisa knows an awful lot,' Jamie had remarked during one of their earliest breakfasts, when earnest discussion had seemed to flow naturally with the coffee. 'Fancy her knowing all about economics. I must ask my tutor if I can read Adam Smith.'

'Never tell me I am attempting to teach a bluestocking!' Hugh had exclaimed in mock-dismay. 'She knows a deal about so many subjects, not to mention the breeding of horses.'

'And the latest developments in farming,' Amelia

had supplied with a sniff. 'I tell her it is most unladylike
to read such earnest books as she does, but she don't
take a bit of notice. I've told her, if she develops brain
fever, she has only herself to blame!'

'I am sure you cannot really believe learning induces
brain fever, Lady Nazeby.' Hugh had smiled. 'Such
out-of-date nonsense! And to believe that women
cannot learn! Elizabeth Montagu and her set of blue-
stockings proved otherwise quite convincingly fifty
years ago!'

'But women's brains are smaller——' Amelia had
begun, only to be interrupted.

'Men's are not all the same size, dear ma'am. But is
a man with a small head necessarily less able to learn
than one with a large one? It is quite obvious that very
often the opposite applies.'

'Well, the large one might be empty,' Amelia had
muttered, not to be worsted in the argument.

Louisa had laughed. 'Really, Aunt! I cannot believe
you truly hold to such fustian ideas! I think you only
advance them because you wish me to emulate certain
feather-brained women who have gained themselves
husbands. Lady Nazeby,' she had explained to Hugh,
'does not believe any man would be willing to burden
himself with an educated wife.'

'It might be inconvenient if *he* was not very clever,'
Jamie, who had been listening with growing interest,
had put in. 'He wouldn't want to be made to look a
fool, even if he *was* light in the attic himself.'

At this the company had dissolved into laughter,
though Amelia, determined to have the last word, had
added, 'What did I tell you, my love?'

'But,' Hugh had murmured to no one in particular,

'think of the boredom of sitting down to breakfast each morning with someone only capable of chattering about clothes and the latest *on dit*.'

'Oh, there's nothing to that,' Amelia had replied carelessly. 'The gentleman simply buries himself behind his newspaper.'

'And never the two minds shall meet!' Louisa had exclaimed with asperity. 'Well, Aunt, I categorically refuse to live my life unable to communicate with my husband! I should,' she'd added less forcefully and with a chuckle, 'rather dwindle into an old maid.'

This reference to previous conversations had brought a gleam of appreciation to Hugh's eyes. 'I cannot believe there to be a great risk of that.'

'You,' Amelia had responded darkly, 'cannot be aware of my niece's obdurate nature!'

'There, ma'am, I think you do me an injustice.'

Louisa had hastily changed the subject, suddenly recognising the intention behind her aunt's voicing of such archaic ideas. She'd appeared far too smug at having elicited such an admission from Lord Hugh. But Hugh had looked no more that amused.

Now, as she went to her room to change from her riding habit into a morning gown of becoming sprigged muslin, she reviewed Hugh's recent behaviour. Since their excursion in the Bois when the broken fences between them had been at least partially repaired he had made no attempt to be alone with her. No attempt to claim the kisses he had threatened on the evening of the ball. He had escorted both her and her aunt to the Tivoli gardens to enjoy the dancing and the lavish and spectacular firework display. But, despite her apprehension—and, she had to admit, her traitorous anticipation—he had spent the entire evening in courteous and proper attendance upon both ladies, claiming only one dance from her and making no attempt to lure her into one of the convenient paths leading to secluded glades.

Louisa knew his attention meant nothing of significance. He had offered and she had accepted his escort before the incident at the ball. He had merely been keeping an engagement already arranged. But her aunt had been quite in raptures, her opinion of the gentleman soaring to excessive heights. Which was, Louisa supposed sourly, why Lady Nazeby had provoked that discussion over breakfast a couple of days later.

Since then he had escorted them on several occasions, as he had proposed during that ride in the Bois. And he had kept his promise to behave. Louisa did not know whether he was exerting self-control, or had lost any desire to dally with her. The uncertainty wore at her nerves.

He had also organised the projected visit to places of interest in Paris, when most of his attention seemed to be directed towards keeping Jamie entertained and informed. They had gone in her curricle, with Hugh driving. Her aunt had been quite unconcerned at the thought of his taking the reins of her precious bays.

'His reputation as a whip is second to none, my love. Of course I shall not object!'

Why she had been forced to discover his ability for herself Louisa could not fathom. Except, she supposed, that in London other, more important things had occupied her attention and any such information concerning a gentleman she did not know had passed over her head. Only his reputed excursions into adultery had

made any impression upon her mind then, due no
doubt to her sensitivity over such matters.

That day had, though, only served to deepen her
admiration for the man. His knowledge proved prodi-
gious and his method of imparting it commanded both
interest and respect. All the places made famous during
the Revolution came under their scrutiny as well as
buildings of more general and cultural interest.

Jamie had returned home almost hopping with
excitement. 'I wish you were my tutor, Lord Hugh!'

'Do not make too great a work of this expedition,'
Hugh had warned quietly. 'You will offend Mr Coynd
who, I have no doubt, is in most ways an excellent
tutor. He cannot be expected to excel in every depart-
ment of his duties.'

Louisa had thought this a generous speech, considering the hostility Mr Coynd had shown.

'Are you to come on Lord Wellington's expedition
to Versailles next week?' Jamie had asked. 'Please do!'

'I believe so, Jamie. Unless some urgent diplomatic
duty prevents my attendance.'

'Capital!'

But for Louisa that had turned out to be an equally
informative but frustrating occasion. Versailles had
demanded her admiration and awe. But Hugh,
although as attentive as ever, had travelled in the
Stuarts' coach and had not once overstepped the
bounds of propriety. She was becoming excessively
frustrated.

But now, what was she to make of his assertion—
although not made in so many words—that he cared
for her? Her hard-won composure in his presence was
under grave threat as she entered the breakfast parlour.

She felt like some foolish chit just out of the school-room, all of a flutter. What could he have meant?

She was to find out after an unusually quiet meal. Of course, Jamie's absence could account for the lack of lively conversation. But even Amelia seemed suscep-tible to some atmosphere pervading the air and con-sumed her coffee and rolls in near silence. Until Hugh suddenly spoke.

'I have news which means I shall be forced to leave Paris within the month. Possibly before the end of the lessons I engaged to give you, Louisa.' He addressed her by her given name now before Amelia or Jamie. 'Of necessity, I fear our wager must be cancelled.'

'News?' exclaimed Amelia. 'What news?'

Louisa simply looked at him, her heart turning several somersaults before sinking to her shoes. Recently, she had been living from day to day, not daring to look to a future which did not include Hugh Deverill. Now she was forced to recognise exactly how bleak such a prospect was. Her expectations, which had been so elevated by his earlier remark, descended with a thump.

'I have been honoured by a considerable promotion. I am to be appointed His Britannic Majesty's Ambassador to Austria.'

Amelia's cries of congratulation obscured Louisa's less voluble and rather unhappy reception of this news. She smiled, tried to look pleased and remarked, 'At least you know Prince Metternich well.'

He inclined his head gravely. 'That will indeed be an advantage. Had he not agreed to my appointment, I doubt it would have been made.'

'So—we are to lose your company.' Amelia sounded

less enthusiastic over the news as its implications sunk in.

'I fear so, ma'am. I shall, of course, return to England periodically and we may renew our acquaintance there.'

'Not,' said Amelia tartly, 'if you continue to ignore London Society as you have done in the past!'

Hugh smiled. 'I shall give myself the honour of calling on you in Grosvenor Square the instant I return to the capital.'

He did not look at Louisa yet she was overwhelmingly conscious that he would be calling to see her rather than her aunt. The thought did little to alleviate the sudden ache of loss which had settled in the region of her heart.

'But we must not be selfish! We do rejoice over your good fortune, do we not, Louisa?'

'Certainly, Aunt.'

Her voice sounded flat, but she could not help it. Somehow she could not summon the reserves of energy needed to put on a brave and sparkling front.

Hugh noticed her sudden loss of spirits and took comfort in the fact. Perhaps his object would not be so difficult to achieve as he had feared.

'If you are ready, Louisa, we could begin the lesson,' he suggested quietly. At Louisa's nod of assent he turned to the older woman. 'But I must beg you, Lady Nazeby, to allow me a few moments alone with your niece before you join us.'

Amelia glanced swiftly from him to Louisa who, surprised as she was at the request, gave another slight nod of assent. She did not think Hugh Deverill had dalliance in mind, although what his object could be in

seeking a private interview with her she refused to
guess. He could have said anything he had to say on
the way back from the Bois. Unless. . . Normally a
gentleman had only one reason for——

Her mind balked.

He held the door for her and she walked through to
another small parlour, where the lessons were usually
given. He shut the door firmly behind them and she did
not protest.

Too agitated to sit, Louisa took up station before the
empty fireplace. She moistened her lips and cleared her
throat.

'You wished to speak with me, Hugh?'

'I did.' As he moved to join her he indicated a chair.
'Will you not be seated, my dear Louisa?'

Because they were alone he was not only calling her
by her given name but adding an endearment. Suddenly
weak in the knees, Louisa sank down on the nearest
elegantly padded chair.

Hugh himself appeared unusually restive. Having
seen her seated, he paced backwards and forwards a
couple of times before swinging round to face her. His
stance became peculiarly aggressive.

'Miss Finsham—Louisa. You must know that my
feelings for you have been growing for months now and
I can resist them no longer. You know how deeply I
admire you. I beg you to do me the honour of accepting
my hand in marriage. Louisa, my dear, dear girl, will
you marry me?'

Oh, those sweetest of sweet words! Yes! cried her
heart. Yes, I will marry you, my dearest Hugh.

But her lips would not form the words.

'No,' she heard herself say. 'I am sensible of the

honour you do me, Lord Hugh, but I regret I cannot marry you.'

He went white. His eyes, almost slate-grey with emotion, held an incredulous, dazed expression. 'Why not?' he demanded. 'Is it because of what I said at the ball? When I asked you to refuse me should I weaken and ask? If so, I release you from your promise forthwith!'

'No!' cried Louisa. 'Of course not!'

'Then why? Is it my lack of fortune? I had not thought——'

'Do not insult me with such an accusation, sir! You know very well it is not! But you have no true desire to wed,' said Louisa, her voice gaining sad conviction with every word. 'You have told me so often enough. Mayhap you need a wife now, for you will require a hostess in your new appointment. But I will not marry you simply for your convenience, my lord.'

'My convenience!' he spluttered. 'Louisa, what are you implying? You know how much I desire you and— I know you did not find my wretchedly improper advances distasteful,' he added, his voice sinking to a rueful growl. He made a helpless gesture. 'Louisa, you must marry me!'

'Indeed, sir, that I must not. I repeat, I will not be wed for convenience, be it for domestic reasons or to gratify a gentleman's carnal needs.'

He showed no shock at her outspoken words. 'But what of your own?' he demanded roughly. 'You cannot, in all honesty, deny your response or tell me you wish to remain forever a virgin! You must know that, together, you and I could share untold delight in a marriage bed!'

'Lust, sir!' snapped Louisa, fighting back a treacherous desire to burst into tears. 'I will not be seduced by lust!'

'No!' he denied passionately. 'My regard for you is not based simply on lust and neither is my proposal. We suit so well. Our minds meet on every point. You long for an outlet for your indisputable abilities. As my wife you would surely be able to find it and I would place no barrier in your way!'

If only he had spoken one word of love. She took a sustaining breath.

'Indeed that is so, my lord, should I wish to become your wife. Unfortunately, I do not.'

He could not leap to his feet in hurt outrage, for he was not on his knees, but he stiffened his spine and raised his chin. 'In that case, there seems little more to be said.'

'No, my lord. Except——' she tried to smile, which wavered '—can we not remain friends, at least until you depart for Vienna?' She seemed always to be asking rejected suitors for their friendship, she thought rather hysterically. Luckily those she liked mostly complied. 'Although I do not wish to marry you I do hold you in great esteem and value our discussions,' she went on, unconsciously pleading. 'I would not wish our lessons to be curtailed unnecessarily. Besides, Jamie will think it strange. . .'

He bowed formally. 'If that is your wish, Miss Finsham. Forget I ever had the temerity to address you. I should have remembered all those others you have refused, your determination to ignore you own nature and to remain a spinster. I can now fully sympathise with those other fellows' feelings.'

A flush spread over Louisa's face at his reference to her nature. Of course she wanted to be wed! And to him! But not without love. How could she make him understand?

'Not all were as honest or as sincere as you, my lord, and the damage was largely to their pride, not their feelings. If I have hurt yours, please forgive me, for I had no desire to do so. But I will not wed without love.'

So that was the trouble. He had not managed to engage her affections. He had at last achieved a position from which he could afford to support a wife and wed without being accused of seeking a fortune, only to be turned down by the one woman who could meet all his needs. Hugh stifled his disappointment and raised a rueful smile. Ignoring her painful reference to love, he said, 'Nor I to offend yours, my dear Louisa. That was ill-spoken. Shall we, then, proceed with the lesson?'

Louisa nodded, unable to trust her voice. She had given him his cue and he had ignored it. So an old tabby she would become.

When Amelia cautiously entered the room five minutes later they appeared to be deeply immersed in German declensions. Only they knew that neither mind could concentrate on the lesson.

'What did he want?' demanded Lady Nazeby the moment Hugh had departed.

Louisa told her.

'To marry you! How wonderful! But why did you not say, you dreadful creature, so that I might offer my congratulations?'

'Because I refused him.'

Amelia slumped in her chair. Visibly. 'Refused him?' she gasped in a strangled voice. 'But why? He is so *right* for you!'

'Except that he does not love me, Aunt. He wants me, he needs me, but he does not love me.'

'Love!' snorted Amelia, not for the first time. 'You are obsessed by the word. What is love but affection, understanding, consideration, the desire to put the other's happiness before one's own? Hugh would give you all those things. And passion, too, I do not doubt.'

'But loyalty? Could I depend upon his not taking a mistress the moment he began to tire of me?'

'As to that, my love,' answered Amelia ruefully, 'I could not say. Many men do, of course, but as many others do not. He admires Lord Castlereagh, I perceive, who is a model husband. You must learn to trust a little, Louisa.'

In the heat of her emotions she would have accepted Hugh had he loved her. But in the aftermath of turmoil all her insecurities flooded back to haunt her, making her glad she had not succumbed to her own feelings.

Her father's lifestyle and her mother's unhappiness had thrown a shadow over her childhood, her father's neglect a cloud over her youth. And Amelia herself had suffered unhappiness in her marriage. So how could the Dowager advocate it so strongly?

Because, Louisa realised, her aunt had made the best of her circumstances, had had the courage to take a lover, had immersed herself in the bringing up of her children, found joy in the love of her family, lavished her love on them and had had enough left over to extend to her niece. Now she was concerning herself over her grandchildren, most particularly at the moment over Jamie, and, as ever, over her.

A wave of affection brought her to kneel at her aunt's side.

'Dear Aunt, you refine too much over me. I know you are right. When the time comes for me to trust a man, I shall know.'

She should trust Hugh. He approved of Castlereagh and disapproved of the Duke and his indiscretions. Could I have managed without his love? she asked herself. Did I make a mistake?

Doubts assailed her constantly from then on but she could not bring herself to be more than politely friendly when she next met Lord Hugh, fearing where it might lead if she allowed herself to behave with all the warmth she still felt towards him. She wanted to make love with him so much. He would lead her into realms of unimaginable delight.

He had been right. She was denying her own nature in refusing to have him as her husband. Yet the barriers of her doubts stood solidly between them.

Jamie rejoined the morning sessions and the lessons continued as before for a few days, until Hugh announced that he must return to England to make a start on setting his affairs in order before taking up his new appointment in November.

He had not needed to make this extra journey. Another visit to London would still be necessary before his departure to Vienna. Officials at the Foreign Office would require to see him, to give him his instructions. And there would be last-minute personal arrangements to make, farewells to be taken from family and friends.

He could have combined all his business into the one trip.

Pacing the deck of the packet carrying him back to France and remembering that other passage, Hugh recognised that his brief visit to the family estates had been an excuse to quit Paris for a time. He had hoped that separation from the first object of his desire might cool the flames of passion, might cure the strange ache he felt whenever he thought of his lovely Louisa. But it had not. He could not wait to see her again.

As it happened his visit had turned out to be opportune. He had discovered himself to be the beneficiary of a childless cousin's will.

'We were about to inform you, my lord,' the solicitor had told him. 'You know the property, of course, a small manor house set in a few acres close by your own father's estates. Your cousin held some investments, too, which bring in an additional income.'

Hugh mourned the passing of a congenial companion. But undoubtedly possession of an estate and private means revolutionised his financial situation. Together with his income from his new appointment he now had all the means at his disposal to wed in security and comfort. An establishment to which he could take his bride, and to which they could return on leave or when his ambassadorship ended.

But Louisa had turned him down. Because she did not love him.

He arrived back in Paris during the second week in October. Louisa had found life exceptionally dull without him. She was so glad to see him when he appeared in the Bois again that she greeted him with more far more warmth than she intended.

His own emotions under tight control, Hugh eyed her gravely, scrutinising the radiant smile on an otherwise rather wan face with suddenly intent eyes.

'You are well?'

'Indeed, my lord. And you?'

He looked tired, and thinner. The journey and intense activity, no doubt.

'I am in capital health, I thank you. Jamie is not riding this morning?'

'Not as yet. He has sent no message, so I expect him at any moment. He has seemed low in spirits recently. His mother has taken up with Prince Boris. He does not like the Russian.'

Hugh's frown deepened while a twisted smile marred the normally pleasant set of his lips. 'A pity. But he is rich and royal. A potent combination for a woman.'

'For some women, mayhap. Do not judge all womankind by such as Amy Thurrock.'

'My apologies, Louisa. I had forgot. Your requirements in a man are rather more complicated.'

Louisa bit her lip. He sounded cynical. It did not suit him. She had not intended to open old wounds. Apart from Hugh's servant, Dutton, riding with Pershaw at a discreet distance behind, they were alone.

'Peace, Hugh,' she murmured. 'I have missed you.'

'Obliging of you to say so.'

The Hugh she had come to know had not been given to cynicism or bitterness. Could it be that he had truly been deeply hurt by her refusal, and not simply piqued? Or were bitterness and pique one and the same thing?

Louisa wallowed in a mire of self-reproach and singularly painful dismals, knowing that whatever she said would simply make matters worse. Etiquette precluded her from broaching the subject of his proposal again. She could attempt to give him every encouragement to renew his offer, but in his present mood she doubted whether that would serve. He had climbed up on his high ropes and it would be difficult to bring him down. And if he did ask her again, was she really willing to abandon her doubts, fling her cap over a windmill and entrust her future happiness to him?

She still wasn't certain, despite missing him so badly while he'd been away and the undisputed effect his close presence had upon her senses, sending her pulse racing so fast that breathing became difficult. So she remained silent, staring straight ahead, the sound of the horses' hooves, muffled by fallen leaves, a dull accompaniment to her mood.

So she did not see the anguish in Hugh's eyes as he gazed at her profile. She had admitted to missing him, and seemed subdued. Her smile on greeting had made him dare to hope that she had changed her mind. But if he did sink his pride and address her again what guarantee had he that her answer would be any different? She seemed determined to turn down every offer she received and remain unwed. He might have suspected her of being cold, of having a disgust of the physical aspects of marriage had he not known differently. Memories sent the blood rushing through his veins, to become an ache.

He shifted in his saddle to ease it as his thoughts swept on. He had suspected she hid a passionate nature under that vivacious manner, for it was betrayed by the wide, sensuous curve of her mouth. He was quite sure she did not yet fully realise her own emotional depths. And he could only imagine the joy of awakening her to the knowledge. The thought of another man teaching her the intimate joys of making love racked him with such jealousy that an inaudible groan escaped him. Kismet, sensing his tension, tossed his head and skittered dangerously on the slippery leaves.

God, he thought as he settled his mount with automatic expertise, I should never have come here this morning! The sooner I leave again for London and Vienna the better! Yet frustration had accompanied him to England and would surely do so to Austria. Despite—or because of—this he had not been able to resist the temptation to see her again, to share precious moments conversing in fractured German. Although, he admitted wryly, she was learning the language with exceptional speed. She would make the perfect ambassador's wife. That was not, however, the reason he had asked her to marry him, whatever she thought. He couldn't exactly explain why he had, except that his circumstances had changed, making it possible, and the thought of life without her left him feeling desolate, even desperate.

The horses seemed to sense their riders' mood and plodded along listlessly. They had had a run, so the edge had been taken from their initial energy. They did not seem to care, any more than their riders did, where they went or how slowly.

They were still progressing in this depressing way when a horse came tearing up behind them. William Coynd pulled on his reins so sharply that his sweating horse reared and staggered before coming to a lurching halt.

'Lord Thurrock is not with you?' he gasped.

Prince Hal had already stopped. Kismet drew along-side to allow Hugh to face Coynd.

'Jamie?' said Louisa sharply, jerked from her reverie by the anxiety on the tutor's face. 'No, he has not put in an appearance this morning. Why?'

Hugh's features had settled into a frown. 'Has something happened to him?'

'I don't know. He's missing. I thought perhaps he'd come here, though according to the stable lad he had his horse saddled up and left very early, before dawn, about five-thirty of the clock, he thinks.'

Hugh brought out his pocket watch. 'It is half of the hour before nine now. He's been gone for three hours. Why did no one miss him before?'

'His servant has gone with him——'

'Ah! So he is not alone.'

'No. And I had no reason to suppose he had not come here, until I went to the stables for my mount and spoke to the boy.'

'His mother knows nothing of his likely where-abouts?' demanded Louisa.

Coynd shifted uncomfortably. 'Lady Thurrock is not at home.'

'Not at home?' Hugh shot Coynd a fierce glance. 'Then where the deuce is she?'

'She has eloped with Prince Boris. They left late last evening.'

'And the boy knew?'

Coynd nodded. 'He discovered his mother's absence when he sent his servant, Milsom, to fetch a drink from the kitchen. The servants were agog.'

'So I should imagine. So she left without saying farewell to her son?'

'Yes, Lord Hugh. She knew he would make a scene, I suspect, and just before her departure she gave me a draft on the bank here with instructions to take his lordship back to England. She also instructed me not to inform him of her departure until this morning.'

Louisa drew a painful breath. 'Typical of Amy Thurrock,' she muttered angrily. 'I do not think she bears any love for her son, only for his title. Hugh, we must find him!'

Hugh had relaxed, any tension in him now being of a different order. He looked like a racehorse straining to be off. 'Certainly. But where should we begin to look? Have you any suggestions, Coynd?'

Coynd hesitated. 'He may have gone after them, my lord.'

'Did he know their destination?'

'He knew they were headed for Russia.'

'The devil! The boy would surely not undertake a journey like that on horseback!'

'He had a bundle with him,' confessed Coynd miserably.

'Why on earth did the stable lad not wake you, his tutor? Surely he knew his young master should not be allowed out alone apart from Milsom at that hour? And what was Milsom thinking of?'

'If he could not dissuade him, Milsom would accompany him rather than let Jamie travel alone,' suggested Louisa quietly. 'Though I would have thought he might notify you of his young master's intention, Mr Coynd.'

Blood suffused Coynd's face. 'I was not there. My charge was safely asleep and is often left alone with servants until the early hours. I spent much of the night with friends.'

'You did not look in on the boy on your return?' asked Hugh.

'It seemed unnecessary. Besides, I needed my bed. I confess to having been a little foxed,' Coynd admitted.

'Hmm,' muttered Hugh. 'I can only regret your neglect, Coynd. It has served to exacerbate this disaster.'

'No one could regret it more than I.'

Louisa, caught up in swinging emotions, cried impatiently, 'We cannot sit here talking! We must do something! Jamie could be in danger! Think of the malcontents and footpads——'

'Quite. But where best to start?' mused Hugh. Pershaw and Dutton had drawn nearer, listening with growing concern to their employers. He turned to them. 'We will go back to Lord Thurrock's. Pershaw, you had best speak to the grooms and the lad who saddled the horses. See if his lordship left any clue as to his destination. We will examine his room. He may have left a note.'

'I did not see one,' muttered Coynd.

'Nevertheless, we will search. Something may present itself.'

'The portrait of his father has gone,' exclaimed Coynd some half an hour later.

Hugh turned from examining the contents of a mahogany military chest, which must have belonged to the late Earl of Thurrock, and Louisa looked round from the clothes press, where she had been attempting to assess what Jamie had worn, what he might have taken with him. It did not appear to be much.

'Where was it?' demanded Hugh.

'On top of his livery cupboard. Which,' added Coynd grimly, 'is empty apart from candles. He took the store of food and drink with him, I collect.'

'And no doubt Milsom obtained more from the kitchen. Did he have money?'

'One or two *louis*, perhaps.'

'Then that has gone, too.' Hugh indicated the chest. 'There is none here. They will not starve, and he will have enough to pay for lodgings at night.' He indicated an open pistol case. 'I believe he must have taken his father's side arm. The balls and primer have gone, too. Unless he was not allowed to have them?'

'He was given the chest intact, on his thirteenth birthday. His sword has gone, too,' supplied Coynd gloomily.

'Well, at least they'll have something to defend themselves with if they're attacked,' offered Louisa brightly. 'If he can't use the gun I am sure Milsom can.'

'Just so long as he does not have some romantic idea of calling the Prince out. . .'

Louisa gazed at Hugh in horror. 'Oh, surely not! He couldn't possibly imagine he would win a duel!'

'A young gentleman of his age does not always stop to think of the consequences of his actions,' said Hugh sadly. 'But I would have credited Lord Thurrock with more sense, young as he is.'

'So would I! So I believe he has taken it for defence only. That would be a sensible decision.'

They were saved further speculation by a discreet tap on the door followed by Pershaw's entry into the room, with Dutton at his shoulder.

'Pershaw, what news?' asked Louisa anxiously.

Frustration was eating at her soul. So much time wasted already!

'Not much, Miss Louisa. But something.'

Pershaw's lined face showed his concern. She suspected there was little he did not know about the relationship between his employer and the young Earl. Jamie, too, had inherited his devotion.

'What, then? Out with it, man!' exclaimed Hugh, revealing his own anxiety by the impatience in his voice.

'I questioned the lad carefully, my lord. At first there seemed nothing to go on, but then he remembered overhearing something Lord Thurrock said to his man. He says he said, "Thank you for understanding, Milsom." And Milsom said, "I do, my lord." And then the Earl said, "Now *she*'s not here, I can go at last." The boy did not think the exchange important, since his lordship did not state where he intended to go, but——'

'Waterloo!' cried Louisa. 'He so wanted to go to the battlefield, to see where his father died. And we would not let him!'

'Then I must be off at once,' said Hugh decisively. 'They will have taken the main road, for certain. My horse is fresh, and I can change him at a post stable along the way. Dutton will accompany me. I should overtake them fairly quickly.'

'I will come with you,' said Louisa briskly. 'Luckily I have fallen into the habit of carrying my papers with me. One never knows, in France, when one will be asked to show them. Pershaw, are you willing to ride with me?' He was not, after all, her servant, although she felt sure he would obey her commands without demur. But in this matter she must offer him the choice.

'Naturally, Miss Louisa, I should not allow you to go without me. Like Lord Hugh's, our horses are fresh enough——'

'You will do no such thing!' interrupted Hugh. 'Louisa, my dear, this is a man's task——'

'Fustian! I can ride as well as you, and am closer to Jamie!'

This exchange, which indicated an unusual degree of intimacy between his lordship and Miss Finsham, elicited various responses from those observing it. Dutton and Pershaw exchanged knowing, satisfied smiles. William Coynd was heard to sigh.

Neither Louisa nor Hugh was concerned with what others thought at that moment, and all antagonism, all reserve had dropped from them in their mutual concern. But Hugh continued to argue.

'My dearest girl, I cannot allow you to accompany me without a chaperon. Your reputation would be in shreds——'

'Fustian!' repeated Louisa. 'It is not so fragile that it cannot withstand my making such a necessary journey as this! Pershaw will be with me——'

'But you need a woman, my dear.'

'Well, there isn't one. I cannot return for Betty without causing Aunt Nazeby unnecessary distress, and in any case she would need to travel in a carriage. So would most women, come to that. Lady Shelley departed for Brussels these weeks past so I cannot ask her. And even were she still here, would you suggest that I invite gossip by asking her to join us? No, I thought not,' she went on triumphantly at Hugh's horrified look. 'So I must rely on Pershaw to chaperon me. I am certain he will do a splendid job!'

Pershaw bowed, trying to hide his amusement and not quite succeeding. 'Indeed, Miss Louisa, I will do my best. It is always difficult to control a filly with the bit between its teeth, my lord,' he murmured. 'Best to let it have its head.'

It was the first time Pershaw had ever ventured such an insubordinate remark and Louisa was astonished. Had it been any other servant she would have dismissed him instantly for insolence, but Pershaw was a friend, as well as a devoted servant, and was trying to help her.

So, 'That will do, Pershaw,' she said briskly.

'I could hire a post chaise,' mused Hugh. 'That might be faster and better for you——'

'No.' Louisa shook her head firmly. 'They are uncomfortable things and Pershaw and Dutton would have to ride alongside anyway—there would not be room inside for us all—so it would not be faster. Besides, we do not want to draw the curiosity of French postillions, and if we used a coach it would be more susceptible to hold up.'

Hugh grinned, and shrugged. Louisa, sensing victory, smiled back.

'I am ready to start without further delay. Are you?'

'I must return to my quarters at the embassy for money. We will need changes of horses and most probably lodgings for at least one night. It will not take long.'

'I shall accompany you,' put in Coynd at this point. He had been standing in the background, forgotten by both Hugh and Louisa as they argued and made their plans. 'The Countess has made me responsible for him in her absence. It is my duty to find his lordship.'

'No doubt,' returned Hugh pacifically, 'but we can do that as well as you, and Lady Thurrock has entrusted Jamie to our care in the past, and would no doubt do so now. You, Coynd, will be more useful here.'

'I cannot see——'

Hugh cut the protest short. 'Lady Thurrock left you in charge. You are the only person with enough authority to direct the household, which is already in a sad state of turmoil and will undoubtedly descend into chaos without you here. And besides, should Lord Thurrock return unexpectedly it would be well if he found you here waiting for him.'

Coynd lifted his shoulders in a resigned shrug, giving way to Deverill's superior authority without further question. 'Very well, my lord. I will bid you farewell and wish you both a successful journey.'

He bowed. They returned the courtesy and Hugh turned to Louisa again, giving her a slightly grim smile. 'Are you ready?'

'Indeed, my lord, I have been ready this age!' She grinned suddenly, her real anxiety for Jamie somewhat mollified by the knowledge of his destination and by a new sense of adventure.

'What are we waiting for?'

CHAPTER TEN

HUGH's clock struck ten before they were ready to
leave his apartments, for he had insisted that they eat
some breakfast before starting out on the gruelling
journey.

Louisa had argued that Jamie was just getting further
ahead, but Hugh had remained adamant. It would do
Jamie no good at all for them to fail in their mission for
lack of sustenance.

Pershaw had only just joined them, having detoured
to the Hôtel des Fleurs with a carefully worded message
for Amelia, telling her merely that Louisa was visiting
Jamie's house and might remain away for several
nights.

'Lady Nazeby will be surprised and wonder at my
missing Lady Castlereagh's drum tonight, but should
not be unduly worried,' Louisa had told Pershaw as she
finished scribbling the note. 'Leave this with Chausson;
don't deliver it yourself; it is too early for her to be up,
but if she was she would want to question you! But do
not forget to collect your own papers, and tell no one
where you are going or why, just that you are remaining
with me. If she sends to the Thurrock establishment for
information Mr Coynd will field her enquiries. In the
end he might have to reveal the truth, but by that time,
if no message has reached him to say Jamie is safe, she
will have to be told. We cannot spare her anxiety for
long.'

Pershaw occupied a snug room over the stables. He would not need to speak to anyone apart from Chausson and possibly a stable lad. 'I will be as quick as I can, Miss Louisa,' he had promised. And had been as good as his word.

Neither he nor Dutton had eaten breakfast, either, Hugh had pointed out. Louisa could not bring herself to deny the servants the chance to eat, and was hungry herself, so in the end she had given in with good grace.

When the small party did at last set off, Hugh having obtained Sir Charles's assent to his absence, the autumnal sun, still rising to its low zenith, was behind them. Overnight rain had left the roads wet, but so early in the year the mud was not deep, as it would surely be by Christmas. Their progress was therefore reasonably fast.

At the end of the first stage they discovered that Jamie had rested his Conker and Milsom's horse before setting off again. The boy and his servant had eaten breakfast and departed on freshly watered horses some four hours earlier.

'We'll take fresh horses,' Hugh told the ostler, 'and leave ours here. We will return for them, of that you may be sure. I'll thank you to see that all four animals are properly cared for in our absence.'

A large sum of money changed hands. The ostler's eyes lit up. Louisa, watching with impatient interest, imagined the man had seldom, if ever, held as much gold in his hand before. But gold need not be the only inducement. She could offer a possibly more effective one. Money alone did not always secure loyalty. She stepped forward and gave the man her most winning smile.

'I am certain you will look after them to perfection.' She patted Hal's sweating neck fondly and kissed his nose. 'See they are well rubbed down, won't you? I should be greatly distressed to find any of the horses, even those ridden by the servants, had suffered harm while in your care.'

Quite overcome by the not inconsiderable battery of the lady's charm, 'You can rely on me, *madame*,' promised the man fervently.

'Lucky man, lucky Hal,' murmured Hugh as he passed her by to leave the stable.

Louisa flushed and followed him quickly, a tingle of anticipation adding an edge to her exhilaration. The job horses were already saddled and waiting. Pershaw stood ready to help her to mount, but Hugh gave him no opportunity. He placed his strong, capable hands on her waist and lifted her easily into her saddle. His fingers lingered momentarily on her thigh as she sought the stirrup. She settled her other leg more comfortably in the hooked pommel and arranged her skirts. When she looked down his eyes were fixed on her face, their expression unmistakable.

She looked away quickly, afraid that hers might reveal her ardent response. It was wonderful to be with him again. But too many unanswered questions hung between them.

Since his abortive proposal Hugh had been holding his emotions under tight control, not allowing Louisa or anyone else to guess how much her refusal had shaken him. The moment he had set eyes on her again this morning he had known his situation to be hopeless.

Pain caught again at his raw emotions. He loved her so deeply. There and then he vowed to do his utmost to win her love in return and then to renew his offer for her hand.

For some time they rode in silence, both lost in their thoughts. At last, while the horses slowed to take a hill, Louisa spoke.

'When do you suppose we might catch him up?'

Hugh had been silently considering that matter, among others, for some time. Brussels lay some one hundred and fifty miles ahead. Jamie had a four-hour start. They stood scant chance of coming up with him that day. Darkness would fall before six. Had he been alone he would have ridden on, but with Louisa in the party to travel after dark was beyond consideration. In this way her insistence on accompanying him would slow him down, but he would not dream of pointing this out. Her company was too precious. As it was they must find a lodging for the night by five o'clock. Time for only one more change of horses, then.

'Not today, I fear,' he answered her after a moment's delay while he carefully guided his mount round a deep pothole filled with muddy water. 'He had too long a start, and has been making good speed. We cannot hope to overhaul him quickly.'

'He seems to command the means to pay his way without stint,' she remarked. 'Mr Coynd must have been mistaken in the *louis* he possessed.'

'True. Although he has not expended money on hiring horses.'

'He would be reluctant to part with Conker.'

'Also true. We cannot be certain what means he has at his disposal. Mayhap he had been hoarding his allowance. And possibly Milsom has some savings and can oblige his master with a loan.'

'He could no doubt obtain credit. With his title——'

'Titles, in France, are not much in favour, even now.'

Louisa gave her reluctant mount an encouraging cluck and a tap with her crop. She did not look at Hugh as she spoke. 'Is that why you do not use yours?'

She had noticed he forbore to prefix his name with 'Lord'. It made little difference, though, for, however surly, the innkeepers and ostlers he addressed automatically responded to his air of easy command. So the prospect of spending the night in a French inn did not daunt Louisa. With Hugh beside her to smooth their path she knew the best rooms would miraculously become available.

'It seems diplomatic,' Hugh responded wryly.

Louisa chuckled, looking at him at last, her eyes dancing. 'My dear Hugh, you have certainly found your vocation!'

She was roasting him! The leap in his spirits seemed out of all proportion to the simple fact. Yet it meant she felt easy with him, that the awkwardness between them following his proposal had disappeared. That perhaps she would be willing to reconsider——

Or mayhap a renewal of his addresses might simply reintroduce the constraint between them. He must be patient. But he had vowed to win her, and he would!

'Then we may not catch up with him until we reach Brussels,' she added seriously, after a moment's consideration.

Hugh's horse shied at some imaginary threat in the hedgerow. Effortlessly, he brought it under control, glad of the diversion while he executed the more difficult task of doing the same for this thoughts. 'That is quite possible.'

'I'm sorry.'

'Sorry?' He sounded genuinely puzzled.

'That you should have to visit a place you dislike so much.'

He remained silent while they filed past a lumbering wagon, its sweating horses struggling to haul their load, encouraged by the carter's whip, then spoke in measured tones.

'I do not dislike Brussels. Neither do I despise the battle or the field upon which it was fought. I rejoice in the victory and admire the men who won it so brilliantly. It is the morbid curiosity I find distasteful. I thought I had already made that plain.'

'Well, yes, you did, but I had thought you would dislike to have to go there yourself. Personally, although I am concerned for him and anxious to see him safe, I shall be glad if we do not catch Jamie before he reaches Waterloo. I think we were wrong to stop him from visiting when he asked. He loved and revered his father. It is natural he should wish to pay his last respects at the place where he fell. There was, after all, no funeral.'

'I hope we do catch him,' returned Hugh sombrely. 'It is no pilgrimage a child of his age should make without support. He would be better served were we with him.'

Louisa could not hide her surprise. 'You would not attempt to prevent him from carrying out his mission?'

'No. You have made me see that for some it is a necessary act of mourning. Without it he may never properly recover from his father's death. Afterwards, he should be able to place his father's memory in its

proper perspective and continue with his life untram-
melled by frustrated longings and regrets.'

The smile Louisa turned on him was so radiant that
Hugh caught his breath. 'You have removed my last
objection to catching him up! I am so glad we feel the
same way about it,' she said fervently. 'I wished Aunt
Nazeby wouldn't insist on going, you know, but at first
I didn't know why she was so set upon it. When she
told me I could understand. And she's been much
consoled by the visit. Since then I believe she has quite
come to terms with her son's death.'

'Her son?'

Hugh's startled query made Louisa realise her indiscretion. Her colour rose to accompany her confusion
and she fiddled with her mount's trappings. 'Oh, dear!'
she said as the horses rose to a canter on the far side of
the hill. 'I should not have said that. She will be so
vexed with me for revealing her secret.'

'It is safe with me,' Hugh assured her.

'Thank you, my lord diplomat! I am certain it is,'
said Louisa with a slight laugh, wondering whether it
would be wise to tell him the whole story later. His
curiosity must be piqued. And the telling would explain
her own rather personal involvement in Jamie's affairs,
which had probably already given him cause to wonder.

After that silence reigned between them as they
urged the tiring horses forward. They could scarcely
expect job horses to be as fast as the splendid animals
they had left behind. But Jamie's speed would be even
more curtailed, for his horses would tire and need
longer periods of rest. By the time they came to an inn
where they could spend the night enquiry of the inn-

keeper elicited the information that the lad was only three hours ahead.

'We are catching up with him, but too slowly for my liking,' mused Hugh.

'We must make the earliest possible start tomorrow.'

'And do you not think he will do the same?' he asked wryly. 'But we can only do our best. You must be tired,' he added, concern informing his voice as he saw again the weariness Louisa was attempting to hide, first noticed as he'd lifted her from her horse. 'You are not used to being so long in the saddle, my dear. Go and rest while I order a meal and it is prepared. It will be at least half an hour, I am told. Water will be sent up and I will see that you are called when supper is ready.'

'This,' admitted Louisa honestly, 'is where I could do with Betty and a change of clothing! But you are right. I am longing to cleanse myself and rest for a while.'

As expected Hugh had obtained the best bed-chambers, together with a private parlour where they could eat.

The innkeeper's wife brought the hot water up herself, and exclaimed over Louisa's lack of a maid.

'I can manage perfectly well,' Louisa assured the woman, 'but I should be grateful if you could lend me a comb and a night shift. I had to leave suddenly, without luggage, you see.'

The woman gave her a knowing wink. 'Eloping, are you, *mademoiselle*? He is a fine gentleman; I cannot say that I blame you——'

'You are wrong!' proclaimed Louisa firmly, annoyed that her colour should rise at the suggestion. '*Monsieur* and I are not eloping, merely travelling together on an urgent mission. He was able to return to his residence for a few necessities and to collect his man, but for reasons I do not intend to explain I was unfortunately not in a position to do the same.'

'I see,' said her hostess, smiling in a friendly fashion but speaking in a tone of voice that said she didn't believe a word of what Louisa said. 'Would you like my daughter Marie to come and attend you, *mademoiselle*? She can bring the things you'll need and you'll find her a capable lady's maid.'

'Thank you, *madame*. I should be most grateful for the service.'

Rested, bathed and refreshed, her hair dressed with dexterity by the innkeeper's daughter, who had lent her a chemise and a cotton blouse so that she could wash Louisa's garments ready for the next day, Louisa went down to the parlour feeling more hungry than she had for many a long day. They had barely stopped for dinner, snatching some cold meat with bread and a glass of wine while fresh horses were saddled.

Once the covers were served and he was assured that they lacked nothing, the innkeeper left them. Dutton hovered about his master, offering further service, but Hugh soon dismissed him, telling him to join Pershaw in the common dining-room, where he could partake of his own supper.

The autumn evening being chilly a huge fire burnt in the grate, its glow filling the little parlour with cheerful warmth. At first Louisa found the intimate atmosphere daunting but told herself not to be so missish. No one here was likely to report back to Paris and if she could not enjoy a meal alone with a gentleman without feeling herself compromised it would be a very poor thing indeed.

'Is this their ordinary?' she asked brightly, sniffing at the delicious bowl of soup steaming on the table near a branch of candles. 'I must confess to being extremely sharp set!'

'With a few extras,' smiled Hugh, watching the soft, flickering light illuminate her face, emphasising the straightness of her narrow nose, revealing the delicate hollows beneath her high cheekbones, the fullness of her lips, the length of the lashes surrounding her lovely eyes, which appeared quite green in that light. The candles brought out the copper tints in her brown curls, simply dressed and without ornament. Heat surged through his body as he studied her delectable person. God, how he loved her!

He worked hard to keep his voice cool. 'The notice was too short for our hostess to prepare much in the way of specialities, but she has baked some fruit tartlets and made a custard. The mutton chops, the cold ham and the savoury pancakes the French make were already on the menu.'

'It all smells delicious, and I see she has not stinted the sauces!'

'They keep a good cellar here, too. The wine is excellent. Shall I pour you a glass?'

'If you please.'

Before she had finished the soup the food and the heat of the room had made Louisa uncomfortably hot. Her thick maroon habit was suited to riding but not to eating in a warm parlour.

'I think I must remove my jacket,' she apologised,

undoing the buttons concealed among the gold frogging.

He was on his feet in a moment. 'Allow me.'

He eased the jacket from her shoulders, his movements a caress. A shiver ran down Louisa's spine, disturbingly pleasurable. This was the first time they had been alone together since his proposal and, apart from the disturbing touch on her thigh that morning, the first time he had touched her in other than a purely impersonal manner since the ball.

Marie's peasant blouse with its little puff sleeves lay low on her shoulders, kept up by a drawstring around the neckline above a band of dainty smocking. Louisa longed for the courage to re-tie the bow, to draw the material up to cover her exposed flesh, for she saw Hugh's eyes drawn to the graceful column of her neck and descend to linger on the gentle swell of her breasts. Yet the blouse was less revealing than the ball gowns and evening dresses she wore every day, and she did not feel embarrassed when men looked at her then!

Had she known the temptation the bow tying the drawstring presented to Hugh's itching fingers she would have lost the last remnants of her composure. She was struggling as it was. She was so acutely aware of him. He had discarded his riding coat, retaining his waistcoat over changed linen. His shirt and immaculate cravat gleamed softly white in the candle-glow, the simple brown waistcoat with brocaded reveres affording a dignified contrast to the buff breeches tucked into his newly polished calf-length boots.

She tucked her own badly cleansed boots further under the protection of her travel-stained skirt. How she envied him his change of apparel! Dutton had probably packed a razor, too, for Hugh appeared to be freshly shaven. She raised a small and silent vote of thanks to Marie, without whose help her own appearance would have been regrettable indeed.

Hugh, having put temptation firmly aside, laid her jacket on a chair and resumed his seat. 'Have some mutton,' he suggested prosaically, although Louisa detected a slight tremor in his hand—one to match that afflicting her entire body. 'The caper sauce is delicious.'

Louisa attempted to divert both their thoughts with bright chatter. 'A small portion, then, for I must sample the pancakes! Do you know what our good landlady has used to fill them?'

Hugh had already consumed his mutton. He transferred a *galette* to his plate and investigated the contents.

'Ham, I believe, and mushrooms.' He took a mouthful and sampled the flavour. 'Cheese, too! The woman is a capital cook.'

'I agree,' said Louisa, savouring the mutton. 'She is wasted here!'

'Not so! Instead of catering to the whims of one family, she gives cheer to countless weary travellers!'

'We were fortunate to find this inn.' She finished the last of her mutton. 'Delicious! And now I shall try one of those pancakes, if you please!' He served her with smooth efficiency and as she cut into the food she thanked him before finishing her opening remark. 'We could have been forced to put up at some flea-infested hovel!'

'The main roads are well served. If Napoleon did nothing else, he kept his communications open.'

'I suppose he did have some good points.'

'Undoubtedly. He did much for France until power went to his head and he tried to subjugate the world and in the process sacrificed the flower of French manhood. In the end, you know, he was calling up sixteen-year-old boys. Those who tried to evade the conscription were sent to the front in chains.'

'Well, he's on his way to St Helena now. He will not escape again, I think.'

'God forbid!'

They completed their meal in an amicable silence only interrupted by polite enquiries as to each other's needs and fancies. The tension between them eased. Louisa sipped her final glass of wine and sighed.

'I must retire and leave you to your brandy.'

'Must you leave? I should not enjoy my brandy sitting here by myself. I have never seen the need for a gentleman to be left to drink at the table alone—unless, of course, he intends to imbibe to excess.' Louisa was already on her feet. He rose at the same time and held out his hand. 'Since we cannot retire to another room, will you not join me by the fire? We may, perhaps, drink tea together, if our hostess is capable of making it!'

'I hope she is! How I long for a dish of tea! But the French do not seem to have embraced the habit, as we have, and make it so poorly!'

He shifted her chair to facilitate her movements and, taking her hand, led her to a chair by the fire, which burnt less brightly now but still gave out a pleasant warmth.

'Are you comfortable? Would you like the tea at once?'

'Quite comfortable, thank you. And I should love to

have my tea now if that would be possible. If we are to make an early start I must seek my bed soon.'

Tempted to say he would be pleased to see that she found it and to join her there, Hugh resisted the wicked impulse in the interests of future progress. In some moods he was certain she would respond in kind to such an improper suggestion, for she was no simpering miss, but he was not sure enough of her at that moment. Instead, 'I will ring and order it,' he murmured prosaically.

He picked up the handbell and strode to the door. A serving girl answered the summons but *madame* herself brought the tray.

'Here you are, then, *monsieur, mademoiselle.*' She put the tray down on its legs and curtsied, giving them a distinctly knowing smile. 'Shall I pour it, or would you prefer to be left alone?'

Louisa did not think she could abide the woman in the room a moment longer, with her looks and innuendoes. All made in good part, of course, but highly embarrassing just the same.

'Thank you, *madame*, I will pour. Will you ask Marie to go to my room and make my things ready for the night? I shall not keep her waiting long.'

'Certainly, *mademoiselle*, though she will not mind how long she has to wait.'

The woman left them with another suggestive smile.

Hugh chuckled. 'I do believe she thinks we are up to no good!'

'She believes we are eloping,' muttered Louisa.

'Well, that's better than——' He broke off abruptly at sight of the mortification mirrored on Louisa's half-averted face. He realised that, far from welcoming the idea, Louisa was upset by it. He crushed down his own disappointment in an attempt to comfort her. 'My dear, I am sorry if you find the idea of eloping with me distasteful, but what does one common woman's mistaken opinion matter? Perhaps we should call in Dutton or Pershaw to chaperon us.'

'No,' protested Louisa fiercely. 'I will not be overset by a peasant's impertinence! I knew there could be misunderstanding when we set out. I was prepared to outface my own kind, so I am certainly able to withstand her insinuations! I will pour the tea if you will bring the tray nearer.'

Hugh did as requested, his mind in new disarray. Was it indeed the idea of marrying him that had caused her distress, or the thought of losing her reputation? He wished he knew. If it were the latter, why had she been so determined to accompany him?

'You should not have come,' he suggested softly.

'No doubt you are right.' She busied herself pouring the tea so that she need not look at him. She was a nuisance; he had not wished for her company. But he did not have the same incentive to catch up with Jamie and see him safe as she did.

'I had to.' Now was the time to explain fully. Then he could not misunderstand and think her motive had been simply to be with him. . . That had only been part of it. She handed him a cup of tea.

'Had to?' he probed.

'Yes. For Aunt Nazeby's sake. He is her grandson. My cousin. Although, of course, he does not know it and must never be told!'

Hugh drew a breath. 'I see! Then Muriel, Countess

of Thurrock, is not his grandparent? Robert was not her son?'

'No. She was and is Aunt Nazeby's dearest friend. They arranged it between them. But of course no one must ever know, because of the succession.'

'But who was his father? And why the deception?'

'I do not know who her lover was, except that he was a man of rank. And as to why, Aunt says the deception kept two marriages together. Perhaps three. Muriel needed a son, Amelia a good home for her bastard. And her lover's marriage was saved from the effects of scandal.'

Hugh put his cup back on the tray and moved to kneel beside her chair. He looked up into her shadowed eyes, his own serious.

'And is this why you have such an aversion to a man taking a married woman as his lover?'

Louisa started. Such a thought had been far from her mind. She gave a slight, negative shake of her head. 'Not particularly. I did not know of it until we reached Waterloo. But it illustrates my reasons for disliking such irresponsible and licentious behaviour. Tell me, Lord Hugh, how many of your bastards are in line to inherit a title?'

Hugh sprang to his feet, his leap reminding Louisa of the effect of an electric shock, an amusing novelty when demonstrated among one's friends. But Hugh was not amused. A smothered curse escaped his lips as he swung round to turn his back on her.

'Do you still believe the scurrilous gossip that has been put about?' he demanded harshly. No wonder she could not love him! But he had thought her more generous-minded.

'I don't know what to think.' How Louisa controlled her voice she did not know. As it was it sounded desperately uncertain. Her deep-seated distrust of all men had led her unruly tongue to run away with her and she had offended him bitterly. She continued almost inaudibly, quite unable to meet his blazing eyes. 'But you must concede that many lofty houses may nurture a cuckoo in their nursery. With all the immorality, the infidelity, rife among the nobility I often wonder whether any ancient line is as pure as its incumbents are pleased to believe.'

'And that concerns you?'

His tone had lost its bitter edge. It had softened, become thoughtful. Emboldened, Louisa looked up and met the full force of his penetrating gaze. It held an arrested expression, yet something like tenderness lurked there too. She shivered slightly, and shrugged.

'I think it a pity. But what concerns me more is the lightness with which people, both gentlemen and ladies, take their marriage vows. They are made before God and should be sacred.'

'Yes. You must believe that, for me,' he averred soberly, 'they would be. That they are not for some men and women concerns me but in the end their conscience is their own.'

'How can they do it?' wondered Louisa.

'For many reasons. Unhappiness. Their spouse's indifference or infidelity. Boredom. Sometimes, especially for men, it is sheer promiscuity, for women, often the promise of luxuries a mean or impecunious husband cannot or will not supply. It does not take much to persuade a woman that an amorous adventure will answer all her problems, will add excitement and glamour to her life. And the acquisition of a lover proves to an older female that she is still attractive.'

Louisa stood up, her scarcely touched tea forgotten. 'I think I must retire to my room.'

Hugh made a last attempt to penetrate the barrier she had erected between them. 'How can I persuade you that I am not the libertine you think me?' he demanded softly.

'Perhaps you already have, my lord, for what it is worth.' She managed a tremulous smile. 'You must understand, though, that I find it difficult to trust any man. My father's behaviour caused my mother such pain.'

'My dear!'

'Goodnight, Hugh.'

He laid a hand on her arm as she went to sweep past him, not trusting herself to remain in his company any longer. She would burst into tears or say something else she would regret if she did.

He looked down into her face, his eyes heavy with a longing he could not disguise. In her face he saw only hostility, in her eyes anguish. He sighed and let her go.

'God grant you a good night's rest.'

Louisa left the room swiftly, before she gave in and cried against his chest. She had been so sure he meant to kiss her. Her lips had parted in anticipation while her mind, whirling with conflicting thoughts and divers emotions, had taken control of her taut nerves. She had not wanted him to see how much she longed for his kiss. Yet the desire had been there.

And now, as she made her way up the dark stairway by the light of a candle picked up and kindled at its foot, all she felt was dismay at what she had done. And acute disappointment over what he had not. Why had he not taken her into his arms and resolved all her doubts with a kiss? For if he loved her——

But she had no reason at all to believe that he did.

CHAPTER ELEVEN

LOUISA descended to breakfast in subdued mood. She should not have quarrelled with Hugh. The disagreement had arisen, she recognised, from a desperate need to resist his lure. To pick a fight had been the simplest way to prevent herself from falling into his arms. But she should not have done it. They had a purpose in common and must work together to achieve its aim, whatever their personal feelings. Of course, Jamie was probably perfectly all right and well able to look after himself with Milsom's help, but they could not rely on that or allow him to continue his impetuous journey without adequate protection.

Hugh was already in the parlour when she entered. He immediately stood and made his devoirs.

'Good morning, Louisa. You are rested, I trust?'

Louisa dipped a curtsy in response. 'Thank you, yes.' Dutton was in attendance. No doubt Pershaw was seeing to the acquisition of fresh horses. But Hugh's wary politeness was not caused by Dutton's presence. No, his manner was a direct result of last night.

She held out an appealing hand. Surprised, he hesitated fractionally before taking it into his firm clasp. Her heart, already drumming, beat faster.

'Forgive me, Hugh. I was tired last evening,' she apologised, with an unconsciously pleading smile. 'Forget the unfair accusations I made. I have no wish to be at odds with you.'

227

His expression softened. All hostility had disappeared from her eyes, which shone up at him like stars. 'Readily.' He turned the hand he held palm up. His lips, dry and warm, lingered on her quivering flesh. He looked up to capture her eyes again with his. 'If you will allow me to offer my sincere regrets for any pain I may have caused in return?'

He retained her hand, smiling crookedly into her tear-sheened eyes. Dutton was busily occupied at the sideboard. She could almost see the man's ears flapping. But she did not mind. She knew that he approved of her. As Pershaw approved of Hugh. Servants really did hold an extraordinary influence over one's life, she thought, when their approval or disapproval could colour one's own judgement! She accepted Pershaw's opinion over so many things. Why not over Hugh?

Because Hugh Deverill was not a horse, she thought wryly. But a good judge of a horse was often a good judge of a man.

Her whole being relaxed. She blinked back her foolish tears and gave him a sunny smile. 'You, my dear diplomat, could charm anyone into anything!'

Now he laughed, captured her other hand and kissed both palms in turn, causing delicious tremors to course through her body. Then he closed her fingers over his kisses and gave her back her hands. 'We should eat. Dawn will be breaking soon.'

Thrown completely off balance by his caresses, Louisa nodded and took her seat. Reluctantly, she uncurled her fingers to break her roll and spread butter. But the feel of those kisses remained upon her palms long after she mounted her horse and took hold of the reins. Beneath her leather gloves the tingle left by his lips continued to remind her of that precious moment when the rift between them had been healed.

There was little sun. A chill wind had sprung up overnight but the rain held off and they scarcely noticed the weather. The regular halts for changes of horses and a quick bite to eat became longed-for breaks in a relentless drive forward. Louisa had never been called upon to ride hard for so long in her life before and exhaustion threatened to overtake her. She pressed on doggedly, determined to die rather than show it and prove Hugh right when he'd tried to dissuade her from coming.

So she ignored her sore seat and aching back and concentrated on keeping up with him. He, ever solicitous, had probably cut down his own pace, she realised. Having her along was slowing down his progress. He made no comment, being too much the gentleman to do so. And Pershaw was really too old for this kind of jaunt. She had done him no favour by asking him to accompany her.

But, steadily, they were overtaking Jamie. By the time they reached Cambray, where contingents of the Allied army had been billeted, he was little more than half an hour ahead, and still riding Conker.

'We should catch him up before nightfall,' said Hugh, relieved. 'He will cross into Belgium and stop at Mons, I should guess. We can hope to find him there.'

Louisa nodded, saving her breath. They were approaching a wooded, winding stretch of road and she was thankful that, although the sun had still not quite broken through, the low, dark clouds had lifted somewhat during the day, making the tunnel through the trees less gloomy.

Determinedly keeping her eyes fixed on potholes and hazards a few yards ahead, she heard Hugh swallow an oath. He put out a warning hand to touch her horse's bridle.

'Slower!' he ordered, just loud enough for the two servants behind to hear him. 'Dutton, Pershaw, cock your pieces!'

Jerked from her concentration on the road immediately in front of her hack's hooves, Louisa focused her eyes ahead.

The scene that met he eyes brought a gasp to her lips. A coach blocked the highway, the four snorting, restive horses harnessed to it restrained by a man at the leaders' heads. Several mounted men surrounded the carriage. At least two figures lay on the ground. Another stood backed up against a wheel with his hands above his head. There seemed to be a couple of loose animals adding to the confusion.

Hugh slowed his party down to a walk as he led a cautious approach. Having assessed the situation, 'Scatter,' he ordered crisply. 'Dutton, Pershaw, follow me. Dutton, fire a warning shot into the air.'

'There are too many——' began Louisa in dismay.

'Keep out of the way!' barked Hugh, spurring his horse forward as Dutton's shot rang out.

The men holding up the coach, realising they had been interrupted, answered fire. A ball whistled past uncomfortably close to Louisa's head. She ducked, heart in mouth, but did not slow down, keeping close behind Pershaw and Dutton, who, riding well apart, followed a length behind Hugh.

He had drawn his sword. Bellowing a challenge, he spurred his horse into a charge. Unfortunately, not being Kismet, the animal responded reluctantly, pounding forward with ears laid back, its eyes rolling in fright. Pershaw and Dutton, flourishing their pistols—Louisa suspected that Dutton's needed reloading—thundered along behind.

Someone shouted from within the carriage and the muzzle of a twin-barrelled fowling piece appeared in the window. The flash of fire as it first spluttered and then went off alarmed everyone, although the single ball went harmlessly up into the trees.

The approach of three armed men and the threat posed by the second barrel of the sporting gun proved too much for the highwaymen. A cry went up to retreat. The one at the carriage cattle's heads released them and sprang into his own saddle. The leader of the band, masked like the rest, grasped the reins of a riderless chestnut horse that, to Louisa, looked alarmingly familiar.

'Conker!' she gasped.

She spurred forward and as she approached the tableau resolved itself further. Three bodies lay on the ground, two on one side of the coach, one on the other. The man who had been standing with his hands above his head moved quickly to bend over the nearest prone figure, which groaned and moved. Louisa was more interested in the small person struggling to his feet on the far side of the coach.

'Jamie!' she cried, flung herself from her mount and rushed to his side, running round the back of the coach out of reach of its plunging horses.

'Louisa!' Utter relief washed over his face. 'We tried to stop them but they knocked me off, and hit Milsom——' He broke off, looked helplessly to where

Milsom lay, one side of his face covered in blood, and then his face crumpled. 'And they've taken Conker!' he ended miserably.

'You stay here with the boy,' Hugh called to her across the backs of the coach horses. 'Dutton, come with me. We'll try to recover the stolen horse.'

'Yes, my lord.'

As though he were used to undertaking this kind of task every day, Dutton accepted the still cocked pistol that Pershaw thrust into his hand and prepared to follow his master. The two rode off without a backward glance as Pershaw sprang to control the horses attached to the coach.

Jamie appeared to be frightened but not seriously hurt, although he had a bruise on his forehead. Milsom she didn't know about. Hugh was riding full tilt into danger. She scarcely hesitated.

'Is your pistol loaded, Jamie?'

'Yes, and primed. I didn't get a chance to fire it or to draw my sword——'

'Good. Give it to me. I know how to use it. Stay here with Pershaw.'

She grasped the gun, ran back to her horse, which, now the excitement was over, was busy munching grass from the verge. 'Help me up,' she threw at the man with the fowling piece, who was just descending from the rocking vehicle.

'My dear young lady——'

'You,' said Louisa, addressing the footman and ignoring the master, since he was arguing. 'Help me to mount and then look to your horses so that Pershaw may attend the wounded.'

Her voice carried such command that the man

obeyed instinctively, albeit with a glance of apology in his master's direction. Louisa rejoiced to see that the coachman, who had caught a ball in his shoulder, was very much alive, sitting propped against a wheel and groaning with pain.

Pershaw would see to everything there, she knew. And, overwhelmingly, it was Hugh who mattered. She had to be with him. To help if possible. Die with him if necessary.

The weariness had dropped from her like a cloak. She felt full of energy, alert, frightened to death and yet driven by some power above and beyond herself to ride to her love's side.

Hugh had a good start, but was not out of sight, for once through the narrow wood the track led straight across the fields. The highwaymen had not so far fired again on their pursuers, no doubt concentrating on speed and conserving their balls. Like Hugh's and Dutton's, her mount was relatively fresh. She made a light burden.

She began to overtake them, just as they were overtaking the fugitives, who found themselves hampered by a fractious Conker. Unused to such rough treatment and disliking being parted from his master, the chestnut was showing his mettle.

Before long Hugh was close enough to be within firing range. 'Stop! *Arrêtez!*' he roared.

They didn't heed his cry. Hugh fired.

Realising the captured horse was slowing them down, the leader let go of Conker's reins; Dutton returned the fire of one of the others but Louisa, clinging on with her knees, cocked Jamie's pistol and aimed for the leader; for, once free of the need to manage Conker, the man had looked over his shoulder and was pointing his pistol at Hugh.

She was too far away really. Her ball smacked harmlessly into the ground at the horse's heels, but the frightened animal leapt forward, almost throwing the man, whose shot went high and wide because of it.

Louisa's mount, frightened out of its wits by the explosion above its head, wheeled sharply, threatening to unseat her. While she struggled to remain in her saddle, handicapped by a pistol she did not wish to abandon since it was precious to Jamie, it took the bit between its teeth and bolted. Hazily, as she concentrated on clinging on and trying to regain control, she saw that Hugh, who had easily captured the loose Conker, had stopped the chase and allowed the miscreants to escape.

Relieved beyond measure to know that he was safe, Louisa was content to let her horse run. It would soon tire and since it had chosen to make straight back towards the road she had no real desire to stop it.

As the animal approached the belt of trees it decided it did not like the darkness ahead and swerved to the left.

Now Louisa did attempt to regain control, resting the hand holding the pistol and a tight rein on its withers and tugging regularly with her other. But the creature still kept the bit firmly between its teeth despite the discomfort caused by her treatment. Years of being ridden by indifferent horsemen had given it a hard mouth.

Hoofbeats from behind were drawing near. Taking a moment to glance behind, she realised Hugh had been chasing after her and that now she had changed course he was cutting across to intercept.

Before he could reach her a troop of scarlet-coated Life Guardsmen appeared from the trees ahead. Her tiring animal spotted them at once. It pricked its ears at the sight of so many other horses progressing steadily towards it, slowed its place, shook its head and responded to the bit. Louisa rode it forward before turning it to face Hugh.

By the time he drew his sweating mount alongside hers the soldiers were only a hundred yards off. They both reined in.

'You foolish creature!' he accused, breathing heavily, his voice unsteady. 'I told you to remain on the road!'

'Would you have preferred me to fall into strong hysterics?' demanded Louisa indignantly. She was panting, too. 'I am sorry, Hugh, that I am not of a fashionable disposition, but I am not in the habit of succumbing to the vapours at the veriest hint of danger.'

'I know, my dear——' he managed a smile '—and I admire you the more for it! But you cannot imagine my feelings when I thought to see you thrown, perhaps killed. . .'

His voice trailed off. Louisa looked into his eyes, saw the anguish he could not hide and a small smile touched her lips.

'But I can,' she assured him huskily. 'Why do you imagine I followed you when you rode off into danger?'

'Louisa——'

There was no time for more. The captain drew his troop to a halt and saluted.

'May I enquire your business here, sir?'

Hugh explained. 'Had you travelled another mile along the road you would have discovered the coach,' he finished.

'The highwaymen made off in that direction, did they?' mused the captain, nodding over the fields. 'I think we might give chase. Sergeant, take six men and see what you can find.'

'One of the horses,' said Hugh, 'is a piebald, and one of the men has a ginger beard.'

'Capital. You heard that? On your way, then, Sergeant. I'll accompany you back to your friends, my lord. We may be able to offer assistance to the wounded. Do you know the identity of the gentleman in the coach?' he went on to ask as he rode between Louisa and Hugh, the remainder of his troop trotting behind.

'No. But he was armed and so was his coachman, I imagine, since he got shot.'

'There was a crest on the door,' put in Louisa, 'but I did not recognise either him or it. He was English, though,' she added as an afterthought, 'I should have thought I might.'

'We shall no doubt soon discover his identity,' murmured Hugh with a grin. 'It is not only members of the *ton* who are entitled to crests, you know.'

'And most unwise of him to flaunt it on these roads,' observed the captain drily.

Chatting and speculating amiably, they at last returned to the road. As Louisa had expected, Pershaw had everything under control—including, it seemed, the rather choleric occupant of the coach.

'Intolerable delay!' he was spluttering as they

appeared. 'My man needs attention and I wish to reach
Paris with all speed!'

'Here comes his lordship now,' said Pershaw stiffly,
obviously relieved. 'You will be able to thank him
personally, my lord.'

So he was ennobled. But she had never seen him in
London or elsewhere and now she heard him speak
properly she could perhaps imagine why. He had the
broadest of country accents. Difficult to place.

Jamie jumped forward eagerly. 'Allow me to present
you, my lord. Lord Hugh, Louisa, this is Lord Cumnor,
of Cumnor Place in Lancashire, who has been visiting
Waterloo on his way to Paris, where he hopes to be
presented to Lord Wellington. He owns a mill and
supplies material for our army's uniforms and believes
Lord Wellington will be grateful.' Hugh and Louisa
dutifully inclined their heads. 'Miss Louisa Finsham,
the niece of Amelia, Dowager Countess of Nazeby,
and Lord Hugh Deverill, of the British Embassy in
Paris, my lord.'

Well done, Jamie, thought Louisa, giving the lad a
smile as Cumnor made a stiff bow. Now everyone knew
exactly who everyone else was!

Hugh indicated the captain. 'Captain Brownhill of
the Life Guards, my lord. His corporal is skilled in
attending the wounded. He will look at your coachman.
Jamie, how is Milsom?'

'He's all right apart from a sore head, I think. He
was knocked out and the wound bled a bit. And the
coachman has been seen to. But, sir, you got Conker
back! Dutton brought him in and said Louisa's horse
had bolted!'

'You took a bump, too, by the look of it,' said Hugh,

ignoring the latter part of Jamie's outburst as he dismounted and assisted Louisa from her saddle. 'Let the corporal take a look at both of you. My lord, your attackers are being pursued by some of Captain Brownhill's men. But they had a good start. I doubt whether they will be caught. You are lucky we all came along when we did.'

'I am grateful to you of course, Deverill, and was asking your man to convey my thanks, but he insisted I wait for your return.'

'Not Lord Hugh's man but Lady Nazeby's groom, my lord.' Louisa thought she had seldom met a less gracious person in her life. 'I imagine he was concerned for our safety and wished you to witness our return before taking your own departure. In certain circumstances your coach could have been essential to our survival.'

Pershaw nodded. 'Precisely, Miss Finsham.'

'Luckily we escaped unharmed,' said Hugh, his polite manner, Louisa realised, concealing considerable anger. 'Now the corporal has inspected your coachman and pronounced him fit to travel I can see no reason to delay you longer. However, I would advise you to hire some armed outriders at the next town. They should accompany you for the remainder of the journey, particularly as your crest is so prominently displayed on your carriage doors. There is safety in numbers. As no doubt Lord Thurrock has discovered.'

Jamie flushed and Louisa wished Hugh hadn't publicly criticised the boy. But Cumnor did not notice.

'I have my fowling piece. I shall not hesitate to use both barrels another time!'

'But you will have only one fit man to protect you,

my lord. Take my advice and do as his lordship has suggested.'

Captain Brownhill had dismounted, too. His clipped voice brought a scowl to Cumnor's heavy face. 'I'll do as I think best. Good day to you, my lords, Captain, Miss Finsham. You will be returning to Paris? Perhaps we shall meet again there.'

Hugh bowed. 'We shall be returning when our business in Brussels is finished. Certainly within the week.'

Jamie's flush of embarrassment turned to one of eagerness. He had not missed the implication of Hugh's words. Louisa gave him an encouraging smile.

'Then I'll be on my way. Thanks again, Deverill, and to you, Thurrock.'

With the prospect of speedy departure, Cumnor was behaving with condescending grace. They watched the coach roll away with some relief.

Captain Brownhill remounted and gathered his troop behind him. He saluted. 'Pleasure to be of service, my lords, ma'am.'

'I hope you catch those rascals,' said Hugh. 'If you need us to identify them we'll be in Brussels for the next couple of days. The Duchess of Richmond will know our whereabouts. After that, we shall return to Paris.'

'I should be glad to welcome you to the barracks at Cambray, my lord, if you have time to stop in passing. We should have news by then.'

'Thank you, Captain. We may well take you at your word.'

With a brisk nod the captain called his men to order and rode off at their head.

'And now, young man,' said Hugh with paternal severity, 'I should ring a peal over your head for being such a sapskull. Not only did you endanger your own life, but that of Milsom, too.'

'I was awfully glad to see you,' confessed Jamie, subdued. 'How did you guess where I'd gone?'

'It was not difficult. And the reason I shall not make a tiresome piece of work of this matter is because Louisa has persuaded me that you should be allowed to see the field upon which your father died if you so wish. We shall therefore escort you there. If that is still your desire?'

There could be no question of that. Milsom, having been complimented for his care of his young master, was helped back on his horse.

'Are you certain you are fit to ride?' asked Louisa dubiously.

'Perfectly, thank you, Miss Finsham. I shall manage,' he said, which was a mixed sort of response, but Louisa admired the man's determination. Conker skittered about when Jamie mounted, glad to be reunited with his master. The hired horses accepted their burdens with resignation and the party proceeded into Belgium.

In view of their exchange just as the Life Guards had ridden up Louisa expected Hugh to seek to be alone with her that evening. She anticipated the moment with intense pleasure. If Hugh proposed again she would accept. He must care for her. Else why had he been so distraught at the mere thought of her being hurt? She knew perfectly well what had caused her concern over his safety. Surely he must love her just a little? Enough for her to work on in the future? And single independence had long ceased to appear as attractive to her as it had when she'd left England.

She was to be disappointed. Jamie, professing himself far from tired and quite able to manage for himself for one night, sent Milsom to bed to nurse his aching head and settled down to monopolise Hugh for the remainder of the evening. Louisa, who was desperately tired, the excitements of the day adding to her exhaustion, retired early herself. Hugh bade her a ceremonious good night, his eyes warm, his lips ardent on her hand.

It was not enough.

Arrived in Brussels, Hugh immediately called on the Duchess of Richmond. Since the Duke and Duchess had taken up residence in Brussels she had naturally become the leader of the *ton* in that city and her ball, thrown on the eve of Waterloo, had become famous. So many of the gay young officers who had danced there and left in the early hours to report for duty had not survived the battle.

Hugh returned to the inn, where the others were taking refreshment, to inform them that Her Grace had offered her hospitality. He had accepted with gratitude. Although conditions in Brussels had improved considerably over the last couple of months the inns were still crowded and the danger of infection lurked within their walls.

'My dear,' cried the Duchess after greeting Louisa, 'so brave of you to undertake such a hazardous journey! And to defy convention to do so! You must know that Lord Hugh—such an excellent young man—has explained the situation and you have my full support! My maid will attend you. She will search out a gown for you to wear—there must be something suitable in my wardrobe and if not then in Jane's or Georgy's. My daughters are in Paris but have left much of their wardrobes behind.'

'You are most kind, ma'am. I have met your daughters, of course. They are in excellent health and spirits. Lady Georgiana is a great favourite with Lord Wellington.'

'They both are! I truly believe he looks upon them as his own daughters! But come, my dear, Brigide shall show you to your room and then see to your needs.'

A bath had never been more welcome. Cleansed, her hair and skin faintly perfumed with some mixture added to the water by Brigide, Louisa gratefully accepted a complete change of linen and donned a low-necked, cream silk gown trimmed with lace, which belonged to Lady Jane. It had been selected from those available as being a good fit and of reasonably suitable design for dining at the Duchess's table. A blue sprigged muslin dress had been set aside for wear the following day.

'I will see to the cleaning of your habit, *mademoiselle*,' promised the lady's maid. 'How would you prefer your hair to be dressed?'

'You decide,' suggested Louisa.

'Well, *mademoiselle*, I think it would suit you a little shorter, with curls drawn down over your forehead and arranged around your ears to frame your face. The style would be soft yet emphasise the fine lines of your jaw.'

Louisa regarded herself in the mirror. Her hair had grown a little long and certainly at that moment, having just been dried, looked untidy. Yet—— An image of Hugh, as though reflected behind her in the mirror, suddenly swam into her vision. His eyes were fixed on her unruly curls and his fingers were stretched out as if to bury themselves in their luxuriant thickness. A *frisson* of awareness ran down her spine, as though in truth his fingers were caressing her. He would prefer her hair longer; she knew it instinctively. Its brown colour was nothing exceptional. Its attraction, if it had any at all, lay in its abundance and vitality.

'No,' she decided. 'I will not have it cut any shorter just yet. But otherwise your suggestion sounds excellent. I usually have it dressed off my forehead. This will make a change.'

Brigide set about her task without further demur. She was more skilled than Betty, of that there could be no doubt. Under her expert ministrations the curls were tamed and a slight decoration to match the satin bow beneath her breasts was fixed.

'Capital!' exclaimed Louisa, rather taken aback by the vision confronting her in the mirror. The woman was a magician! 'Thank you, Brigide!'

The Duchess's maid acknowledged the praise with a curtsy and departed to minister to her mistress.

Brigide had of necessity dressed her early, so Louisa had an hour to spare before dinner. The afternoon sun made the small parterre beneath her window appear especially inviting. She did not imagine the Duchess would object to her taking a stroll along its paths. She felt restless. As though she was on the edge of some great adventure. Mayhap she was, for Hugh must surely renew his proposal before long. And she would accept him this time. With or without any declaration of love. Of one thing she was now fairly certain. Once wed, she would have no reason to doubt his fidelity.

She had worried herself needlessly on that score. Unless, of course, she failed him as a wife.

That did seem rather unlikely, unless childbirth rendered her delicate, which was not an unknown eventuality. She had to hope she would survive the dangers of that condition and emerge in good health. For who could blame a man whose wife was unable to receive him in her bed for seeking release elsewhere? She would never be so foolish as to choose to banish him. Given her health she would love him so much that he would never wish to look at another woman while she lived!

Having carefully placed a bonnet over her new *coiffure* and wrapped a thin shawl about her bare shoulders, Louisa went downstairs to seek a door leading to the garden. Directed to one by a passing servant, she strolled towards the far end of the parterre, drawn by the sight of colourful blooms and the aroma of herbs. Those which had scented her bath must have been gathered here. She drew in an appreciative breath, revelling in the mixed perfumes of the garden, at their most pungent as evening approached.

Finding a seat, she sat down to enjoy a few moments of quiet reflection, so welcome after three days of energetic action.

Jamie was safe and well. Hugh had sent an express message back to William Coynd the previous evening, from Mons. Aunt Nazeby should hear the whole story soon and be reassured, knowing them all to be together. What she would think of her own part in the business Louisa dared not imagine. That her aunt would try to stop wagging tongues she did not doubt.

Of course, Hugh might think he now had to ask her

to wed him. She was, in the eyes of many, hopelessly compromised. But—oh, dear God, if he asked her for that reason she would feel obliged to refuse him again!

The complications of the situation had not occurred to her before. Her mind had been set on rescuing Jamie and she had dismissed all the consequences of her impulsive action in accompanying Hugh without the presence of a proper chaperon as of little account. Now she stopped to think clearly on the matter it had been a foolish thing to do. But surely, as she had protested at the time, her reputation would be strong enough to withstand the malicious gossip which would undoubtedly ensue?

For years Hugh had chosen to ignore the society which so ruled her life. Until, in fact, that society had temporarily moved to Paris and his position there had forced him into taking his place in it. He would depart for Austria shortly, leaving all the gossip behind. As usual, it would be the woman who suffered censure, although Hugh might be criticised for not coming up to scratch.

Footsteps on the path brought her head up. Hugh was striding purposefully towards her. Her recent thoughts seemed suddenly most pertinent. Had he come to propose, to regularise their relationship because their presence presented an embarrassment to the Richmonds? Not that the Duchess had appeared in the least overset. . .

Her thoughts made her uneasy in his presence. He did not appear to notice. He made his bow and indicated the space on the seat beside her.

'May I sit?'

Louisa moved a little to make more room. 'Of course. This garden is most pleasant, is it not?'

'A veritable haven of peace. I saw you sitting here and hoped you would not mind my joining you. We are within clear sight of the house.'

So he had the proprieties in mind. Louisa did not know whether to be glad or sorry. The tension inside her grew as he settled himself on the seat, his thigh mere inches from her own.

'Jamie would like to visit the battlefield tomorrow. Do you wish to accompany us?'

His abrupt words restored much of Louisa's calm. He had not sought her out to propose!

'Yes,' she said immediately. 'I see it as my duty. But you have no need——'

'Like you, I consider it a duty. Very well, we will all go. I will hire a coach which Pershaw may drive. It will make a change from horseback riding and give Conker and Milsom's horse a much needed rest.'

Louisa noded. 'When shall we begin our journey back to Paris?'

'The following day, I suggest. I must return with all speed, for I have many neglected duties awaiting my attention. If you would prefer to travel by chaise——'

Louisa cut him off. 'No. We have no luggage and may as well take advantage of the fact. We shall be a sizeable party and hardly likely to attract the attentions of highwaymen. Besides, if we hired a chaise, what would Jamie do about Conker?'

'Both horses would have to be brought back by a groom.'

'That would not please Jamie!'

Hugh grinned. 'No. I have the greatest admiration

for that boy. I wonder whether his mother will return to see to his welfare?'

This question had been exercising Louisa's brain. 'If the Prince marries her I should think not. If he does not, she is ruined and will scarcely dare. I think she has abandoned Jamie.'

'She must be a most unnatural mother!'

'She could not gain sole control of his fortune, you see. The other trustees—his grandmother and a firm of lawyers—must also be consulted whenever anything over and above his allowance is to be spent. They must approve expenditure on the estates, too. She has her jointure, of course, but that was not enough. She did not like the trust arrangements, but the Thurrock fortune has always been well hedged against dissipation by anyone other than the Earl himself—once he comes fully into his inheritance, of course.'

'So what will he do?'

'I have been thinking. I imagine the old Dowager will take up residence at Thurston, his favourite estate, and do her best to see he is happy. Lady Nazeby will always be welcome and between them the old ladies will thoroughly spoil him!'

'I can imagine,' chuckled Hugh. 'It sounds an ideal solution.'

'And should anything happen to either of them I shall step in to ensure that Jamie's welfare does not suffer.'

'If you are able.'

'I can see nothing to stop me.'

That was his cue. Louisa waited, scarcely breathing, for him to protest that there could be everything to prevent her. Instead, in a leisurely manner, he rose to his feet.

'It is growing a little chilly. I believe you should return indoors. It must be almost time for dinner.'

CHAPTER TWELVE

A FRUSTRATING evening loomed, probably to be followed by another early night. What were Hugh's intentions? wondered Louisa impatiently, toying with her food while listening with half an ear to the wide-ranging conversation he was conducting with their intelligent hosts. He had been betrayed into displaying more concern than was strictly necessary after the incident on the road the previous day. This had raised her hopes enormously. She had thought an impassioned declaration imminent. Yet it had not materialised and now his behaviour towards her, though undoubtedly attentive, remained strictly correct in every way.

Of course, while staying in the Richmond's residence their conduct must be above reproach. Louisa recognised and regretted the fact. Hugh had shown in the garden that he respected their hosts too much to attempt to snatch a few stolen moments of forbidden privacy and thus give cause for offence. So, in fact, did she—respect their hosts. But appreciating the limitations on their freedom did nothing to lessen her present puzzlement over Hugh's true feelings.

Leaving the men to sit on at the dining-table over their port and brandy, the Duchess led her guest into the drawing-room. Having settled her comfortably in an armchair, she proceeded to ply her with questions. Louisa was happy to talk about her friendship with James Grade, the new Earl of Thurrock, explaining how they enjoyed riding in the Bois de Boulogne together, where Lord Hugh Deverill, like many others, including Lord Wellington, often joined them. And how the intimacy between all three had deepened during Lord Hugh's instruction of both herself and Jamie in the German language, so that when the Countess eloped with the Russian prince, enabling Jamie to set off on his longed-for mission to Waterloo, it had seemed natural for them to ride together to his assistance.

'Hasn't Deverill offered for you yet?' asked the Duchess when Louisa stopped.

Louisa simply could not prevent the blush that rose to stain her cheeks. 'Why do you ask, ma'am?'

'You are manifestly attached to each other. It is obvious he cherishes a *tendre* for you, as, I suspect, you do for him.'

Louisa's fingers began to tremble as the import of the Duchess's words sunk in. Were her feelings really plain for all to see? And since the Duchess was correct about her, could she be right about Hugh?

She smoothed a crease in the skirt of her gown and prevaricated. 'Neither of us has any wish to marry. Especially Lord Hugh.'

'Devil take me if I ever heard such nonsense! True, as Chadford's younger son Deverill has no duty to produce heirs, but most men, sooner or later, become persuaded that they need a wife and a nursery of their own.'

'Lord Hugh will need a wife, as Ambassador to Austria.' Louisa met her hostess's eyes bravely. 'Yes, my lady, he has asked me to marry him. I refused.'

'May I be permitted to enquire why?'

Louisa suddenly felt that she could confide in this kindly, experienced woman, the mother of two young girls, one still unmarried. 'I did not wish to be wed as a matter of convenience, ma'am. I have fortune enough to render me independent for life. I have no cause to tie myself in wedlock with a man who does not love me.'

The Duchess snorted. 'You sound like my Georgie! She is hanging out after some romantic ideal, won't consider any of the matches we propose for her!'

'But you do not force her into matrimony, dear ma'am.'

'No. Unfashionable, I know, but can't bring ourselves to do it. I suppose she will marry one day,' sighed the Duchess, 'probably just before it is time for her to say her last prayers! You should do the same, Louisa. What makes you think Hugh Deverill does not love you, my dear?'

The sudden question forced Louisa to lower her eyes, unable at that moment to meet the Duchess's sharp gaze. 'He has never said so.'

'Is that all?' Her Grace sounded somewhat derisive. 'Actions speak louder than words, child, you should remember that! Some men find it difficult to put their emotions into words. Yet they are displayed for all to see in their behavior. Mayhap Deverill is such a one.'

'Perhaps, ma'am.' Louisa doubted the truth of this supposition. He was excellent at expressing himself on other intimate matters. 'But I am not inexperienced in the way of gentlemen. Others who have asked me to marry them have protested their devotion.'

'Did you believe 'em?'

'Not all of them, no.'

And the one she had had not been speaking the truth.

'So there you are!' For the Duchess that admission seemed to vindicate her argument. 'To some men a declaration of love comes as easily as a snatched kiss in the dark! To others, the emotion is too deep, perhaps even too precious a feeling to be put into words. It may not even be recognised as love.'

Louisa digested this piece of wisdom in silence. 'I hope he will not feel *obliged* to ask me again,' she said at last.

The Duchess immediately recognised the oblique reference to the present unorthodox situation in which the pair found themselves. She shrugged her elegant shoulders. 'If he possesses the fine sensibilities I believe him to, he will realise that the best way to lose you would be to allow you to imagine any such thing. Be patient, my dear Louisa, and if he dallies too long then take steps to bring him to the point again!'

'Steps, ma'am?' Louisa's eyes opened wide in seemingly innocent surprise.

'Don't play the green girl with me, my dear,' chuckled the Duchess, 'it won't wash! I've known you since you first appeared at St James's, too long to suppose you do not know what I mean! But take my advice. Wait until you are back in Paris and the scandal of your headlong rush after young Thurrock with only a groom to chaperon you has had time to be forgotten. I would wager Deverill will have spoken of his own accord by then. But if by chance he has not, you must make sure he does.'

'He leaves Paris in a few weeks,' observed Louisa despondently.

'My dear Louisa, I have never known you to be defeatist before! Depend upon it, the man loves you! But he will not address you again if he thinks another refusal likely.'

Louisa sat up straighter, a new determination written on her face. 'You are right, ma'am! I am indulging in unnecessary dismals! And,' she added ruefully, 'I have given him little enough cause to renew his offer!'

The gentlemen joined them soon after this and Louisa tried hard to enliven her thoughts. Lady Richmond was correct. She was not usually so ready to sink into gloom. But nothing, ever, had seemed so important to her as discovering whether Hugh truly loved her or not. Whether he intended to renew his offer or not. Time was so short. All her future happiness was at stake. How could she not be apprehensive?

The party set off for the battlefield after breakfast the following morning. Dutton sat on the box with Pershaw while Louisa, Jamie and Hugh rode inside the coach. Milsom had been left behind to nurse his sore head.

'We need not meet many of those who are merely sightseers,' remarked Hugh as they set off, the coach rumbling through the busy streets of Brussels, now happily almost cleared of wounded derelicts. 'The hired coachmen take their customers to Mont St John and the scene of Wellington's final victory. I propose that we travel on to La Belle Alliance, where the major met his death at the hands of Napoleon's reserves. I have instructed Pershaw accordingly.'

'Such a waste!' mourned Louisa. 'If only they had retreated in good order after routing the French *cuirassiers* and not charged on through the infantry and into Napoleon's reserve lines!'

'It was the Union Brigde that did it.' Jamie had clearly studied the reports with precocious interest. 'Lord Uxbridge—he was the commander of the cavalry, and he led the Household Brigade himself, you know—couldn't stop them. My papa died trying to cover the retreat.'

'The troopers had been served with rum to stiffen their nerve. It made them reckless,' observed Hugh grimly.

Silence reigned as the coach gathered speed along the less crowded road south out of the city. The coach lurched and bumped into potholes despite Pershaw's excellent driving. Hanging on to the strap, Louisa considered that the long journey on horseback had been preferable to one confined within a bouncing carriage. However, if the weather changed and became wet she supposed Hugh would insist upon their travelling back to Paris by coach or chaise. Either way the long journey promised to be tedious.

'I'd quite like to look across from Mont St John first,' said Jamie suddenly, jerking her thoughts back to the present. 'If there are not too many other people already there,' he added apologetically. 'It's where the charge began.'

Hugh smiled a trifle wryly. 'I collect that you will not be satisfied until you have seen everything.'

'Well, sir, he was my father.'

'I know, Jamie. You shall see whatever you wish. I'll tell Pershaw.'

Hugh thrust his head out of the window to draw the coachman's attention and gave the order to divert. He

was sitting opposite Louisa and Jamie, who were facing
the horses. As he drew his head back inside his eyes
met Louisa's. Understanding flowed between them.
Neither relished the next few hours, but Jamie deserved
their support.

They passed the village of Mont St John and then the
deserted farmhouse, which brought them to the ridge
behind which Wellington had hidden most of his army.
They descended from the coach and climbed the hill.
Louisa had seen the battlefield before, but not quite
from here. She had been slightly below the top of the
ridge on her previous visit, on the road on its far side,
unable to see what lay behind. In any case, she had not
wanted to look.

Having reached the crest, Jamie stood and slowly
turned full circle. 'Yes,' he said, 'I can see it now. Only
the nine-pounders and a few advance troops were
deployed to the south, hidden among the corn. Papa
and the remainder of the army waited back there.' He
waved a hand towards the ruined farmhouse.

Louisa looked about her, too, less reluctant than she
had been on her first visit. She had heard enough
discussion of the battle in the drawing-rooms of Paris
to arouse her interest. The fields in every direction had
been flattened, their crops lost, trampled into the mud
by thousands of feet and hooves. Visible evidence of
the carnage had been removed. The ground had begun
to recover. Only the shells of the buildings remained as
a reminder of the men who had died there.

Hugh had also become absorbed in the scene as he
followed Jamie's explanation. It was surprising how
compelling the place could become when one's interest
was personal, mused Louisa. He must have read and

listened to the accounts of the battle too, for he nodded his head. 'And here, behind the ridge, was where the men endured Bonaparte's eighty-gun bombardment and held the line until Blücher's Prussian reinforcements could arrive.'

Louisa tried to imagine lying in the corn on wet, muddy ground with shot and shell continually falling around her, watching comrades being killed and injured and simply having to endure. And after that to face the terrorising panoply of a Napoleonic offensive, hear the threatening beat of drums advancing at the head of a formidable army, the bearded grenadiers marching four hundred abreast and shouting at the top of their voices, the elusive *tirailleurs* running and firing ahead. It did not bear thinking about.

'And I suppose,' said Jamie after some moments of silent contemplation, 'that must be La Belle Alliance.'

He pointed across the flattened fields to the south to another ridge.

'That is what I understood from the guide when I was here before.' Louisa was glad to remove her eyes from the devastated fields near by to a point so distant that detail was obscured. 'And that knoll there is the one from which Bonaparte conducted the battle.'

'May we please go and see it?' asked Jamie.

Just below where they stood the carriages of sight-seers had begun to arrive. Both Louisa and Hugh turned thankfully back to rejoin their coach.

There was little more to be seen than further devastated buildings and flattened fields on arrival at the spot from which Napoleon had directed the battle. The two great commanders had never joined directly in battle before. On that day, as so often before in his career, the Duke had proved that sound defence could break the resolve of the attacking army and win the day. It had been the Peninsula story all over again. Napoleon had rejected the advice of his veteran marshals and used his normal tactics. And been beaten.

Jamie did not have much to say as he contemplated the field on which his father had died. Eventually, hand on sword hilt, he turned to Hugh and smiled, a rather strained smile but a smile nevertheless.

'Thank you for coming with me, Lord Hugh.' He swivelled to where Louisa stood. 'You too, dear Louisa. I can imagine it all now, the noise and the smoke and the fury of battle. I should like to follow my father and purchase a commission in the cavalry when I am older.'

Louisa opened her mouth to protest that he should consider no such thing but Hugh silenced her with a look.

'That will be your privilege, my lord. Are you ready to leave now?' As he assisted Louisa over the rough ground he murmured, 'At that age I wanted to be a mail-coach driver!'

Louisa understood. There would be plenty of time for Jamie to change his mind without her lecturing him now.

'Well,' said the Duchess over dinner, 'what did you think? Such a sad, brave sight! When I think of all those gallant young men who left my ball to die on that field I sometimes wonder how I can bear it! I had asked Wellington if I should cancel the affair, for we all knew a battle must be imminent, but he said no. We were all so gay that night! Not least Wellington himself!'

'Or so he wanted it to appear. He had made his dispositions, my dear. There was nothing more he could do except to receive messages and write new orders. Although with the messages pourin' in, he did confess to me that Napoleon had humbugged him, had gained four and twenty hours' march on him. He had not expected the enemy to advance to rapidly.' The Duke of Richmond laughed slightly, wryly reminiscent. 'He asked to borrow my local map.'

'Very soon the officers took their leave, the trumpets sounded and the drums beat to arms. Brussels was alive with troops.' The Duchess shuddered. 'Then, when the wounded began pouring in. . .! My dears, it was quite frightful!'

'We need not dwell on it any longer, my love. Thankfully it is all over and that monster is safely on his way to St Helena, if he has not already arrived. He will be able to do no more harm.'

The Duke having deftly diverted the conversation, Hugh followed his lead. 'With the American war ended we may hope for a period of peace at last.'

'Indeed, my boy, and you are just the person to see to it that we do! Off to Vienna, eh? Ever been there?'

'No, Your Grace. During much of the Congress of Vienna I was engaged in assisting those sent to negotiate peace with America. The Treaty of Ghent was signed only last December. After that I spent a few months in England.'

'Well-earned rest, eh? And then they sent you over to Paris. Done an excellent job there, by all accounts. Castlereagh can't speak highly enough of you. Deserve an embassy of your own. We are not entirely cut off from news here, you know! And you, young lady, are you goin' to marry the fellow and go with him?'

Louisa could have sunk with mortification but instead she tilted her chin. How could he? As blood flooded her face she dared not even glance in Hugh's direction. What possible answer could she give?

She was saved by the Duchess. 'Really, Richmond!' exclaimed that lady. 'Don't be such a bumble! Leave the young people alone to settle their own affairs!'

Jamie, however, blurted out, 'Are you to be married? How famous! I may visit you in Vienna!'

Goaded, Louisa spoke before she thought. 'No,' she declared fiercely, 'we are not! And now, everyone, may we please change the subject?'

'Sorry,' mumbled the Duke, looking rather shame-faced but allowing a twinkle to remain in his eyes. 'Delicate subject, eh? Should've realised. Well, my dear, you'd better leave us soon, or we'll never be ready to leave for the Countess's drum. Glad you're coming, Deverill. Still a few of us left in residence here for you to meet.'

Thus prompted, the Duchess rose to lead Louisa from the room. Louisa avoided looking at Hugh. She could not imagine what his reaction to the Duke's words had been.

'I have ordered an early tea tray, my dear, and then we may be off. You will know most of the English people there, but you will meet some of the local first circle as well.'

After the Duke's unfortunate remarks Louisa did not feel she could face Hugh again that day. Let alone suffer all the curious looks and questions both strangers and acquaintances were certain to throw in her direction. She simply could not go!

'If you will excuse me, dear ma'am, I would beg your leave to remain in my room this evening. We begin our journey back to Paris tomorrow and I shall need to rest.'

'Nonsense!' declared the Duchess roundly. 'It is essential for you to come! You must realise that appearing under my patronage will scotch the gossip surrounding your arrival in Brussels. If I indicate my approval of your presence here no one else will dare to criticise. At least not openly! And the news will soon travel to Paris. Your presence tonight will secure your future acceptance in Society.'

Wise in the ways of the *ton*, Louisa had recognised the fact earlier and then forgotten it in her desperation to avoid an embarrassing confrontation with Hugh. She smiled wryly.

'Of course you are right, ma'am. It was foolish of me to forget.'

'But you feel so mortified by what my dear husband the Duke said that you wonder how you may keep your countenance in the presence of Deverill.' At Louisa's half-hearted attempt at denial, the Duchess merely smiled. 'Depend upon it, he will be feeling exactly the same. So you must both put on a brave front and behave with impeccable propriety. In that manner you may retrieve the situation, especially as I intend that you should travel back in my coach, accompanied by one of my maids.'

'Your Grace, you must not put yourself to so much trouble——'

'I can do as I like with my own coach and staff, you'll

allow? We have another carriage we may use meanwhile.'

Louisa could do nothing but accept with gratitude. She wondered what Hugh would have to say to the gesture.

The evening passed off without serious incident. Louisa, still wearing Lady Jane's dress and consequently not feeling up to scratch in her appearance, did her best to appear her usual lively self. Under the auspices of the Duke and Duchess both she and Hugh were welcomed to the informal evening's entertainment given by one of the Duchess's firmest friends.

Hugh behaved with impeccable courtesy, hovering behind the ladies while they were seated, plying them with drinks as requested and asking Louisa to stand up with him for the prescribed two sets. Otherwise he did not dance, remaining with the Duchess, seating himself when Louisa's chair became available beside her, at other times standing elegantly propped against the wall, always chatting amiably to those who came to pay their respects to his hostess. The Duke had disappeared in search of the card tables.

The gathering was relatively small and the dancing informal. Louisa did not lack for partners, for some army detachments were still stationed in Brussels. All the time she danced she was acutely aware of Hugh. On the occasions when she found the courage to look, his eyes seemed to be following her. Yet he had said nothing of importance during their dances. Had shown no embarrassment, either. Gradually, under his calming influence, her own discomfort had lessened. Plainly he intended to ignore the Duke's unfortunate remarks. She would therefore do the same.

Hugh found it impossible to take his eyes from Louisa's graceful figure as she danced with lively abandon. Not the frenetic abandon of those early days in Paris, he noted thankfully, and, although she laughed with and smiled at her partners, coquetry was quite absent from her manner.

She had been truly moritifed by the wretched Duke's question. But for Hugh, busy biding his time before laying his heart at her feet, the Duke's indiscretion had proved equally distressing. For Louisa had rejected the prospect of marriage to him as though it was the last thing in the world she wished to contemplate. He had been so confident, after her words after the hold-up, that her feelings for him had deepened. He could no longer deny the true nature of his own attachment. Physical desire had exploded upon him like one of Congreve's rockets almost from the first, but love had crept up like a thief in the night, stealing his heart and soul. Without Louisa, his life would be worth nothing. Persuading her of this, after his former irregular conduct, he had expected to prove difficult. Now he wondered whether he could ever succeed and, even if he did, whether it would make any difference if her heart had not been touched. She had declared that she would not wed without love. And had sounded so entirely opposed to the idea of marrying him and accompanying him to Vienna!

The Duchess, watching his grim profile and detecting the direction of his gaze, decided not to interfere further. She had done her best to reassure Louisa. If Hugh Deverill was half the man she thought him to be

he would not appreciate the advice of anyone, let alone
an interfering woman's. He knew exactly what he
wanted and would go his own way about getting it.

The party departed next morning after an early breakfast. One of the Duchess's personal maids, an older
woman named Rhoda, travelled inside the carriage
with them. The Duke's second coachman held the
reins, with Pershaw beside him to take his turn if
required. Dutton and Milsom rode on the seat behind.
Jamie's two horses had been tethered to the rear of the
carriage. Without the weight of riders on their backs
they would be able to stay fresh much longer and
should prove little drag on the speed of a coach drawn
by four post horses. All six men, including Jamie,
carried pistols.

Louisa bade their hosts an affectionate farewell. She
had always had an admiration for the Duchess of
Richmond and although the Duke had caused her so
much mortification she could not long hold him in
disgust. She liked him and he had meant no harm.

A slight drizzle soon cleared away and those riding
outside had a more pleasant journey than anticipated,
despite a decidedly autumnal chill. Luckily the weather
had, on the whole, been kind. Jamie and Milsom had
brought a change of clothing and a caped riding coat
each, as had Hugh and Dutton. Pershaw, however, had
been forced to borrow a suitable garment and Louisa
was glad of the travelling rugs draped over her
shoulders and tucked in about her knees.

Rhoda sat beside her, with Jamie and Hugh opposite.
As the coach rocked and swayed onwards Louisa
listened idly to Jamie's chatter, her real attention

centred on the man sitting opposite, whose knees bumped hers every time the carriage lurched and threw him forward. Whenever this happened a shock ran through her body and it was not pleasant. It should have been, of course, but it was not, for it meant nothing. Hugh was not affected by the contact. His eyes rested upon her from time to time, serious and remote. Both her own instinct and Lady Richmond must be mistaken. He could not love her.

How she longed for the brisk but unhurried journey to end, her torture to be over! Only one thing relieved the monotony—a brief visit to the barracks at Cambray.

The Life Guard captain greeted them warmly, but had no news of the miscreants they had encountered on the road.

'My men chased them for several miles, following their hoofprints until they came to a crossroads,' Captain Brownhill told them. 'Since there was no sign of the horses or of the men and they could have gone in any direction, the Sergeant abandoned the search. But my patrols are keeping a sharp eye open for them, you may be sure.'

Louisa and Jamie were fascinated by all the comings and goings, the incredible mixture of uniforms, the sight of companies of different armies all drilling in the barrack square at the same time.

'What a splendid sight they make!' Louisa commented.

Jamie's eyes were fixed on a troop of Life Guards drilling on their horses.

'There is talk of moving the Allied headquarters here,' smiled the captain, fully aware of their interest.

'Discipline must be maintained, for the Commander in Chief may visit at any time.'

'I wish the same could be said of the troops in and around Paris,' sighed Louisa. 'The Prussians and even the Russians and Austrians still leave a trail of shattered homes and ruined fields behind them. No wonder Madame de Staël and others plead so earnestly with the Duke of Wellington to reduce the numbers of the army of occupation!'

'He will not, of course,' put in Hugh, 'for we must remember, even if they find it convenient to forget, how ready some parts of the French army and many of its citizens were to welcome Bonaparte back last March. Wellington will keep a sizeable presence here until the new French leaders have proved themselves capable of ruling a peaceful country. He himself intends to remain in Paris for some time yet.'

'Such requests are regarded by those at headquarters as causing trouble. Such people will find themselves unpopular if they persist in their demands,' stated Captain Brownhill.

'Do not fear, Captain, their Lordships Wellington and Castlereagh, ably assisted, may I say, by Lord Hugh Deverill——' Louisa risked a small smile in his direction '—are constantly putting their views on the matter to those that matter in Paris. If only discipline could be introduced into the conduct of the occupying forces I believe everyone would accept its presence as a regrettable necessity.'

'Lord Wellington does his best, of that you may be sure,' said the captain. 'But he lacks disciplinary authority over any but his own army.'

Hugh made a helpless gesture. 'No, and Blücher and

the other commanders, being victorious, consider themselves justified in allowing their troops licence. There, too, persuasion is the only answer. But, Captain, we must not take up more of your time. We still have some distance to travel before nightfall.'

'I am glad to see you are well protected,' said the captain as he bade them farewell, 'and that the crest on your coach is unobtrusive. I pray you will not meet with trouble on the way.'

'Much as she enjoys ostentation, the Duchess of Richmond has an even greater regard for survival,' grinned Hugh. 'She is keenly aware of the likely consequences of blazoning her arms too obviously on continental roads.'

'I suppose,' said Louisa ruefully as the coach gathered speed, 'we shall be forced to recognise that dreadful creature, Lord Cumnor.'

'We owe him civility, no more,' responded Hugh.

'He owes you much more,' said Jamie indignantly, 'and so do I! I could not have borne to lose Conker! He was Papa's last present to me and he carried me so well on the journey.'

'You should have used post horses,' commented Louisa with a smile. 'Did it not occur to you, Jamie?'

'Yes, but I didn't think my funds would stretch to the cost, you see. As it was I had to borrow from Milsom. I do hope I can repay him when I get back.'

'Your mother left some funds with Mr Coynd, but if you find you cannot lay your hands on ready money I will stake you until your affairs are settled,' promised Hugh. 'Did your mama say nothing, Jamie? Will she marry this Prince?'

Until then they had kept a discreet silence over the

circumstances surrounding Jamie's abrupt departure. Hugh obviously thought it time to clear up a few matters before they arrived back.

'No, she didn't, and I hope she doesn't!' muttered Jamie rebelliously. 'If she sends for me I shan't go. She can't make me if my other trustees say I need not.'

'You must consult your grandmother at the earliest possible moment,' advised Louisa.

'Yes.' Jamie seemed to hesitate. 'I suppose I shall have to continue to obey Mr Coynd. But I shall insist he takes me back to England shortly.'

'Those were your mother's instructions and it would certainly seem to be the best plan,' agreed Hugh. 'I must return there myself in a few weeks. Perhaps we may travel together.'

'Capital!' exclaimed Jamie. 'Mr Coynd could have no objection to that!'

Hugh's smile was rather wry. 'I trust not.'

And that was how matters stood when at last they entered Paris, with Pershaw, leading Prince Hal, Kismet and Dutton's horse, following on behind. The animals had seemed in fine fettle when they'd recovered them at the last stage. Conker had appeared quite content to continue trotting along behind the carriage so he and Milsom's horse remained tethered to it. The sight of all the riderless animals following the coach brought a smile to Louisa's face. 'What a splendid sight we make!' Then she sobered. 'But conspicuous. No one will be able to miss our return.

'No one should be allowed to do so,' mumured Hugh. 'We have done nothing of which we need feel ashamed.'

'I shall tell everybody how you came to my rescue!' cried Jamie. 'You'll be the greatest of heroes!'

'No need to make a great piece of work of it, my boy,' cautioned Hugh. 'You will be facing scandal enough as it is, with your mother eloping and you disappearing as you did. Best to play the entire episode down.'

'Oh.' Jamie looked quite disappointed. 'I was looking forward to telling everyone about the hold-up.'

'Of course you may tell anyone who asks. But keep your account brief and do not exaggerate.'

'I'll try,' muttered Jamie.

Louisa privately thought it would be a miracle if he succeeded.

scarred to parade his conquest before his wife his previous year. How terribly tempting for her to have to watch him escorting beautiful, talented women while she herself stayed until sent back to obscurity at home. But she had not been able to hold his partiality for other women by now. She could not possibly be

CHAPTER THIRTEEN

THE sensation occasioned by Miss Louisa Finsham's scandalous behaviour quickly died. The Duchess of Richmond had entertained the couple in her home and presented them to Brussels Society; and admiration for their prompt action in riding to the rescue of the young Earl of Thurrock, so unscrupulously abandoned by his mother, won the day. Besides, since the pair concerned seemed entirely composed over the whole affair, other, more rewarding subjects for gossip soon occupied the gabble-grinders' attention.

For one thing the Duchess of Wellington was expected in Paris, informed at last by her husband that he was ready to receive her, perhaps hoping her presence would quell the rumours still rife concerning his relationship with Lady Frances Wedderburn-Webster.

For a week or so the previous year, before returning home, Kitty had tried very hard to be a duchess and fulfil the functions of an ambassador's wife in Paris. But she was not suited to the station to which her husband's success had elevated her, being altogether too homely, uninterested in his affairs, too much in awe of her famous husband to succeed. She annoyed him in almost every way, particularly by her inability to manage money, thus ending up in debt. Her arrival was therefore awaited expectantly. Would the Duke continue his addresses to La Grassini? He had not scrupled to parade his conquest before his wife the previous year. How terribly lowering for her to have to watch him escorting beautiful, talented women while she herself sat ignored until sent back to obscurity at home! But she must surely be inured to his partiality for other women by now. She could not possibly be ignorant of the string of beautiful and gifted women he had courted, trailing back through the Peninsula to India. Though of course she hadn't been married to him while he was in India.

Making her curtsy to the Duchess, Louisa could only feel sorry for the dowdy, middle-aged woman. She was making a brave effort. She adored her distinguished husband but was overawed by him. The hem of her unusually splendid gown had become torn. Doing her best to hide the damage, she cried, 'Do not tell the Duke! I pray you, do not draw his attention to it! He will be so vexed!'

Why she should think he would concern himself over such a trifle defeated Louisa. But she could see that poor Kitty could offer him no sparkling conversation, no radiant beauty, no outstanding horsemanship, no particular talent of any kind. Not even passion, by the looks of her; she was too timid. He must feel his marriage a disaster, apart from the two healthy sons Kitty had borne him.

Louisa made an effort to keep the Duchess company, to direct her myopic gaze away from the sight of the Duke paying open court to Madame Grassini and talking animatedly with the other admiring women gathered about him. She was scarcely surprised when, on several such occasions, Hugh strolled over, made his bow and proceeded to engage Kitty in conversation on mundane matters, asking after her sons and how things did in London. He had no need to consult Kitty, he had been there so recently, and the embassy was kept well abreast of the latest news from the capital. Louisa loved him the more for his kindness. He drew her into the conversation and, together, they managed to divert Kitty's attention from the Duke's neglect.

In the midst of all the speculation following Duchess Kitty's arrival, news came of Jamie's mother. The Countess of Thurrock was now a princess. Her elopement had caused enough stir. Her marriage became the subject of the latest on-dits.

James determinedly resisted her undoubtedly cool suggestion that he join her in Russia for the summer.

'I don't like him,' he confided to Louisa and Amelia, who had been in transports of relief over the safe return of both her loved ones. 'I shall never acknowledge him as my father! I am going to return to England with Lord Hugh. Grandmama Thurrock will see to it that I do not have to obey Mama's summons!'

'We all will,' declared Amelia. 'We shall return with you. We have no reason to remain in residence here for the winter. I shall prefer to be in London for the last of the Little Season and to retire to Minchingham for Christmas. Do you not agree, Louisa?'

'Of course, Aunt.'

Louisa's insides churned at the prospect of the journey. Not only would she be travelling with Hugh, but she must endure the sea crossing again, perhaps making another exhibition of herself in front of him.

Contrary to the Duchess of Richmond's prediction he made no move to declare himself again. In fact he seemed so occupied with neglected embassy business that she saw little of him. When they did meet in drawing-room or salon he held himself aloof, impeccably polite but never, by so much as a look, hinting at any intimacy between them, past or present. Only his eyes, when they rested upon her, held a look she could not fathom.

Neither Paris nor London could hold any attraction for her without Hugh's presence. The only person she would be sad to leave was Fanny d'Arblay. Otherwise she did not care whether she went or stayed, although going would prolong the bittersweet agony of seeing him for a little longer. And as for taking the Duchess's advice and precipitating matters between them—well, so far the opportunity simply had not arisen. And if it did she doubted she would have the courage to act. Hugh's apparent indifference had seriously diminished her self-confidence.

So it was with anxious foreboding that Louisa embarked upon the journey home. Hugh's taking up of his appointment in Vienna had been delayed until the New Year. He would spend what was left of November and part of December at the Foreign Office being briefed and remain in England for Christmas. She supposed he would leave his rooms in St James's and retire to the family estate, Kidderslake Hall in Hampshire, for the festival, there to take final leave of his parents and family. She would be at Minchingham in Berkshire, some twenty miles distant as the crow flew, but it might just as well be two hundred.

He travelled with Jamie. William Coynd occupied the third pull-out seat of that hired chaise. She shared a similar conveyance with Lady Nazeby. Pershaw, his lad and Jamie's groom, Percy, were bringing all the horses separately, while the other servants followed their masters and mistresses in two post chaises, required to change vehicles as well as horses at every stage. Yet another vehicle had been hired to carry the overflow of their considerable luggage. Four chaises and sixteen sweating horses driven by postilions plus a coach and coachman with another four horses pulling that had rendered their progress quite impressive. It did not, however, bring any meaningful communication between Louisa and Hugh, who maintained his pleasantly reserved manner during all their stops and overnight halts.

At Calais Louisa eyed the packet boat with grave misgiving. Shelter on the deck was non-existent, yet she dreaded having to descend into the dark, smelly cabin. She wore her thickest pelisse and carried a large, warm travelling rug, prepared to endure the cold rather than the discomfort of the cabin, since although the day was dull it was not raining. Their luggage was being carried aboard, the process overseen by Hugh and Dutton on the quay and Jamie, with Mr Coynd and Milsom in attendance, on board. She watched it disappear into the hold with abstract interest. The surly *douaniers*, their faces still scowling under their large cocked hats, had let it through without much trouble. Everyone's papers had been in order and they were free to board. Amelia and the maids, escorted by Dench, had already begun to cross the gangplank. Louisa hung back, savouring her last moments on solid ground.

A quiet voice spoke in her ear.

'The sea is tolerably calm today and the captain does not expect the weather to worsen. We have a fair breeze and the crossing should be a fast and pleasant one.'

Louisa turned impulsively. This was the first sign of other than polite concern Hugh had shown since Brussels. His words had not been extraordinary but his tone had changed.

'You remember my weakness,' she accused wryly. 'How I wish I were a good sailor!'

'How could I forget?' His smile lit a small flame in her heart. 'You were unfortunate to experience a storm on your first voyage. This one may enable you to face future crossings with greater fortitude.'

Louisa grimaced. 'Possibly, if I am ever persuaded to make such a journey again! But I cannot sit in that stuffy cabin!'

'Then you need not. The true joy of the sea can only be experienced on deck, in the wind and the spray. Come, my dear Louisa. Take my arm. We must board soon or be left behind!'

Oh, the dear feel of him! Louisa trembled and the slight feeling of sick fear disappeared in excitement. If Hugh did not. . .then she would. . . Or would she?

The deck rocked gently beneath her feet but she scarcely noticed it. Hugh had left her to speak again with the ship's captain. Amelia, with the maids, had already climbed down below, to obtain the best seats, Louisa surmised. Jamie, watched over by a diligent William Coynd, was exploring the deck. Dench, Milsom and Dutton leant on the rail some distance away, chatting with a number of other deck passengers.

'Come,' said Hugh, returning. 'The ship is about to sail. We must join the deck passengers behind the mast while the sailors attend to their work. Afterwards, we may go where we will.'

'You are to remain on deck, too?'

'Did you think I would leave you alone?'

He smiled at her in a way that set her heart beating faster. This was the old Hugh, attentive and charming, his smile and the expression in his eyes holding something more than friendship.

They made themselves as unobtrusive as possible while the ship was warped out of the harbour and the sails hoisted and set. The shouts of the men, the noise of creaking timbers, the sound of flapping canvas all combined to bring a sense of adventure Louisa had missed on the outward voyage, confined as she had been in the cabin below deck. Afterwards she had felt too ill to give the sweating sailors' activities more than passing attention. But now she had to admire their energy and skill as they hauled on ropes and secured the ends. The wind filled the sails and the ship heeled, sending her reeling into Hugh's ready arms.

He laughed. 'Enthralling, isn't it? They've finished now, see? They're settling down to wait for their next order and the ship is on a steady keel. Come to the weather side, here, where there is no tackle to worry us. It'll be breezy but dry.'

Louisa clutched the rug round her shoulders with one hand as she leant on his arm with the other. It was chilly, but so exhilarating! The feathers and ribbons on her bonnet blew wildly and she answered his laugh with one of her own.

The up-and-down motion now seemed no more than a gentle rocking as the ship's bow cut through the waves, sending white spray to drench the foredeck. A little drifted back to where they stood, but not enough to concern either of them.

Hugh's arm went about her shoulders and she did not object. Propriety might demand that she should, but the feel of it there was too precious. For several minutes they stood in silence, braced against the bulwarks. Despite his easy manner Louisa could feel tension in the arm across her shoulders. Hugh was not as relaxed as he appeared. She wondered what he was thinking. Her nerves responded to his rigidity by producing butterfly sensations in her stomach. She hoped she wouldn't feel sick again. But this fluttery sensation was due to pleasurable anticipation, not motion or fear.

He stirred at last, though he did not speak. Instead, he lifted her chin with his free hand and bent his head. She closed her eyes as he insinuated his head beneath her brim, knowing what was coming before ever his mouth touched hers.

They seemed to fuse together, those two pairs of lips. His tenderly demanding, hers sweetly yielding. And despite all the layers of thick clothing separating them Louisa's body, with a will of its own, melted into his. Place, time, everything was forgotten as she enjoyed the delight of his kiss. She had waited so long for him to carry out his threat that she had almost forgotten what his mouth felt like, yet instantly it was familiar, as though he had never stopped kissing her at all. His heart thudded under her hand. A small groan of pleasure escaped her and the beat quickened.

And then a loud laugh from one of the deck passengers penetrated her consciousness. She stiffened, tore her lips from his and made a feeble attempt to push him away.

'Hugh! Remember where we are! Everyone will see!'

'Capital,' said Hugh calmly, although his eyes and the give-away clenching of his jaw told her he was far from calm. His hold did not relax at all. 'If I have managed to compromise you before all these people then you will have to marry me.'

'Hugh!'

Her shocked tone brought a twinkle to his grey-blue eyes, a mischievous smile to those fascinating lips. 'My love, you were going to marry me anyway, so what does it matter?'

Stunned by his words and slightly incensed by the manner of his declaration, Louisa bridled, despite the sudden singing of the blood in her veins. 'I was not!' she denied. 'And of course it matters! A lady's reputation——'

'Yours, I confide, is not so fragile as to be damaged by so small a matter in such a public place. You said yourself, in Paris——'

'I know what I said in Paris!' Louisa's colour had heightened to a hectic red. Wretched man! To throw her own words back in her face! Then, suddenly, she had to ask. 'Why have you waited all this time to carry out your threat?'

'Threat?'

His innocent expression denied the laughter in his eyes. He would force her to say the words.

'To kiss me whenever opportunity presented itself,' she muttered.

He smiled down at her, certain now that his doubts had been groundless. That her vehement denial of any question of marriage between them had been

defensive, designed to hide her true feelings. He shifted
the arm about her downwards and tightened his hold.

'Because,' he said softly, serious now, 'I discovered
that I could not treat you with such disrespect.'

'So you asked me to marry you instead.'

'Yes,' he admitted soberly. 'Of course, having been
promoted and so being in a position to do so helped,
but I did not realise, then, how much I loved you. I
only knew I desired you and wanted to protect you,
from yourself if necessary.'

'But I,' sighed Louisa regretfully, 'had no wish to be
protected!'

'Unfortunately, no.' He grinned, but then his
expression became passionate and his emotions spilled
over into speech. 'My dearest girl! You must know that
I adore you! You are become the first object of my
heart and I find I cannot live without you!'

Louisa gazed up at him, stunned by the ardent nature
of his declaration. 'But——' she took refuge in the past
'—you said you did not wish to wed. You were so set
against it!'

'Because I had always sworn to myself not to wed
before I had the means to support a wife in style. My
pride would not allow it, and I had no wish to be
branded a fortune-hunter,' he admitted. 'I was absolutely determined not to wed an heiress until I had a
fortune of my own! And you, my love, not only
possessed such a fortune but appeared to be rather
flirtatious. How could I know what your feelings were?
Even after I lost my heart I denied it to myself, afraid
to admit it because it made me vulnerable. I was
jealous.' He gave a slight, self-deprecating laugh. 'I

could not begin to contemplate the prospect of losing you to another.'

Louisa eyed him steadily. 'My excessive flirtatiousness was occasioned by your attitude! I should not have cared, but I did.'

'I wonder why?' he murmured, his lips finding one corner of her mouth.

'I considered you horribly stuffy, quite overbearing and distinctly arrogant.'

'Charming,' he murmured, kissing the other corner.

'But I couldn't help falling in love with you,' she whispered.

He sucked in his breath sharply. 'Yet you said you did not.'

At a loss, Louisa frowned. 'When?'

'When I asked you to marry me. You said you would not wed without love.'

'Your love,' she told him softly, smiling contentedly. 'Now I know I have that, there is no problem.'

'And your mistrust of all men?' he probed. 'Do you now feel able to trust me?'

'I trust you,' she assured him earnestly. 'Love has quite overcome my fears. I realise that Papa never loved Mama.'

'As I most assuredly love you!' he declared again, and kissed her to prove it.

'And I love you,' Louisa asserted once she was able. 'Although,' she added provocatively, 'I do find your arrogant assumption that I would wed you, while still believing I did not love you, quite incomprehensible.'

'But I knew you did, after your horse bolted. Or at least I thought I knew it until you denied so roundly any intention of marrying me, at the Richmonds'. Your attitude sunk me in despondency but I could not quite forget that moment when you confessed your concern for my safety. And then, just now on the quay. You smiled at me,' he said simply.

'After weeks of polite coldness your voice held warmth,' she whispered. 'I had hoped your concern for my safety meant you loved me, Hugh, but then your attitude changed. I quite despaired.'

'I felt I must keep my distance, for your reputation's sake. Had you shown some enthusiasm for our union I would have explained my attitude to you. But I did not think you cared.'

'Oh, Hugh! Not care? My love, you cannot imagine how much I care!'

They searched each other's eyes and neither could see anything but sincerity and love reflected there. Hugh broke the spell by drawing a deep breath.

'Oh, my love! I find in you all I could ever wish for in a wife. Beauty, poise, passion, brains, an unrivalled ability to take your place in Society and a definite gift for languages. Besides all that you can ride like a dream and Pershaw tells me you know almost as much about breeding as he does. What more could I possibly desire, except your love? If I have that then I am rich beyond measure.'

'You forgot my modest fortune,' teased Louisa, snuggling closer into his arms.

The wind had whipped colour into her cheeks. Her bonnet, which she had thought so securely fixed, had become dislodged and her curls blew carelessly about her face. Hugh saw the happiness, the laughter filling her gorgeous eyes and could not resist another kiss.

'But that is yours. Lady Nazeby informed me so,' he

remarked after a while. 'It will not become mine. Unlike the rest of you. And it is you I want, my love.'

'The traitor!' gasped Louisa, part annoyed, part relieved that he already knew the truth and still wanted to marry her. Then she smiled up at him. 'I wish you could have my fortune too, my love.' She discovered that she would have trusted him implicitly to look after it. He would never squander money, though his spending could be lavish at times and like all men he gambled, but in moderation. And because she loved him she wanted to keep no part of herself back. Never before had she regretted the terms of her inheritance. 'We shall need a home of our own in England,' she added as an afterthought.

'I have one!' He grinned triumphantly into her surprised face. 'It is not widely known yet, for I only discovered it for myself while I was in London, but I inherited a small estate quite near to the family acres from a bachelor cousin. There is a modest income to accompany it. I believe the house will please you and we can extend it if it grows too small. But——' his arms tightened yet again as he crushed her to him '—the trust you show in wishing you could offer me your fortune overwhelms me.'

Without her realising it Louisa's arms had risen to encircle his neck. 'I could never have married a man I could not trust with it. That is why I kept its nature secret. The revelation was to be my final test of any suitor's integrity! Aunt quite spoilt it for me!' she teased.

'Wretch!'

'I know. And I cannot tell you how glad I am that she did, for she saved me from severe embarrassment.

How could I have sprung such knowledge on you without feeling ashamed of my deception? But you can possibly appreciate why I preferred to remain independent. I had no need to marry for security. Only for love, and the hope of a family.'

'The first you have, the second I shall do my best to give you,' vowed Hugh.

The kiss which followed was interrupted by a bellow from the captain followed by intense deck activity as the sailors rushed for the ropes. Hugh still had his arm about her waist as though to steady her as they made for safety behind the main mast, but Louisa knew it was because he did not want to let her go. Poker-faced servants greeted their arrival. Jamie and Mr Coynd joined them from another part of the deck. Jamie's grin almost split his face. Only then did Louisa realise that their every move must have been avidly watched. She blushed.

'Should we congratulate you, my lord?' enquired Dutton solemnly, attempting to hide his grin. 'If I might be allowed to say so, miss, Mr Pershaw will be that pleased to hear the news.'

'What news?' demanded Louisa blandly.

'Why, of your engagement, miss!'

'His lordship has not yet asked me to marry him,' responded Louisa demurely.

Hugh's brows almost disappeard into his tumbled hairline. His hat, like hers, had suffered dislodgement. It was perched at a precarious angle on the back of his head. 'Have I not?'

'No, my lord. You told me that I should marry you.'

'Ah!' exclaimed Hugh. 'I collect that I should make my offer in form. I shall do my best, though I absolutely decline to go down on one knee on the wet deck.' He glanced around the circle of the servants' studiously blank faces and beyond them to the deck passengers, whose expressions held avid interest. Without the slightest sign of either annoyance or embarrassment he turned to Louisa and made an elaborate bow. 'My dear Miss Finsham, will you do me the inestimable honour of accepting my hand in marriage?'

'Why, Lord Hugh! I do declare, you quite take me by surprise!' Louisa entered into the spirit of the thing. If the proposal was destined to be made a public spectacle, why not make it a good one? 'But since our servants are so happily disposed to anticipate our union, how can I possibly refuse you?'

'How indeed, you little tease!'

He held out his hand and Louisa placed hers in it. He drew her nearer.

'And I'm glad, too!' Jamie's excited voice broke the threatened spell. 'It's capital news, Louisa! I must go and tell Lady Nazeby! She'll be quite in raptures!'

'Not so fast, my lord! If you will allow, I should like to be the first to inform her ladyship of my intentions.'

'Oh! Yes, of course. Are you going now?'

'Not quite yet.' Hugh looked down into Louisa's radiant face. 'My love, can you wed me before Christmas? I shall not wish to leave for Austria without you.'

'Whenever you like, my lord,' murmured the future Lady Hugh Deverill meekly.

'Capital,' murmured Hugh. And, bracing his legs against the movement of the ship, he took her in his arms and bent his head to kiss her again, ignoring the amused expressions of almost everyone present. The servants managed to maintain some semblance of gravity.

The sniggers and chuckles, the shouted words of encouragement and Jamie's cheer were quite lost on the couple swaying together on the heaving deck, each aware only of the other.

'Now,' murmured Hugh, reluctantly releasing her soft lips, 'you are, I think, sufficiently compromised. Jilt me at your peril!'

'Why, sir,' she murmured in return, 'you leave me no choice. I fear I must bow to your wicked demands.'

The rush of wind and water and the creaking of the timbers drowned their lowered voices.

'Wicked?' He gazed down into her face. The flare of his nostrils, the flame in his eyes made her shiver in happy anticipation. 'Whatever we do together, my dearest love, will never be wicked.'

'I know,' she acknowledged. 'You have given me a glimpse already. You will lead me to paradise.'

This time when they kissed no one laughed or cheered. William Coynd, a rueful smile on his face, tugged Jamie away. Everyone else, as of one accord, turned their backs to allow them privacy. A moment of such obvious tender commitment demanded nothing less.

Paperback Writer...

LEGACY *of* LOVE

Coming next month

THE LAST ENCHANTMENT
Meg Alexander
Brighton 1813

To prevent her niece, Caroline, from marrying the notorious Duke of Salterne, Aurelia Carrington took the girl away to Brighton. As a means of escape, it was a failure, for Salterne followed them. Deeply, if unwillingly, attracted to him, Aurelia suspected he preferred her company to Caroline's, so what had made him offer marriage? By the time she found out, more was at risk than Aurelia's heart.

MARRIAGE RITES
Pauline Bentley
Essex 1694

Laura Stanton could lose Fairfield Manor on her grandfather's death—and he was dying. In sheer desperation she undertook a Fleet marriage with a prisoner, Matthew Thorne, only to find her simple plan was fraught with problems. Her grandfather unexpectedly rallied, and her 'marriage' *had* to seem real. But Matthew had his own demons to fight, and answers to find, before he could think about any future with Laura. Once he had his ship back, he would be off to sea, and Laura wouldn't leave Fairfield...

LEGACY of LOVE

Coming next month

FORTUNE HUNTER
Deborah Simmons
Regency England

To save his inheritance, Leighton Somerset, Viscount
Sheffield, badly needed a wealthy wife, and lovely Melissa
Hampton was his target. Her coolness towards suitors had
earned her the name of Lady Disdain but, somehow,
Leighton slipped under her guard, even though hard
experience had taught Melissa to evade charmers like him.

Leighton wasted no time in manoeuvring her straight into
matrimony and, accepting her fate, Melissa was tempted to
lose her heart. But she was in more than one kind of danger,
for someone was stalking her—in deadly earnest—and it
appeared to be her husband…

HEAVEN'S GATE
Erin Yorke
Ireland 1567

Banished to Ireland, Regan Davies arrived at her new estate
ready for anything—except it's former owner! Connor
O'Carroll had sworn to kill the man responsible for taking his
lands, until 'he' turned out to be a woman. Unable to bring
himself to exact revenge on Regan, Connor planned to regain
his home by marriage. Simple enough—as long as Connor
didn't ruin all by giving his heart to his enchanting enemy…